Recall Zero

Books by Jack Mars

LUKE STONE THRILLER SERIES

ANY MEANS NECESSARY (Book #1)

OATH OF OFFICE (Book #2)

SITUATION ROOM (Book #3)

OPPOSE ANY FOE (Book #4)

PRESIDENT ELECT (Book #5)

OUR SACRED HONOR (Book #6)

HOUSE DIVIDED (Book #7)

FORGING OF LUKE STONE PREQUEL SERIES

PRIMARY TARGET (Book #1)

PRIMARY COMMAND (Book #2)

PRIMARY THREAT (Book #3)

AN AGENT ZERO SPY THRILLER SERIES

AGENT ZERO (Book #1)

TARGET ZERO (Book #2)

HUNTING ZERO (Book #3)

TRAPPING ZERO (Book #4)

FILE ZERO (Book #5)

RECALL ZERO (Book #6)

ASSASSIN ZERO (Book #7)

Recall Zero

(An Agent Zero Spy Thriller—Book #6)

Jack Mars

Jack Mars

Jack Mars is the USA Today bestselling author of the LUKE STONE thriller series, which includes seven books. He is also the author of the new FORGING OF LUKE STONE prequel series, comprising three books (and counting); and of the AGENT ZERO spy thriller series, comprising seven books (and counting).

ANY MEANS NECESSARY (book #1), which has over 800 five star reviews, is available as a free download on Amazon!

Jack loves to hear from you, so please feel free to visit www.Jackmarsauthor.com to join the email list, receive a free book, receive free giveaways, connect on Facebook and Twitter, and stay in touch!

FILE ZERO (BOOK #5) – SUMMARY

As an international crisis threatens to spark a new world war, shadows within the highest levels of the US government work to further their own plot. The only person outside their ranks that knows about it is CIA Agent Kent Steele, who makes a desperate bid to save the lives of millions while keeping those close to him out of the hands of those whose interests would be served.

Agent Zero: His lost memories now restored, Zero took what he knew from years earlier to the highest level, the President of the United States—which only inspired those working behind the scenes to target the president and blame the assassination on Iran. Zero successfully stopped the assassination attempt, and in the process discovered that his friend and ally, Agent John Watson, was the one that killed Zero's wife and the mother of his children, at the behest of CIA superiors.

Maya and Sara Lawson: Both of Zero's daughters have grown keen and capable in the wake of multiple threats on their lives, but they are unaware of the harrowing details surrounding their mother's demise that their father recently discovered.

Agent Maria Johansson: Maria's cooperation with the Ukrainians was based on discovering whether her father, a high-ranking member of the National Security Council, was involved in the conspiracy. She discovered that he was not, and after helping Zero stop the assassination attempt, broke ties with the Ukrainian FIS. Her father was named as interim CIA director in the wake of the scandal and ensuing arrests.

Alan Reidigger: Zero's best friend and a fellow CIA agent that all thought was long dead, Reidigger reappears under the guise of Mitch, the burly mechanic that helped Zero previously. His appearance has been drastically altered, but with Zero's memories back, he was quickly able to recognize his old friend.

Deputy Director Shawn Cartwright: Though Zero was dubious about Cartwright's innocence in the plot to initiate a war in the Middle East, Cartwright proved himself loyal when he helped Zero escape from The Division. However, Cartwright was gunned down in a basement while holding the mercenaries off.

Deputy Director Ashleigh Riker and Director Mullen: The two heads of the CIA that were involved in the plot and actively working against Zero were both arrested in the wake of the assassination attempt, along with dozens of others that included much of the president's cabinet.

Table of Contents

Prologue

Karina Pavlo watched as the two men on either side of her at the conference table rose from their seats. She rose as well, because she knew she was supposed to, though her legs felt weak and tremulous. She watched as they smiled amiably at one another, these two men in expensive suits, these starkly contrasting heads of state. She said nothing as they concluded their business by shaking hands across the table.

Karina was still in shock over what she had just heard; over the words that had spilled from her own lips.

She had never been to the White House before, but the part of the structure that she was visiting was one rarely in the public eye. The basement (if it could even be called that, since it hardly resembled anyone's idea of a basement) beneath the North Portico contained all manner of impedimenta, including but not at all limited to a bowling alley, laundry facilities, carpenter's shop, dental office, the Situation Room, the president's workspace, three conference rooms, and a comfortable waiting area into which Karina had been ushered upon her arrival.

It was there in that waiting room that a Secret Service agent had taken her personal items, her cell phone and a small black clutch, and then asked that she remove her dark blazer. The agent had checked it thoroughly, every pocket and seam, and then performed a thorough yet mechanical pat-down with her arms held out at ninety degrees. He asked her to open her mouth, to lift her tongue, to remove her shoes, and to remain still while he ran a metal-detecting wand over her.

The only things Karina had been allowed to bring into the meeting were the clothes on her back and the pearl stud earrings she wore. Yet the rigor of the security was not out of the ordinary; Karina had been an interpreter for some years now, had served in chambers of the United Nations and translated for multiple heads of state. Born in Ukraine, Russian-educated in Volgograd, and having spent enough time in the US to qualify for a permanent visa, Karina considered herself a citizen of the world. She was fluent in four languages and conversational in three more. Her security clearance was as high as any civilian's could be.

Yet this was the big time. The opportunity to visit the White House to interpret a meeting between the new presidents of both Russia and the United States had seemed, not twenty minutes earlier, as if it would become the new pinnacle of her career.

How very wrong she was.

To her left, Russian President Aleksandr Kozlovsky buttoned the topmost button of his suit jacket, a fluid and practiced gesture that appeared irrationally casual to Karina, considering what she had just heard uttered only moments prior. At six-foot-three, Kozlovsky towered over the both of them, his thin build and long-limbed gait giving him the appearance of a cellar spider. His features were bland, his face smooth and wrinkle-free, as if it were still a work in progress.

Eighteen months ago, the former Russian president, Dmitri Ivanov, had retired. At least that's what they were calling it. In the wake of the enormity of the American scandal, it was simultaneously discovered that the Russian government had been colluding, not only lending their support to the US in the Middle East, but biding their time and waiting for the world's focus to be on the Strait of Hormuz so they could seize Ukrainian oil-producing assets in the Baltic Sea.

No arrests had been made in Russia. No sentence handed down, no prison time served. Under pressure from the UN and the world at large, Ivanov simply resigned from his position and was summarily replaced by Kozlovsky, who Karina knew was far more of an understudy than he was any sort of political rival, as the media made him out to be.

Kozlovsky smiled smugly. "A pleasure, President Harris." To Pavlo, he simply gave a curt nod before turning sharply and striding out of the room.

Twenty minutes earlier, the Secret Service man had escorted Karina to the smallest of three conference rooms in the White House basement, inside which was a long dark table of some exotic wood, eight leather chairs, a television screen, and nothing else. Not a soul. When Karina had been tasked as interpreter, she had assumed the meeting would involve cameras, news reporters, members of both governments' cabinets, the press and media.

But it had been only her, and then Kozlovsky, and then Samuel Harris.

President of the United States Samuel Harris, standing to her right, was seventy years old, half bald, his face creased with age and stress and his shoulders perpetually slumped from a back injury he had sustained while serving in Vietnam. Yet he moved with great purpose, and his husky voice was far more commanding than anyone would have assumed he could muster.

Harris had easily defeated the former president, Eli Pierson, in the election the previous November. Despite some sympathy from the public due to the assassination attempt on Pierson's life eighteen months earlier, as well as the former president's fairly noble efforts to rebuild his cabinet in the wake of the Iranian scandal that had come to light, America had lost their faith in him.

To Karina, Harris was reminiscent of a vulture, made all the more apt by the way he had swooped in and stolen the votes from Pierson like a carrion bird tearing entrails from the carcass of far too many mistakes and trust in the wrong people. Harris, as the Democratic candidate, had barely had to make any promises other than to unearth and promptly end any further corruption in the White House. But as Karina Pavlo had only just discovered, the further corruption in the White House was entrenched firmly—and perhaps solely—in the office of the presidency.

The visit from Russian President Kozlovsky was well publicized, covered by nearly every media outlet in the US. It was the first time since the deceitful cabal in both governments had been revealed that the two new world leaders had met face to face. There had been press conferences, constant media coverage, meetings with a hundred cameras in the room to discuss how the two nations might move forward from near catastrophe in an amiable and aligned manner.

But Karina now knew it was all a sham. The last several minutes that she had spent with the two world leaders, the spider and the vulture, had proven that. Kozlovsky's English was rudimentary at best and Harris spoke not a lick of Russian, so her presence had been warranted and their speech became hers.

It had started off innocently enough, pleasantries exchanged, English passing from Harris to her and then from her to Kozlovsky in Russian as if Karina were a translating automaton. The two men held each other's gaze, not once asking her questions or even acknowledging her presence once the meeting began. She mechanically regurgitated their words like a processor, entering her ears in one language and exiting her throat as another.

It was not until the sinister motivation for the private meeting unveiled itself that Karina realized that this—this handful of minutes in a locked room in the subterranean level of the White House with only the two of them and an interpreter present—was the real reason for the Russian president's visit to the United States. It was all she could do to translate as dispassionately as possible and desperately hope that her own expression hadn't betrayed her.

Suddenly Karina Pavlo became quite aware that she was unlikely to leave the White House basement alive.

With Kozlovsky having exited the room, President Harris turned to her, flashing his leering smile as if the conversation she'd been privy to hadn't just happened, as if this was nothing more than a formality. "Thank you, Ms. Pavlo," he said paternally. "Your experience and expertise have been appreciated and invaluable."

Perhaps it was the shock of what she had just learned that prompted her to force a smile of her own. Or perhaps it was the ease with which Harris seemed to summon such a polite demeanor while full well knowing that the interpreter had just heard every single word, and in fact had repeated each and every one of them to the other party. In any case, Karina found her lips curling upward against her will and her voice saying, "Thank you for the opportunity, Mr. President."

He smiled again. She did not like it, his smile; there was no mirth in it. It was more leering than cheerful. She had seen it a hundred times on television, on his campaign trail, but in person it was even more awkward to witness. It made it seem as if he knew something that she did not—which was certainly true.

An alarm blared in her head. She wondered how far she might get if she shoved him and made a run for it. Not far, she imagined; she had seen at least six Secret Service agents in the corridors of the basement, and she was equally certain that the route she'd taken down there would be guarded.

The president cleared his throat. "You know," Harris told her, "there was no one else in this room for good reason. As I'm sure you can imagine." He chuckled slightly, as if the threat to global security of which Karina had just been apprised was a joke. "You are the only one in the entire world that is aware of the content of this conversation. If it were to leak, I would know who leaked it. And things would not go well for that person."

The smile remained on Harris's face, but it was in no way reassuring.

She forced her lips to smile graciously. "Of course, sir. Discretion is one of my best qualities."

He reached over and patted her hand. "I believe you."

I know too much.

"And I trust you'll remain silent."

He's placating me. There's no way they're going to let me live.

"In fact, I'm certain I'll have a need for your skills again in the near future."

There was nothing Harris could say to dissuade her instincts. The president could have asked for her hand in marriage right there on the spot and still the prickling sensation at the nape of her neck that told her she was in imminent danger would linger.

Harris stood and buttoned his suit jacket. "Come along. I'll walk you out." He led the way out of the room and Karina followed. Her knees felt weak. She was in one of the most secure places on the planet, surrounded by trained agents of the Secret Service. As they reached the corridor she saw that the half dozen agents were posted there, standing with their backs to the walls with their hands clasped in front of them, waiting for the president.

Or possibly for her.

Stay calm.

"Joe." Harris motioned for the agent who had first retrieved her from the waiting room. "See to it that Ms. Pavlo here gets back to her hotel safely, yes? Best car we've got."

"Yes sir," said the agent with a slight nod. A strange nod, to her. A nod of understanding.

"Thank you," she said as graciously as she could muster, "but I can take a cab. My hotel is not far."

"Nonsense," Harris said pleasantly. "What's the point of working for the president if you can't enjoy some of the perks?" He chuckled. "Thank you again. It was a pleasure meeting you. We'll be in touch."

He shook her hand. She shook his. His smile lingered, but his eyes betrayed him.

Karina had little choice. She followed the Secret Service agent, the man called Joe (if that was his real name), through the White House sublevel. Every muscle in her body was taut, anxious, ready at a moment's notice for fight or flight to kick in. But to her surprise, the agent actually escorted her up a set of stairs and down a hall and to another door that led outside. He guided her wordlessly to a small parking garage with a private fleet of vehicles, and then he opened the passenger door of a black SUV for her.

Don't get in.

She got in. If she fought now or tried to run she'd never even make it to the gate.

Two minutes later they were off of White House property, driving down Pennsylvania Avenue. *He's taking me somewhere to do it. They'll get rid of me elsewhere. Somewhere no one will ever find me.*

"You can just drop me off at the downtown Hilton," she said casually.

The Secret Service agent smiled coyly. "We're the US government, Ms. Pavlo. We know where you're staying."

She chuckled lightly, trying to keep the nervous edge out of her voice. "I'm sure. But I'm meeting a friend for dinner at the Hilton."

"Even so," the agent replied, "the president's orders were to take you back to your hotel, so that's what I have to do. For security reasons." He sighed then, as if he commiserated with her plight even though she was fairly certain he was going to kill her. "I'm sure you understand."

"Oh," she said suddenly. "My things? My phone and my clutch?"

"I have them." Joe patted the breast pocket of his suit.

After a long moment of silence Karina followed up with, "May I have them ...?"

"Of course," he said brightly. "Just as soon as we arrive."

"I'd really like them back now," she pressed.

The agent smiled again, though he kept his eyes forward on the road. "We'll be there in just a few minutes," he said placidly, as if she were a petulant toddler. Karina very much doubted that he had her things in his jacket.

She settled into her seat, or at least gave the appearance of doing so, trying to seem relaxed as the SUV eased to a stop at a red light. The Secret Service agent dug around in the center console for a pair of black sunglasses and put them on.

The light turned green.

The car in front of them started forward.

The agent took his foot off the brake, pressed the gas.

In one swift movement, Karina Pavlo pressed the release of her seat belt with one hand while shoving open her door with the other. She leapt out of the moving SUV, her heels hitting the asphalt. One of them broke. She lurched forward, hitting pavement with her elbows, rolling, and then staggered to her feet. She kicked both shoes off and sprinted down the street in her stockings.

"What the hell?!" The Secret Service agent slammed the brake, threw the vehicle into park right there in the middle of the street. He didn't bother shouting for her to come back, and he certainly didn't just let her go—both indicators that she was absolutely right about her notion.

Drivers honked and shouted as the agent leapt out of the car, but by that time she was more than half a block away, practically barefoot as her stockings tore, ignoring the occasional stone that stung the soles of her feet.

She turned the corner sharply and darted down the first opening she saw, not even an alley but rather just a walkway between two storefronts. Then she made a left, running as fast as she could, glancing over her shoulder every now and then for the agent but not seeing him.

As she came out on the next street, she spotted a yellow cab.

The driver nearly spat his coffee, a Styrofoam cup to his lips, when she all but hurtled into his backseat and shouted, "Drive! Please drive!"

"Jesus Christ, lady!" he scolded. "Scared the hell outta me…"

"Someone is chasing me, please drive," she pleaded.

He frowned. "Who's chasing you?" The irritating driver actually glanced around. "I don't see anybody—"

"*Please just fucking drive!*" she screeched at him.

"Okay, okay!" The cabbie shifted and the taxi veered into traffic, eliciting a new fusillade of honks that would no doubt tip the agent off to her relative location.

Sure enough, as she twisted in the seat to look out the rear windshield she saw the agent rounding the corner at a full sprint. He slowed to a trot, his eyes meeting hers. One of his hands briefly snaked into his jacket, but he seemed to think twice about pulling a gun in broad daylight and instead put a hand to his ear to radio someone.

"Turn left here." Karina directed the cabbie to make the turn, drive a few more blocks, take a right, and then she jumped out again as he shouted after her for payment. She ran down the block and did that three more times, jumping into cabs and out of them until she was halfway across DC in such a serpentine manner she was certain there was no way that Joe the Secret Service agent would find her.

She caught her breath and smoothed her hair as she slowed to a brisk walk, keeping her head down and trying not to look frazzled. The most likely scenario was that the agent had gotten the cab's license plate number and the unfortunate (though somewhat slow-witted) cabbie would be stopped, frisked, and background-checked to make sure he wasn't part of some preconceived getaway plot.

Karina ducked into a bookstore, hoping no one would notice she was shoeless. The store was quiet and the shelves were tall. She quickly navigated her way to the back, headed into a restroom, splashed water on her face, and struggled to keep herself from breaking down into heaving sobs.

Her face was still sheet-white from the shock of it all. How quickly everything had gone wrong.

"*Bozhe moy*," she sighed heavily. My god. As the adrenaline wore off, the full gravity of her situation struck her. She had heard things that were never supposed to leave the White House basement. She had no identification. No phone. No money. Hell, she didn't have shoes. She couldn't go back to her hotel. Even showing her face in any public space where there might be a camera was risky.

They were not going to stop pursuing her for what she knew.

But she had the pearls in her ears. Karina absently touched her left earlobe, caressing the smooth stone there. She had the words that were spoken in the meeting—and in more than just her memory. She had proof of the dangerous knowledge that the American president, an alleged Democratic liberal who had earned the country's admiration, was being puppeteered by the Russians.

There in the ladies' room of a downtown bookstore, Karina looked at herself in the mirror as she murmured desperately, "I'm going to need some help."

CHAPTER ONE

Zero sat on the edge of the queen-sized bed and wrung his hands nervously in his lap. He'd been through this before, had seen it in his mind a thousand times. Yet here he was again.

His two teenage daughters sat on the bed adjacent to his, a narrow aisle between them. They were in a room at the Plaza, an upscale hotel just outside of DC. They had decided to hole up there instead of going home in the wake of the assassination attempt on President Pierson's life.

"There's something I need to tell you."

Maya was on the brink of seventeen. She had her father's brown hair and facial features, and her mother's sharp wit and biting sarcasm. She regarded him passively, with a shadow of trepidation over such a dramatically foreshadowing statement.

"It's not easy to say. But you deserve to know."

Sara was fourteen, still round-faced with youth, teetering at a conflicted age between clinging to childhood and burgeoning womanhood. She had inherited Kate's blonde hair and expressive face. She looked more like her mother with every passing day, though at the moment she looked nervous.

"It's about your mother."

They had both been through so much, kidnapping and witnessing murders and staring down the barrel of a gun. They had stayed strong through it all. They deserved to know.

And then he told them.

He'd played it in his mind so many times before, but still the words were difficult to summon to his throat. They came slowly, like logs drifting on a river. He'd thought that once he started it would get easier, but that wasn't at all the case.

There in the Plaza hotel, with Alan out getting pizza and a sitcom muted on the TV mere feet from them, Zero told his daughters that their mother, Kate Lawson, had not died of an ischemic stroke as had been reported.

She had been poisoned.

The CIA had called a hit on her.

Because of him. Agent Zero. His actions.

And the person who carried out the sentence …

"He didn't know," Zero told his daughters. He stared at the bedspread, the carpet, anything other than their faces. "He didn't know who she was. He had been lied to. He didn't know until later. Until after." He was rambling. Making excuses for the man who had killed his wife, the mother of his children. The man Zero had sent away instead of killing him outright.

"Who?" Maya's voice came out hoarse, a harsh whisper, more of a sound than a word.

Agent John Watson. A man who had saved his daughters' lives more than once. A man they had come to know, to trust, to like.

The silence in the next few moments was crushing, like an invisible hand squeezing his heart. The hotel room's air conditioning unit rattled to life suddenly, loud as a jet engine in the otherwise vacuum.

"How long have you known?" Maya's tone was direct, almost demanding.

Be honest. That was the stance he wanted with his girls. Honesty. No matter how bad it hurt. This admission was the last barricade between them. He knew it was time to tear it down.

He already knew it would be what broke them.

"I've known for a little while that it wasn't an accident," he told her. "I needed to know who. And now I do."

He dared to look up then, to look at their faces. Sara cried silently, tears streaming down both cheeks, not making a sound. Maya stared at her own hands, expressionless.

He reached for her. It was the only thing that made sense in the moment. To connect, to hold a hand.

He remembered exactly how it had actually happened. As his fingers closed around hers, she pulled away violently. She scrambled backward, leapt off the bed. Sara jumped, startled, as Maya told him she hated him. Called him every name in the book. And he sat there, and he took it, because it was what he deserved.

But not this time. As his fingers closed around hers, Maya's hand disintegrated beneath his in a wisp of fog.

"No..."

He clambered for her, a shoulder or an arm, but she vanished under his touch like a column of ash in a breeze. He turned quickly and reached for Sara, but she only shook her head ruefully as she too evaporated before his eyes.

And then he was alone.

"Sara!"

Zero woke with a start and immediately groaned. A headache roared through his forehead. It was a dream—a nightmare. One he'd had a thousand times before.

But it had happened that way, or nearly so.

Zero had saved the day. Thwarted a presidential assassination attempt. Stopped a war before it began. Uncovered a conspiracy. And then he and his girls had gone to the Plaza; none of them wanted to go home to their two-story house in Alexandria, Virginia. Too much had happened there. Too much death.

It was there that he'd told them. They deserved to know the truth.

And then they left him.

That was... how long ago now? Nearly eighteen months, by his best recollection. A year and a half ago. Still the dream plagued him most nights. Sometimes the girls evaporated before his eyes. Sometimes they screamed at him, hurling curses far worse than had actually happened. Other times they silently left, and when he ran out into the hallway after them they had already vanished.

Though the ending varied, the real-life ramifications were the same. He woke from the nightmare with a headache and the grim, despairing reminder that they really were gone.

Zero stretched and rose from the sofa. He couldn't remember falling asleep in the first place, but it wasn't surprising. He didn't sleep well at night, and not just because of the nightmare about his daughters. A year and a half ago he had recovered his memories, his complete memories as Agent Zero, and with them came harrowing nightmares. Recollections would shoulder their way into his subconscious while he slept, or tried to. Heinous scenes of torture. Bombs dropped on buildings. The impact of hollow-point bullets on a human skull.

Worse still was that he didn't know if they were real or not. Dr. Guyer, the brilliant Swiss neurologist who had helped him recover the memories, warned that some things might not be real, but a product of his limbic system manifesting fantasies, suspicions, and nightmares as reality.

His own reality felt barely just so.

Zero trudged into the kitchen for a glass of water, barefoot and groggy, when the doorbell rang. He jumped a little at the sudden break in silence, every muscle tightening instinctively. He was still pretty jumpy, even after all this time. Then he glanced at the digital clock on the stove. It was almost four thirty. There was only one person it would be.

He answered the door and forced a smile for his old friend. "Right on time."

Alan Reidigger grinned as he held up a six-pack, a thumb and forefinger looped in the plastic rings. "For your weekly therapy session."

Zero snorted and stepped aside. "Come on, we'll go out back."

He led the way through the small house and out a sliding glass door to a patio. The mid-October air was not yet cold, but crisp enough to remind him that he was barefoot. They took a seat in a couple of deck chairs as Alan liberated two cans and passed one to Zero.

He frowned at the label. "What's this?"

"Dunno. The guy at the liquor store took one look at my beard and flannel shirt and said I'd like it." Alan chuckled, popped the tab, and took a long sip. He winced. "That's... different. Or maybe I'm just getting old." He turned somberly to Zero. "So. How are you?"

How are you. It suddenly seemed like such a strange question. If anyone other than Alan had asked it, he would have recognized it as a formality and answered with a simple and hasty "Fine, how about you?" But he knew that Alan genuinely wanted to know.

Yet he didn't know how to answer. So much had changed in eighteen months; not just in Zero's personal life, but on a macro scale. The US had averted a war with Iran and its neighbors, but tensions remained high. The American government had seemingly recovered from the infiltration of conspirators and Russian influence, but only by cleaning house. President Eli Pierson had remained in office for another seven months after the attempt on his life, but was ousted in the next election by the Democratic candidate. It was an easy victory after Pierson's cabinet was revealed to have been a veritable nest of snakes.

But Zero hardly cared. He wasn't involved in any of that anymore. He didn't even have an opinion about the new president. He barely knew what was going on in the world; he avoided the news whenever possible. He was just a citizen now. Whatever was unfolding in the shadows did so without his influence.

"I'm fine."

He was stagnating.

"Really. I'm good."

Alan took another sip, obviously dubious but not mentioning it. "And Maria?"

A thin smile crossed Zero's lips. "She's doing well." And it was true. She was taking to her new position swimmingly. In the wake of the conspiracy coming to light, the CIA had been completely restructured; David Barren, high-ranking member of the National

Security Council and Maria's father, was named interim director of the agency and oversaw vetting of each and every person under its banner until a new director was named, a former NSA director named Edward Shaw.

Maria Johansson had been appointed as deputy director of Special Activities Division—a job that had been formerly held by the now-deceased Shawn Cartwright, Zero's old boss. She in turn named Todd Strickland as Special Agent in Charge, a position formerly held by one Agent Kent Steele.

And she was good at it. There would be no corruption under her watch, no renegade agents like Jason Carver, and no shadowy conspirators like Ashleigh Riker. It was obvious, though, that she still missed the fieldwork; it wasn't often, but occasionally she would accompany her team on an op.

Zero, on the other hand, had not gone back. Not to the CIA, not even to teaching. He hadn't gone back to anything.

"How's the shop?" he asked Alan, for want of changing the subject from something other than himself and his morose introspection.

"Keeping busy," Reidigger replied casually. He ran the Third Street Garage, which despite Alan's background in espionage and covert operations was, in fact, a garage. "Not much to say there. How's the basement coming?"

Zero rolled his eyes. "It's a work in progress." After the falling out with his girls, he just couldn't stay in the Alexandria house alone. He put it on the market and sold it to the first offer that came along. He and Maria had made their relationship official by then, and she too was seeking a change of scenery, so they bought a small house in the suburbs of the unincorporated town of Langley, not far from CIA headquarters. A "Craftsman bungalow"—that's what the real estate agent had called it. It was a simple place, which was good for them both. One of the many things he and Maria had in common was that they yearned for simplicity. They could have afforded something bigger, more modern, but the little one-story house suited them just fine. It was cozy, pleasant, with a big picture window in the front and a master suite loft and an unfinished basement, all smooth concrete walls and floor.

About four months earlier, at the beginning of summer, Zero had the idea that he'd finish the basement, make it into usable living space. Since then he'd gotten as far as framing out the walls with two-by-fours and stapling up some strips of fluffy pink insulation.

Lately, just the thought of going back down there exhausted him.

"Anytime you want me to come by and help out, say the word," Alan offered.

"Yeah." Alan made the same offer every week. "Rome wasn't built in a day, you know."

"It might have been if they hired contractors who knew what they were doing." Alan winked.

Zero scoffed, but smirked. The can in his hand felt light, too light. He shook it and was surprised to find it empty. He didn't remember even taking a sip, let alone registering the taste. He set the can down on the patio beside him and reached for another.

"Careful," Reidigger warned with a grin. He gestured toward Zero's midsection and the speed-bump of a paunch that was developing there.

"Yeah, yeah." So he'd gained a few pounds in his semi-retirement. Ten, maybe fifteen. He wasn't sure and certainly wasn't about to step on a scale to find out. "Look who's talking."

Reidigger laughed. He was a far cry from the round-faced agent Zero had known four years earlier, with his boyish looks and stubbornly thick torso. In order to obscure his appearance after his faked death, and to assume his alias of a mechanic named Mitch, Alan had put on at least forty pounds, grown out a bushy beard flecked with gray, and perpetually wore a trucker's cap pulled low on his forehead, the brim of it permanently stained with both sweat and dark oily thumbprints.

The cap had become such an omnipresent accessory that Zero wondered if he wore it to bed.

"What, this?" Reidigger chuckled again and slapped his stomach. "This is all muscle. Y'know, I go down to the gym twice a week.

They've got a boxing ring. The young kids, they love to talk trash to the older guys. Right before I whip their asses." He took a sip and added, "You should come sometime. I usually go on—"

"Tuesdays and Thursdays," Zero finished for him. Alan made that offer every week too.

He appreciated the effort. He appreciated that Alan came by so often to sit around on the patio with his old friend and shoot the breeze. He appreciated the check-ins and the attempts to get him out of the house that were growing more halfhearted with every visit.

The truth was that without the CIA or teaching or his daughters around, he didn't feel like himself, and it had led to a sort of sickness settling into his brain, a general malaise that he couldn't seem to overcome.

The sliding glass door opened suddenly then, and both men turned to see Maria step out into the October afternoon. She was dressed smartly in a crisp white blazer with black slacks and a thin gold necklace, her blonde hair cascading around her shoulders and dark mascara accentuating her gray eyes.

It was strange, but for the briefest of moments it was jealousy that swept through Zero at the sight of her. Where he had stagnated, she had flourished. But he pushed that down too, pushed it down into the murky swamp of his stifled emotions and told himself he was glad to see her.

"Afternoon, boys," she said with a smile. She seemed in good spirits; her mood upon arriving home from work tended to be as varying as the odd hours she kept. "Alan, it's good to see you." She bent at the waist to give him a hug.

"Astonished" wasn't quite the term that came to Zero's mind when Maria discovered that Alan was not only still alive, but holed up in a garage not thirty minutes from Langley. But she took the news in stride—a bruising punch to his shoulder and a harsh rebuke of "you should have told us!" was seemingly all the catharsis she needed.

"Hi, Kent." She kissed him before grabbing a beer from Alan's sixer and joining them. "Good day?"

"Yeah." He nodded. "Good day." He didn't elaborate, because the only elaboration he could have offered was that he'd spent the day watching old movies, napping, and vaguely thinking about returning to the waiting and still unfinished basement. "You?"

She shrugged. "Better than most." She tended not to talk too much about work with him—not only because of security clearance, of which Zero currently had none, but also out of the unspoken fear (at least Zero presumed) that it might trigger him, jar some old memory, or otherwise inspire him to get back in the game. She seemed to like him where he was. Though his suspicion about that was another matter entirely.

"Kent," she said, "don't forget that we have dinner plans."

He smiled. "Right, of course." He hadn't forgotten about the guest they'd be hosting that evening. But he was actively trying not to think about that.

Kent.

She was the only one who still called him that.

Agent Kent Steele had been his alias in the CIA, but now that was nothing but a memory. Zero had been his call sign, started as a joke by Alan Reidigger—who still called him Zero. And ever since he'd gotten his memories back, that was the name that he usually thought of himself by. But he wasn't either of those anymore, Kent or Zero, not really. He wasn't Professor Lawson anymore. Hell, he barely felt like himself, his real self, Reid Lawson, father of two and history professor and covert CIA operative and whatever other thing he identified himself as. Even though eighteen months had passed, he still bitterly recalled the shadowy conspirators dragging his name through the mud, releasing his image to the media, calling him a terrorist and attempting to pin the would-be assassination attempt on him. He was, of course, completely exonerated of those charges, and he had no idea if anyone else even remembered it. But he did. And now the name felt foreign to him. He avoided being known as Reid Lawson whenever possible, to the extent that the house, the bills, even the cars were all in Maria's name. No mail came for him with his name on it. No one ever called asking for Reid.

Or Kent.

Or Zero.

Or Dad.

So just who the hell am I?

He didn't know. But he knew that he had to discover it for himself, because the life he was leading was no life worth living.

Chapter Two

Zero was glad he didn't have to talk about them. But Alan knew better than to ask about the girls.

Reidigger stuck around for about forty-five minutes before rising from the deck chair, stretching, and in his usual fashion, announcing he'd better "hit the ol' dusty trail." Zero gave him a brief hug and waved as he pulled the pickup truck out of the driveway and silently thanked him for not asking about his daughters, because the truth was that if Alan had asked how they were, Zero couldn't answer.

He found Maria in the kitchen, wearing an apron over her work clothes as she chopped an onion. "Good visit?"

"Yeah."

Silence. Just the rhythmic tock of the knife against the cutting board.

"You ready for tonight?" she asked after a long moment.

He nodded. "Yeah. Definitely." He wasn't. "What are you making?"

"*Bigos.*" She dumped the cutting board's contents into a large pot on the stove that already contained simmering kielbasa, cabbage, and other vegetables. "It's a Polish stew."

Zero frowned. "*Bigos.* Since when do you make *bigos*?"

"I learned from my grandmother." She smirked. "There's still a lot you don't know about me, Mr. Steele."

"I guess so." He hesitated, wondering how best to broach the subject on his mind, and then decided direct was best. "Um… hey. So tonight, do you think you could maybe try not to call me Kent?"

Maria paused with the knife hovering over a dried mushroom. She frowned, but nodded. "Okay. What do you want me to call you? Reid?"

"I…" He was about to agree, but then realized that he didn't really want that either. "I don't know." Maybe, he thought, she should just avoid calling him anything.

"Huh." It was obvious from her expression that she was concerned, wanted to push further into whatever was going on in his head, but it wasn't the time to unpack all that. "How about I just call you 'pookie'?"

"Very funny." He grinned in spite of himself.

"Or 'cupcake'?"

"I'm going to get changed." He headed out of the kitchen even as Maria called after him, laughing to herself.

"Wait, I got it. I'll call you 'honeybunch.'"

"I'm ignoring you," he called back. He appreciated what she was trying to do, attempting to diffuse the situation with humor. But as he reached the top of the short staircase that led to the loft, the anxiety bubbled up within him again. He'd been glad for Alan's visit because it meant he didn't have to think about it. He'd been glad Alan didn't ask about the girls because it meant he didn't have to face facts or memories. But there was no avoiding it now.

Maya was coming to dinner.

Zero inspected his jeans, made sure they were free of holes or errant coffee stains, and traded his lounging T-shirt for a striped button-down.

You're a liar.

He ran a comb through his hair. It was getting too long. Slowly turning gray, especially at the temples.

Mom died because of you.

He turned sideways and inspected himself in the mirror, pulling his shoulders back and trying to shrink the slight paunch that had gathered around his belly button.

I hate you.

The last meaningful exchange he'd had with his eldest daughter was vitriolic. In the hotel room at The Plaza when he'd told them the truth about their mother, Maya had stood from the bed. She'd started quietly, but her voice rose quickly by the octave. Her face growing redder as she cursed at him. Called him every name he deserved. Telling him exactly what she thought of him and his life and his lies.

After that, nothing had been the same. Their relationship had changed instantly, dramatically, but that wasn't the most painful part. At least she was still there physically, at the time. No, the slow burn was so much worse. After the admission in the hotel, after they had returned home to their Alexandria house, Maya went back to school. She was ending her junior year of high school; she'd missed two months of work but she hit the books with an intensity Zero had never seen in her before.

Then that summer came, and still she exiled herself to her room, studying. It didn't take long for him to figure out what was going on. Maya was fiercely intelligent—too smart, he'd often say, for her own good. But in this case, she was too smart for *his* good.

Maya studied and worked hard and, thanks to a little-known bylaw in her school district's charter, she was able to test out of her senior year of high school by taking and passing every AP exam. She graduated from high school before the end of that first summer—though there was no ceremony, no cap and gown, no walking with classmates. No proud, smiling photos next to her father and sister. There was just a form letter and a diploma in the mail one day, and Zero's abject astonishment as he realized what she was trying to do.

And then, only then, was she gone.

He sighed. That was more than a year ago now. He'd last seen her just this past summer, around July or August, not long after his fortieth birthday. She rarely came down from New York these days. On that occasion she'd come back to get some of her belongings out of storage, and had hesitantly agreed to have lunch with him. It had been an awkward, tense, and mostly silent affair. Him asking questions, prodding her to tell him about her life, and her giving him succinct answers and avoiding eye contact.

And now she was coming to dinner.

"Hey." He hadn't heard Maria come into the loft bedroom, but he felt her arms around his midsection, her head resting against his back as she hugged him from behind. "It's okay to be nervous."

"I'm not nervous." He was very nervous. "It'll be good to see her."

"Of course it will." Maria had organized it. She had been the one to reach out to Maya, to invite her over the next time she was in town. The invitation had been extended two months earlier. Maya was in Virginia this weekend to visit some friends from school, and reluctantly agreed to come. Just for dinner. She wouldn't be staying. She made that very well known.

"Hey," Maria said softly behind him. "I know the timing isn't great, but..."

Zero winced. He knew what she was going to say and wished she wouldn't.

"I'm ovulating."

He didn't respond for a long moment, long enough to realize that the silence was becoming uncomfortable as it yawned between them.

When they first moved in together, they had agreed that neither of them was terribly interested in marriage. Kids were not even on his radar. But Maria was only two years younger than him; she was rapidly approaching forty. There was no longer a snooze button on her biological alarm clock. At first she would just casually mention it in conversation, but then she ceased her birth control regiment. She started keeping keen track of her cycle.

Still, they'd never actually sat down and discussed it. It was as if Maria simply assumed that since he'd done it twice before, he would want to be a father again. Though he never said it aloud, he secretly suspected that was why she hadn't pushed for him to return to the agency, or even to teaching. She liked him where he was because it meant there would be someone to care for a baby.

How can it be, he wondered bitterly, *that my life as an unemployed civilian could be more complicated than as a covert agent?*

He'd waited too long to reply, and when he finally did it sounded forced and lame. "I think," he said at last, "that we should put a pin in that for now."

He felt her arms fall away from around his waist and hastily added, "Just until we get past this visit. Then we'll talk, and we'll decide—"

"To wait longer." She practically spat the words out, and when he turned to face her she was staring at the carpet in undisguised disappointment.

"That's not what I'm saying."

Yes, it is.

"I just think it warrants a serious discussion," he said.

So I can man up enough to admit I don't want it.

"We should at least deal with what's in front of us first."

Like the fact that the two children I already raised hate me.

"Yeah," Maria agreed quietly. "You're right. We'll wait longer." She turned and headed out of the bedroom.

"Maria, wait..."

"I have to finish dinner." He heard her footfalls on the stairs and cursed himself under his breath for mishandling that so badly. It was pretty much par for the course in his life lately.

Then the doorbell rang. The sound of it sent an electric tingle through his nervous system.

He heard the front door open. Maria's cheerful voice: "Hi! It's so good to see you. Come in, come in."

She was here. Suddenly Zero's feet felt like lead weights. He didn't want to go downstairs. Didn't want to face this.

"And you must be Greg..." Maria said.

Greg? Who the hell is Greg? Suddenly he found the willpower to move. One stair at a time, she slowly came into sight. It had only been a few months since he'd last seen her, but still she took his breath away.

Maya was eighteen now, no longer a child, and it was showing more rapidly than he cared to admit. When they'd met for lunch the past summer, her hair was still long and curled into the military-requisite donut bun, but she had since had it cut shorter, a pixie cut, short on the sides and back and sweeping across her forehead, accentuating her lean face, which was growing mature and angular. She looked stronger, the muscles in her arms developing, small but dense.

She was looking more like him every day, while he was looking and feeling less like himself every day.

Maya glanced up at him as he came down the stairs. "Hi." It was a passive greeting, not bright but not flat. Neutral. Like someone greeting a stranger.

"Hi, Maya." He moved in to hug her and the slightest hint of apprehension shadowed her face. He settled for a half-embrace, one arm around her shoulders while her hand patted his back once. "You look … you look well."

"I am." She cleared her throat and addressed the elephant in the room. "This is Greg."

The boy, if he could be called that, stepped forward and stuck out an enthusiastic hand. "Mr. Lawson, a pleasure to meet you, sir." He was tall, six-two, with short blond hair and perfect teeth and tanned arms that were testing the limits of his polo shirt's sleeves.

He looked like the high school quarterback.

"Uh, nice to meet you too, Greg." Zero shook the kid's hand. Greg had a firm grip, firmer than was necessary.

Zero disliked him immediately. "You're a, uh, friend of Maya's from school?"

"Boyfriend," Maya said unflinchingly.

This guy? Zero disliked him even more now. His smile, his teeth. He found himself incensed with jealousy. This grinning idiot was close to his daughter. Closer than Zero was allowed to be.

"What are we all standing around here for? Come in, please." Maria closed the door and led them toward the living room. "Have a seat. Dinner isn't quite done yet. Can I get you something to drink?"

They responded, but Zero didn't hear it. He was too busy examining this relative stranger in his house—and he didn't mean Greg. Maya was flourishing into a young woman, with her new hair and pressed clothes and boyfriend and school and career trajectory... and he wasn't a part of it. Not any of it.

Despite everything that had happened, Maya hadn't deterred from the goal she had set for herself almost two years earlier. She wanted to be a CIA agent—more than that, she wanted to become the youngest agent in the CIA's history. But it had nothing to do with following in her father's footsteps. She had been through some harrowing experiences of her own, chief among them being kidnapped by a psychopathic assassin and handed over to a human trafficking ring, and she wanted to be among the protectors who would keep such things from happening to other young women.

After testing out of her senior year of high school, and unbeknownst to Zero, Maya applied to the military academy West Point. Even though her grades were excellent, she had no ROTC experience and no plans for military service, and therefore wouldn't have made the most attractive candidate. But she had a plan for that too.

In an act of cunning and guile that foreshadowed an illustrious career in covert operations, Maya went over her father's head to fellow agent (and friend) Todd Strickland. Through him, and under the pretense of being Agent Zero's daughter, she managed to secure a letter of recommendation from then-president Eli Pierson, who thought he was doing Zero a personal favor. She was accepted into West Point, and moved to New York before the end of that first summer after discovering the truth about her mother.

Zero found out all of this while she was packing her bags. By then it was too late to stop her, though not for lack of trying. But no amount of pleading would dissuade her.

She was in her second year now, and even though the ties between father and daughter were nearly severed, Maria kept tabs on Maya as best she could and updated Zero. He knew that she was top of her class, excelling in everything she did, and earning admiration from the faculty. He knew that she was heading toward great things.

He just wished that it wasn't the same career path that had gotten her mother killed and ruined the relationship with her father.

"So." Greg cleared his throat, sitting beside Maya on the sofa while Zero sat across from them in a recliner. "Maya tells me you're an accountant?"

Zero smiled thinly. Of course Maya would choose such a bland occupation as his cover. "That's right," he said. "Corporate finance."

"That's... interesting." Greg forced a smile in return.

What a sycophant. What does she see in this guy? "And what about you, Greg?" he asked. "What do you plan to do? Become an officer?"

"No, no, I don't think that's for me." The kid waved a hand as if swatting away the notion. "I plan to go into the NCAVC. Specifically, the BAU..." He trailed off and chuckled lightly to himself. "Sorry, Mr. Lawson, I forgot I was talking to a civilian. I want to be an FBI agent, with their Behavioral Analysis Unit. Violent Crime Division. You know, the guys who hunt serial killers and domestic terrorists and such."

"Sounds exciting," Zero said flatly. Of course he knew what the NCAVC was, and the BAU—just about anyone who turned on prime time television knew that—but he didn't say so. In fact, he had little doubt that if this smarmy kid across from him knew who *he* was, Agent Zero, he would wipe that unctuous grin off his face and devolve into a slobbering fan in point-five seconds flat.

But he couldn't say any of that. Instead he added, "Sounds ambitious, too."

"Greg can do it," Maya chimed in. "He's top of second class."

"That means 'junior,'" Greg offered to Zero. "But we don't call them that at The Point. And Maya here is the best in third class." He reached over and gently squeezed Maya's knee.

Zero had to physically restrain himself from his lip curling in a snarl. Suddenly he understood why Maya brought this boy with her; he was more than just a buffer between them. With him there, they couldn't talk openly. There would be no talk of the CIA, no talk of the past. Hell, he wasn't even sure he could ask the one thing he wanted to ask the most, which was about Sara.

Maya leaving for school crushed him. But Sara…even after all this time, it felt like that nail in the coffin had pierced straight through to his heart.

Greg was still talking, saying something about the FBI and cleaning house in light of the scandal that had rocked the former administration, and how his family had connections, or something of the like. Zero wasn't listening. He looked over at her, his daughter, the young woman he had raised, given everything he could. He had changed her diapers. Taught her to walk and talk and write and play softball and use a fork. He'd grounded her, hugged her when she cried, brightened her day when she was feeling down, put Band-Aids on scraped knees. He'd saved her life and gotten her mother killed.

When he looked over at her, tried to catch her eye, she looked away.

And in that moment, he knew. There would be no reconciliation, at least not tonight. This was a formality. This was Maya's way of saying *you deserve to know that I'm alive and well, but not much more than that.*

She stared at the carpet while Greg droned on about something or other, her gaze pensive. Her smile faltered, and as it vanished, so did Zero's hope of getting his daughter back.

Chapter Three

Maya dipped a crust of sourdough into the Polish stew and chewed it slowly. It was delicious, better than the food that the academy served, but she didn't have much of an appetite. Her dad was seated across from her at the small dining table, with Maria on her left and Greg to the right.

He was staring at her again.

She wished she hadn't come. She didn't owe him anything. And she knew that she couldn't bring herself to look up, to look into his eyes and see the unmasked pain of their rift. So instead she stared at a mottled chunk of kielbasa in her bowl.

Being here, in this new house and seeing him living with Maria, dark circles forming under his eyes and weight pinched around his midsection, her own father felt like a stranger to her. He no longer had the youthful, playful light in his eyes like he did when they were growing up. She hadn't heard his laugh in more than a year. She missed their sarcastic, quipping exchanges and at times heated debates.

"Isn't that right, Maya?"

"Hmm?" She looked up at the sound of her name to find Greg gazing at her expectantly. "Oh. Yeah. That's right." *Good god, is he still talking?*

Greg was not actually her boyfriend. At least she didn't think of it like that. They were being casual about it, unofficial. She knew he liked her—they'd made out a few times, though she wouldn't let him get any farther than that—yet she couldn't help but think it was more of a status thing for him than anything else. He came from a good family, a mother in politics and a father high up in the NSA. She was top of her class and (depending on who asked) likely better than him at most things, particularly academics. Some of the other cadets in second and third class made jokes about the two of them being "the prom king and queen of West Point."

He was cute. He was athletic. He was generally nice enough. But he was also a blowhard, self-centered, and completely oblivious to his faults.

"If you ask me," Greg was saying, "Pierson should have done hard time. My mother says—my mother was the mayor of Baltimore for two years, did I mention that? Anyway, she says that his negligence was enough to impeach him, or at least indict him when he left office..."

Stop staring at me. She wanted to blurt it out, to shout it even, but she held her tongue. She could *feel* how desperate her father was to talk to her. That was part of the reason she brought Greg, so that they couldn't open any cans of worms during this visit. She knew he wanted to ask about Sara. She knew he wanted to apologize, to try to make amends, to put all the ugliness behind them.

The truth was, she didn't hate him. Not anymore. To hate someone required energy, and she was putting everything she had into school. To her, he was a non-issue. This visit was not reconciliatory; it was bureaucracy. Decorum. Etiquette. The values that the academy instilled in its cadets were not entirely applicable to Maya's unique situation, but her takeaway was that she should at least have a check-in with the man who raised her, this shell of his former self. If for no other reason than to prove to herself that she could still stand to be in the same room as him.

But now she wished she hadn't.

"So," Maria said suddenly. Greg had stopped talking long enough to spoon some stew into his mouth, and Maria was taking full advantage of the temporary reprieve. "Maya. Have you spoken to your sister lately?"

The question took her off guard. She had expected it from her dad, but not from Maria. Still, it was as good a time as any to practice the skills she'd been developing on her own time. She fought the instinct to display any betraying expressions and instead smiled lightly.

"I have," Maya replied. "Just yesterday, in fact. She's well." Only half of that was a lie.

"You have a sister?" Greg asked.

Maya nodded. "Two years younger. She's in Florida on a work-study program. Very busy." Another lie, but she told it with ease. She was getting better at that all the time, and often told small, off-the-cuff fibs just for practice—and, admittedly, for a bit of a thrill.

"And, uh…" Her dad cleared his throat. "She's getting by okay? She has everything she needs?"

"Mm-hmm," Maya answered curtly without looking at him. "Doing great."

Greg simpered as he turned to her father. "You ask that like you don't talk to her, Mr. Lawson."

"It's like Maya said," her dad answered quietly. "Sara is very busy."

Maya knew that her own sudden departure was a blow to him. But if that was the case, then Sara leaving was a death stroke.

In that first summer, just a few months after their father saved President Pierson's life, after he told them the truth about their mother and the tension in their home was sky-high, Maya confided her plans in her sister. She told Sara that she had tested out of her senior year of high school and was running down admission to West Point.

As long as she lived, she would never forget the panicked expression on her little sister's face. *Please. Please don't,* Sara had begged her. *Don't leave me alone with him. I can't do it.*

As much as it broke her heart, Maya had made her plans and intended to see them through. So Sara made some of her own. She went online and found a lawyer who would take her case pro bono. Then she filed for emancipation. She knew it was a long shot; there was no proof or evidence of neglect, abuse, or anything like that.

But in a turn that shocked both sisters, their father did not fight it. Less than two weeks after Maya left for military school in New York, her dad attended the court date and, in front of a judge, told his then-fifteen-year-old daughter that if she wanted freedom from him enough to do this, to take him to court for it, she could have her freedom.

That same night came another event that Maya would not soon forget. Her father called her. She ignored it. She still hated him back then. He left her a voicemail that she didn't listen to for two days. When she finally did, she wished she hadn't. His voice wavering, breaking even, he told her that Sara was gone. He admitted that he deserved all of it and then some. He apologized three times, and told her he loved her.

It would be another six months before they spoke again.

But Maya did keep up with her sister. Upon emancipation, Sara packed up what she could carry and got on a bus. She ended up in Florida and took the first job she found, as a cashier in a thrift store. She still worked there. She lived in a co-op, a rented house with five other people. She shared a bedroom with a girl a couple years older than her, and a bathroom with everyone else.

Maya made sure to call her sister at least once a week, and more when her schedule allowed. Sara always promised that she was doing fine, but Maya wasn't sure she could believe it. She'd left high school with the assurance that she'd go back, but she never did. These days Maya didn't bother trying to convince her to return; instead, she pushed for Sara to test for her GED. Just another thing Sara claimed she'd do. Someday.

Maya lived at the academy year-round, and was given a stipend every semester for uniforms, books, food, and the like. She usually didn't have much left over, but she sent her sister some money when she could. Sara was always appreciative.

Neither of them needed anything from him anymore. They didn't *want* anything from him anymore.

They really had talked the day prior; that part wasn't a lie. Sara was sixteen now, and one of the girls in her co-op was teaching her to drive. It pained Maya that she was missing out on such important parts of Sara's life, but she had her own goals and was determined to meet them.

Simply put, the truth about their mother's death and their father's lies had driven a wedge between not only them and their father, but the two girls as well. They were on separate paths, and though they could keep in touch and help each other when able, neither was about to go too far out of their way to disrupt their own lives.

"Would anyone like some more?" Maria offered. "There's plenty."

Maya's attention snapped back to the dinner table. She'd been lost in her own thoughts, and when she looked around she saw that everyone else was finished eating. Still she set the spoon down. She just wanted this visit to be over, to thank them and get the hell out of there. "No thank you. It was very good."

"Agreed," said Greg enthusiastically. "Absolutely delicious." And then the blond idiot went and opened his big mouth yet again. "Thank you, Mrs. Lawson."

A flash of anger combusted inside her like a swelling backdraft. The words forced their way out of Maya's mouth before she even thought about them. "She is *not* Mrs. Lawson."

Maria did a double-take. Her father continued to stare, but now his eyes were wide in surprise and his mouth slightly open.

Greg cleared his throat nervously. "Sorry," he muttered. "I just assumed..."

More anger welled inside her. "I told you that on the ride down here. You wouldn't *have* to assume anything if you stopped talking about yourself for five damn minutes!"

"Hey," Greg bristled. "You can't talk to me like that—"

"Why not?" she challenged. "Is your mommy going to do something about it? Yeah, Greg, I know, she was the mayor of Baltimore for two years. You only mention it every other sentence. No one gives a shit!"

His throat flexed and his face flushed red, but he said nothing in return.

"Maya." Maria spoke softly, yet firmly. "I know you're upset, but it was just an accident. There's no reason to be rude. We're all adults here—"

"Oh." Maya scoffed. "I think there's *every* reason to be rude. Would you like me to enumerate them for you?" She was smart enough to know what was happening, but angry enough not to care. The truth was evident; she was still very angry with her father, despite telling herself she wasn't. But she had channeled all of that hostility and ire into school and her goals. Here and now, without any of that and sitting across from the man who had done this to her, it all came bubbling back to the surface. Her face felt hot and her heartbeat had doubled its pace.

She was suddenly keener than ever that she could not conjure a single happy memory from her childhood without the stabbing realization that her father's life, and by extension much of her own, was one big lie wrapped in a thousand smaller lies. The brightest light in her young life, her mother, had been cruelly and coldly extinguished because of it, at the hands of a man Maya had been foolish enough to put her own trust in.

And her father not only knew about it. He let that man, John Watson, walk away.

"Maya," her father started. "Please just—"

"You don't get to speak!" she snapped. "She's dead because of you!" She surprised even herself with the intensity of it, and was then surprised again that her dad did not have a burst of anger in response. Instead he clammed up, staring down at the table like a kicked pup.

"Look, I don't know what's going on here," Greg said gently, "but I think I'm going to bow out…"

He started to rise, but Maya stuck a threatening finger in his face. "Sit down! You're not going anywhere."

Greg immediately lowered himself back into his chair as if she were a drill sergeant ordering a private. Maria regarded her aloofly, one eyebrow arched slightly, as if waiting to see how this was going to play out. Her father's shoulders slumped and his chin nearly touched his collarbone.

"Goddammit," Maya muttered as she ran her hands over her short hair. She thought she was past all this, past the emotional surges that crashed on her like an errant wave, past the attempts to reconcile the smiling, humorous professor that she called Dad with a deadly covert agent who had been responsible for the trauma she would carry with her for the rest of her life. Past the late-night sobbing bouts when she changed her clothes and saw the thin white scars of the message she had carved into her own leg, back when she thought she was going to die and used her last ounce of strength to give him a clue to her sister's whereabouts.

Don't you dare cry.

"This was a mistake." She rose and started for the door. "I don't ever want to see you again."

She was too angry to cry, she realized. At least she was past that.

Maya slid behind the wheel of the rental car and turned the key in the ignition before Greg came jogging out after her.

"Maya!" he called. "Hey, wait!" He tried to pull the handle of the passenger side, but she'd already locked the doors. "Come on. Let me in."

She started backing down the drive.

"This isn't funny!" He slammed a palm on the window. "How am I supposed to get back?"

"Your mom sounds useful," she shouted at him through the closed window. "Try giving her a call."

And then she drove away, down the street, with a tiny version of Greg standing in the rearview mirror with his hands on his head in disbelief. She knew she'd catch hell for that back at the academy, but in the moment she didn't care. Because as the foreign house of her father grew smaller behind her, it felt like a weight was lifting from her shoulders. She'd gone there that day out of some sense of family, a sense of responsibility. A burden, really.

But now, she realized, if she never saw them or that house again, it would be okay. She was fine on her own. There was no closure, and there never would be. Her mother was dead, and her father was dead to her.

Chapter Four

Karina Pavlo sat at the furthest corner of the bar, obscured by beer taps but with a clear view of the front entrance. She'd chosen a place that no one in their right mind would ever think to look for her, a seedy dive bar in the southeast quadrant of DC, not far from Bellevue. It was not the best of neighborhoods, and the day was quickly becoming dusk, but she was not concerned about petty thieves or would-be muggers. She had bigger problems than that.

Besides, she had just done some petty theft herself.

After eluding the Secret Service agent and hiding out in the bookstore for a short while, Karina risked heading back out onto the street for less than a block before ducking into a department store. Aside from the fact that she was shoeless, she was still well dressed and, holding her head high and walking confidently to avoid scrutiny, looked the part of any upper-middle-class businesswoman.

She headed straight to the women's department and grabbed some casual clothing off the rack, items that wouldn't draw a lot of attention. She left her skirt and blouse and blazer in the dressing room, pulled on a pair of sneakers, and walked back out a different entrance of the store without anyone looking twice at her. Two blocks later she stopped in at another store and, after pretending to browse for a few minutes, walked out with a pair of stolen sunglasses and a silk scarf that she tied over her dark hair.

Back on the street, she targeted a chubby man in a striped polo with a camera hanging around his neck. He couldn't have been more of a tourist if he was wearing a sandwich board that said so. She bumped into him roughly as they passed, gasping and immediately apologizing. His face turned red and he opened his mouth to shout at her, until he saw that she was a slight, pretty brunette. He muttered an apology and scurried along on his way, unaware that his wallet was missing. Karina had always been quick with her hands. She did not condone stealing, but this was a time of necessity.

The wallet had a little less than a hundred dollars in cash in it. She took the money and dropped the rest of it, ID and credit cards and photos of kids, into a large blue postal box on the next corner.

Finally she took a cab east, across town, where she headed into the dive bar, its windows darkened and the place smelling like cheap beer, and took a seat at the bar and ordered a soda.

The television suspended over the beer taps was on and tuned into a news station, the current story an update on sports scores from the night prior. She sipped her soda, calming her nerves and wondering what she would do next. She couldn't go back to the hotel; that would be a fool's errand. Besides, there was nothing for them to find there but clothes and toiletries. She had one phone number memorized, but she was hesitant about finding a pay phone. They were getting rarer, even in the cities. The Secret Service had her cell phone, and they might be watching the pay phones.

She was considering asking the bartender to use their phone, but her contact was an international number and that might draw undue attention.

The next time Karina glanced up at the television, the story had changed. A male anchor she didn't recognize was talking at her, and though the volume was too low to hear she could clearly see the words on the black ticker across the bottom of the screen: HARRIS AND KOZLOVSKY HOLD PRIVATE MEETING.

"*Korva*," she sighed. Shit. Then in English: "Can you turn this up, please?"

The bartender, a Latino man with a handlebar mustache, scowled at her for a moment before turning his back to show just how blatantly he was ignoring her.

"*Zalupa*," she muttered, an unkind curse in Ukrainian. Then she leaned over the bar, located the remote, and turned the volume up herself.

"...anonymous source inside the White House has confirmed that a private meeting was held earlier today between President Harris and Russian President Aleksandr Kozlovsky," the anchor declared. "The two days since Kozlovsky arrived in the United States have been highly publicized and well documented, yet the notion of a closed-door meeting held in a conference room of the White House basement has many people nervously reminiscing on the events from nearly a year and a half ago.

"In response to the leak, the press secretary issued this statement, and I quote: 'Both presidents have been under a veritable microscope these past two days, due largely to the indiscretions of their predecessors. President Harris and his guest simply wanted a brief reprieve from the limelight. The meeting in question was less than ten minutes in length, and the subject of this meeting was for each leader to become better acquainted with the other without the pressure of media presence or scrutiny. I can assure each and every person here and tuning in that there was no clandestine agenda. This was simply a closed-door conversation, and nothing more,' end quote. When questioned further about the specifics of this meeting, the press secretary joked, 'I wasn't privy to details, but I believe the meeting was largely about their mutual love of scotch and dachshunds.'

"Though the true nature of the meeting remains shrouded in secrecy, we have confirmed through our anonymous source that there was only one other person present in the room with the two leaders—an interpreter. Though her identity has not been released, we have confirmed that she is female, and a native to Russia. Now the world wants to know: were the two leaders discussing drinks and dogs? Or does this unidentified female interpreter hold the answer to a question that many Americans have on their—"

The television suddenly flickered out, the screen turning black. Karina looked down sharply to see that the Latino bartender had grabbed the remote and turned it off.

She was about to call him an asshole in plain English but stopped herself. There was no point picking fights; she was supposed to be incognito. Instead she mulled over the report. The White House had not released her identity, at least not yet. They wanted to find her and silence her before she could tell anyone what she had heard. What the two presidents were planning. What Kozlovsky had asked of the American leader.

But Karina had an ace in the hole—two of them, in fact. She again absentmindedly caressed the pearl studs in her ears. Two years earlier, she had been translating for a German diplomat who had accused her of misinterpreting his words. She hadn't, but it had almost landed her in some real trouble. So with some help from her sister and her contacts in FIS, Karina had the earrings made. Each of them contained a tiny unidirectional microphone that recorded a speaker on either side of her; together, the two earrings combined would capture any conversation that Karina interpreted. It was, of course, highly illegal, but also very handy, and since she had begun using them she hadn't found any reason to need the recordings and subsequently deleted them.

Until now. Every word that had been spoken between her, Harris, and Kozlovsky was contained in those two studs. Getting them into the right hands was all that mattered now.

She slid silently off the stool and stole toward the rear of the bar, making a beeline for the bathroom, but then kept on going down a dingy corridor and pushed out through a metal security door and into a rear alley.

Out on the street, Karina tried to look as cool and casual as possible, but inside she was terrified. It was bad enough that the Secret Service was looking for her—and no doubt had the police involved, possibly even the FBI—but when Kozlovsky found out, he would send his own people to find her, if he hadn't already.

And worse, any John Doe citizen who heard the news might look twice at her and wonder. Americans were not the most open-minded when it came to foreigners. Luckily she could do a decently passable American accent. At least she hoped it was passable; she'd never had to use it in any serious situation before. So far she had gotten by just fine pretending to be Russian.

I need a phone. She couldn't risk a pay phone. She couldn't steal a cell phone; the victim would report it and the Secret Service could easily run down the device's location and last-called number, which would put Veronika at risk as well.

Think, Karina. She pushed the sunglasses up the bridge of her nose and looked around—*a-ha.* The answer was right there in front of her, half a block away and across the street. She glanced both ways and trotted over to the cellular store.

The shop was tiny, smelled of disinfectant, and harshly lit by too many fluorescent tube lights. The young black man behind the counter couldn't have been more than twenty, poking idly at a phone in front of him with his chin in his hand. There was no one else in the store.

Karina stood there for a long moment before he looked up at her, his gaze flat.

"Yeah?"

"Do you jailbreak phones here?" she asked.

He looked her up and down. "We're not allowed to sell that service."

Karina smiled. "That's not what I was asking." She hoped her American accent wasn't betraying her. It sounded rough to her ears, tinged with a Ukrainian lilt. "I'm not a cop, and I don't have a phone. I want to use one. I need to make a call on an off-network device via Wi-Fi. Preferably through a third-party app. Something that can't be traced."

The kid blinked at her. "What do you mean, you gotta make a call?"

She sighed curtly, trying not to grow irritated. "I don't know how to make it any clearer than that." She leaned over the counter and lowered her voice conspiratorially, even though there was no one else in the store. "I'm in some trouble, okay? I need five minutes with the type of phone I just described. I can pay. Can you help me or not?"

He eyed her suspiciously. "What kind of trouble you in? Like with the police?"

"Worse," she said. "Look, if it was the kind of thing I could tell you, do you think I'd be here at all?"

The kid nodded slowly. "All right. I got what you need. And you can use it. Five minutes... fifty bucks."

Karina scoffed aloud. "Fifty dollars for a five-minute call?"

The clerk shrugged. "Or you can try someplace else."

"Fine." She pulled the wad of cash she'd stolen from the tourist, counted out fifty, and slid it across to him. "There. The phone?"

The kid rummaged around under the counter and came out with an iPhone. It was a few years old, one corner of the screen cracked, but it powered on just fine. "This one here is off-network, and has a Chinese calling app on it," he told her. "It reroutes through a randomized out-of-service number." He slid it over to her. "Five minutes."

"Great. Thank you. You have a back office here?" To his frown she added, "Obviously this is a private call."

The kid hesitated, but then jerked a thumb over his shoulder. "Go ahead."

"Thanks." She headed into a tiny back office with wood-paneled walls and a melamine table as a desk, covered in invoices and assorted other paperwork. She opened the calling app on the phone, dialed the number she knew by heart, and waited as it rerouted. It took several seconds, and for a moment she thought it wouldn't work, that the call wouldn't go through, but at last it rang.

Someone answered. But they did not speak.

"It's me," she said in Ukrainian.

"Karina?" The woman on the other end of the line sounded confused. "What are you doing calling this number?"

"I need help, V."

"What's wrong?" Veronika asked urgently.

Karina did not know where to begin. "There was a meeting," she said. "Between Kozlovsky and Harris..."

"I saw the news." Veronika sucked in a breath as she realized. "You? You were the interpreter in that meeting?"

"Yes." Karina quickly recounted what had happened, from her time with the two presidents to fleeing from the Secret Service agent. She tried to keep her voice steady as she concluded, "If they find me, they will kill me, V."

"My god," Veronika said breathily. "Karina, you need to tell someone what you know!"

"I'm telling you. Don't you see? I cannot take this to the media. They will stifle it. They will deny it. You are the only one I can trust with this information. I need to get the earrings to you."

"You have them?" Veronika asked. "You recorded the meeting?"

"Yes. Every word."

Her sister thought for a long moment. "FIS has a liaison in Richmond. Can you get there?"

Veronika, Karina's older sister by two years, was a top agent of the Foreign Intelligence Service, Ukraine's version of the CIA. It was no secret to Karina that FIS had several sleepers in the United States. The thought of being under their protection was an attractive one, but she realized she could not risk it.

"No," she said at last. "They will expect me to flee. I'm certain they'll be watching the airports and highways carefully."

"Then I will tell him to come to you—"

"You are not understanding, Veronika. If they find me, they will kill me. And anyone who is with me. I will not be responsible for that." Her voice caught in her throat. Standing there in the dim back office of a shady cellular store, the events of the past few hours finally caught up with her. But she would not let her emotions get the best of her. "I'm scared, V. I need help. I need a way out."

"I will not let anything happen to you," her sister promised. "I have an idea. I will have our liaison make an anonymous tip to DC Metro that the meeting was recorded—"

"What? Are you insane?" Karina snapped.

"And I will have him tell the media as well."

"Christ, V, you have lost your mind!"

"No. Listen to me, Karina. If they believe you possess a recording, then you have a bargaining chip. Without it you are as good as dead. This way, they will want you alive. And if the tip comes from Richmond, they will believe you have fled the city. In the meantime, I will work on an extraction and get you the hell out of here."

"The heat is too much for you to send one of your own to retrieve me," Karina said. "I won't have anyone compromised or killed because of me."

"But you can't do this alone, *sestra*." Veronika was silent for a moment before adding, "I think I might know someone who can help."

"FIS?" Karina asked.

"No. An American."

"Veronika—"

"He is former CIA."

That clinched it. Her sister had truly lost her mind, and Karina told her so.

"Do you trust me?" Veronika asked.

"A minute ago I would have said yes…"

"Trust me now, Karina. And trust this man. I will tell you where to go and when to be there."

Karina sighed. What choice did she have? V was right. She could not elude the Secret Service, the Russians, and anyone else they sent by herself. She needed help. And she did trust her sister, even if this plan sounded ludicrous.

"All right. How will I know this man?"

"If he is still good at his job, you won't," Veronika said. "But he will know you."

Chapter Five

Sara inspected herself in the bathroom mirror as she adjusted her ponytail. She hated her hair. It was too long; she hadn't had it cut in months. Her ends were split badly. About six weeks earlier she'd let Camilla dye it red with a box from the drugstore, and though she'd liked it at the time her bright blonde roots were showing through the first inch from her scalp. It wasn't a good look.

She hated the dark blue polo she had to wear to work. It was a size too big for her slight frame, with the words "Swift Thrift" screen-printed on the left breast. The letters were faded, the edges chipped from repeat washings.

She hated going to the thrift shop, with its constant odor of mothballs and stale sweat, pretending to be nice to rude people. She hated that nine bucks an hour was the best she could do at sixteen without a high school diploma.

But she had made a decision. She was independent.Mostly.

The bathroom door swung open suddenly, forced from the other side. Tommy slid to a halt when he saw her standing in front of the mirror.

"What the hell, Tommy!" Sara shouted. "I'm in here!"

"Why didn't you lock the door?" he shot back.

"It was closed, wasn't it?"

"Well, hurry up! I have to take a piss!"

"Just get out!" She shoved the door closed and left the older boy cursing on the other side of it. Life in the co-op was anything but glamorous, but she'd gotten used to it in the year that she'd been living there. Or had it been more now? Thirteen months or so, she reasoned.

She brushed some mascara on her eyelashes and inspected herself once more. *Good enough,* she thought. She didn't like to wear a lot of makeup, despite Camilla's best efforts. And besides, she was still growing into her looks.

She exited the bathroom, which opened onto the kitchen, just in time to see Tommy leaning away from the sink and zipping up his fly.

"Oh my god." She winced. "Tell me you did *not* just pee in the sink."

"You were taking too long."

"God, you're disgusting." She crossed to the old beige refrigerator and took out a bottle of water—no way she was drinking tap water now, that was for sure—and as she closed it again, the whiteboard caught her eye.

She winced again.

On the refrigerator door was a magnetic dry-erase board with six names in black marker, each of the tenants of the co-op. Written beneath each name was a number. The six of them were responsible for a share of the rent and equal part of the bills each month. If they couldn't pay their share, they had a three-month grace period to wipe out their debt, or else they would have to leave. And the number under Sara's name was the largest.

The co-op was far from the worst place to live in Jacksonville. The old house needed some repairs, but it wasn't a disaster. There were four bedrooms, three of them occupied by two people each and the fourth used as storage and workspace.

Their landlord, Mr. Nedelmeyer, was a German guy in his early forties who had a bunch of properties like this one in the Jacksonville metro area. He was pretty laid back, all things considered; in fact, he insisted that they simply call him "Needle," which to Sara sounded like something you'd call a drug dealer. But Needle was an easy man to deal with. He didn't care if they had friends over, or threw the occasional party. He didn't even care about the drugs. He had only three major rules: If you get arrested, you're out. If you can't pay after three months, you're out. If you assault another tenant, you're out.

At the moment, staring at the whiteboard on the fridge, Sara was worried about the second rule. But then she heard a voice right in her ear that made her worry about the third rule.

"What's the matter, little girl? Worried about that big scary number under your name?" Tommy laughed like he'd told a great joke. He was nineteen, lanky and bony, with tattoos up both arms. He and his girlfriend Jo shared one of the co-op's bedrooms. Neither of them worked; Tommy's parents wired him money every month, more than enough to cover their co-op expenses. The rest they spent on coke.

Tommy thought he was some kind of badass. But he was just a suburban kid on vacation.

Sara turned slowly. The older boy was nearly a whole foot taller, and standing only a few inches away he towered over her. "I think," she said slowly, "you should take a couple of steps back and get out of my face."

"Or what?" He grinned maliciously. "You gonna hit me?"

"Of course not. That would be against the rules." She smiled innocently. "But you know, the other night I took a little video. You and Jo, doing a line off the coffee table."

A flash of fear crossed Tommy's face, but he stood his ground. "So? Needle doesn't care about that."

"No, you're right. He doesn't." Sara lowered her voice to a whisper. "But Thomas Howell, Esquire, down at Binder & Associates? He might care about that." She cocked her head to one side. "That's your dad, isn't it?"

"How do you...?" Tommy shook his head. "You wouldn't dare."

"Maybe not. That's up to you." She walked past him, bumping her shoulder roughly against his as she did. "Stop pissing in the sink. That's gross." And she headed upstairs.

Sara had left Virginia more than a year earlier as a frightened and naïve fifteen-year-old girl. It was hardly more than a year later, but she'd changed. On the bus between Alexandria and Jacksonville, she'd made two rules for herself. The first was that she was not going to ask anyone for anything, least of all her dad. And she stuck by it. Maya helped her out a bit from time to time, and Sara was grateful—but she never asked for it.

The second rule was that she was not going to take shit from anyone, period. She'd been through too much. She had seen things that she could never talk about. Things that still kept her awake at night. Things that a guy like Tommy could never imagine. She was beyond pettiness, past teenage angst. Past her own past.

Upstairs she pushed open the door to the bedroom that she and Camilla shared. It was set up like a dorm room, two twin beds sitting against opposite walls with a lane between them and a shared nightstand. They had a small vanity and a closet that they split. The roommate in question was still in bed, lying awake on her back and scrolling through social media on her phone.

"Hey," she said with a yawn as Sara entered. Camilla was eighteen, and thankfully pleasant. She was the first friend Sara had made in Florida; it was her online ad for a roommate at the co-op that had brought Sara there in the first place. They'd gotten along well. In fact, Camilla was teaching her to drive. She'd taught her how to put on mascara and how to pick out clothes that flattered her narrow frame. Sara had picked up a lot of new terms and mannerisms from her. Kind of like a big sister.

Like the kind of big sister that doesn't abandon you with a man you can't stand.

"Hey yourself. Get out of bed, it's almost ten." Sara grabbed her purse from the nightstand and made sure she had everything she'd need.

"I had a late night." Camilla worked as a waitress and bartender at a local seafood place. "But hey, look at this stack." She flashed a thick wad of cash, tips from the night before.

"Great," Sara muttered. "I got to get to work."

"Cool. I'm off tonight. You want me to do your hair again? It's looking a little haggard."

"Yeah, I know, it looks like shit," Sara snapped irritably.

"Whoa, hostile." Camilla frowned. "What's got your panties twisted?"

"I'm sorry. Just Tommy, being an ass."

"Forget that guy. He's a poser."

"I know." Sara sighed and rubbed her face. "Okay. I'm off to the mines."

"Wait up. You seem pretty high strung. You want a bar?"

Sara shook her head. "No, I'm okay." She took two steps to the door. "Screw it, yeah."

Camilla grinned and sat up in bed. She reached over for her own purse and took out two items—an orange prescription bottle with no label and a small plastic cylinder with a red cap. She shook out a single oblong blue Xanax from the bottle, dropped it into the pill grinder, and screwed the red cap tightly, crushing the bar into powder. "Hand."

Sara held her right hand out, palm down, and Camilla shook out the powder onto the fleshy bridge between her thumb and forefinger. Sara brought her hand to her face, plugged one nostril, and sniffed.

"Attagirl." Camilla smacked her lightly on the butt. "Now get outta here before you're late. See you tonight."

Sara flashed a peace sign as she closed the door behind her. She could taste the bitter powder at the back of her throat. It wouldn't take long for it to kick in, but she knew that one bar would barely get her through half the day, if that.

It was still hot out, even for October, like the Indian summers they sometimes experienced in Virginia. But she was getting used to the weather. She liked it, the almost year-round sunshine, being close to the beach. Life wasn't always great, but it was a far sight better than it had been two summers ago.

Sara was barely out the door when her phone rang in her purse. She already knew who it would be, one of the only people who ever called her.

"Hey," she answered as she walked.

"Hi." Maya's voice sounded quiet, strained. Sara could tell right away that she was upset about something. "Got a minute?"

"Uh, a few. I'm on my way to work." Sara looked around. She didn't live in a bad neighborhood, but it got a little rougher as she neared the thrift shop. She'd never had a problem herself, but she also stayed alert to her surroundings and kept her head up while she walked. A girl distracted by her phone was a potential target. "What's up?"

"I, uh..." Maya hesitated. Being sullen and reluctant was unusual for her. "I saw Dad last night."

Sara stopped in her tracks, but said nothing. Her stomach tightened instinctively as if she was preparing for a punch to the gut.

"It... didn't go well." Maya sighed. "I ended up shouting some things, storming out—"

"Why are you telling me this?" Sara demanded.

"What?"

"You know that I don't want to see him. I don't want to hear about him. I don't even want to think about him. So why are you telling me this?"

"I just thought you might want to know."

"No," Sara said forcefully. "You had a bad experience, and you wanted to talk to someone that you think might understand. But I'm not interested. I'm done with him. Okay?"

"Yeah." Maya sighed. "I think I am too."

Sara hesitated a moment. She'd never heard her sister sound so defeated. But she stood by her position. "Good. Move on with your life. How's school?"

"School's great," Maya said. "I'm top of my class."

"Of course you are. You're brilliant." Sara smiled at that as she resumed her walk. But at the same time, she noticed movement on the sidewalk near her feet. A shadow, stretched long with the midmorning sun, was keeping pace with her own. Someone walking not far behind her.

You're being paranoid. It wouldn't be the first time she mistook a pedestrian as a pursuer. It was part of the unfortunate fallout of her experiences. Even so, she slowed as she reached the next intersection to cross the street.

"But seriously," Maya said through the phone. "You're doing okay?"

"Oh, yeah." Sara paused and waited for the light. So did the shadow. "I'm doing great." She could have turned and looked at them, made them aware that she was aware, but she kept her eyes forward and waited for the signal to cross to see if they would follow.

"Good. I'm glad. I'll try to send you a little something in a couple weeks."

"You don't have to do that," Sara told her. The light changed. She strode briskly across the crosswalk.

"I know I don't have to. I *want* to. Anyway, I'll let you get to work."

"I'm off tomorrow." Sara reached the opposite corner and continued on her way. The shadow kept pace. "Call you then?"

"Definitely. Love you."

"Love you too." Sara ended the call and stuck her phone back in her purse. Then, without warning, she made an abrupt left turn and jogged a few paces, just to get out of his line of sight. She turned, folded her arms across her chest, and put on her very best stern expression as her pursuer rounded the corner after her.

He practically skidded to a stop when he saw her there waiting for him.

"For a supposedly covert operative, you're shit at this," she told him. "I smelled your cologne."

Agent Todd Strickland smirked. "Nice to see you too, Sara."

She did not return the smile. "Still keeping tabs on me, I see."

"What? No. I was in the area, working an op." He shrugged. "I saw you on the street, figured I'd come say hi."

"Uh-huh," she said flatly. "In that case, hi. Now I have to go to work. Bye." She turned and walked away briskly.

"I'll walk with you." He trotted to catch up to her.

She scoffed. Strickland was young for a CIA agent, not yet thirty years old—and, she realized, irritatingly handsome—but he also reminded her too much of her father. The two were friends, going back nearly two years when Sara and her sister had been kidnapped by the Slovakian traffickers. Strickland had helped rescue them, and at that time he'd made a promise that no matter what happened, he would do whatever he could to keep the two girls safe.

Apparently that meant using CIA resources to keep abreast of Sara's whereabouts.

"So things are good?" he asked her.

"Yup. Peachy. Now go away."

But still he walked beside her. "That guy in your building still giving you grief?"

"Oh my god," she groaned. "What, did you bug the place?"

"I just want to make sure you're okay—"

She spun on him. "You're not my dad. We're not even friends. Once upon a time, maybe you were a…I don't know. Glorified babysitter. But now you're coming off like a fucking stalker." She had known that he was tracking her for some time; this was not the first occasion in which he'd suddenly appeared in Florida. "I don't want you here. I don't want to be reminded of that life. So how about you tell me what you want from me, and we can go our separate ways?"

Strickland barely reacted to the outburst. "I want you to be safe," he said plainly. "And, if I'm being honest, I want you to quit the drugs."

Sara's eyes narrowed and her mouth fell open a little. "Just who do you think you are?"

"Someone who cares. It would break your father's heart if he knew."

If he knew? "Oh, you mean you're not hand-delivering him weekly reports?"

Strickland shook his head. "Haven't seen him in months."

"So you're just following me out of some misguided sense of duty?"

The young agent smiled sadly and shook his head. "Whether you like it or not, there are still a lot of people out there that remember

Agent Zero. I hope the day never comes that you have to thank me for keeping an eye on you. But until then, I'm going to keep doing it."

"Yeah. I bet you will." She looked straight up, squinting at the bright sky. "What is it, a satellite? Is that how you watch me?" Sara stuck one arm over her head and flashed a middle finger to the clouds. "There's a photo for you. Send it to my dad as a Christmas card." Then she turned and started away.

"Sara," he called after her. "The drugs?"

Christ, why won't he go away? She turned to face him. "So I smoked a little weed. Who cares? It's practically legal here."

"Uh-huh. And the Xanax?"

The Xanax. Her first question was, how did he know about that? The second that crossed her mind was, why hadn't it kicked in yet? But she knew the answer to the latter already. Her body was getting too accustomed to a single bar. It wasn't enough anymore.

"And the coke?"

She laughed at him then, a bitter and caustic laugh. "Don't do that. Don't try to make me feel like some kind of criminal deviant because I tried something once or twice at a party."

"Once or twice, huh? You have these parties every night?"

Sara felt her face grow hot. It wasn't just because he had offended her; it was because he was right. It had started out as once or twice at a party, but then quickly became a bump after work. A little something to take the edge off. But she wasn't about to acknowledge that now.

"It must be so easy for you," she said. "Standing there, clean cut, Boy Scout, Army Ranger. CIA agent. Must be so easy to judge someone like me. You say you know what I've been through. But you don't understand it. You can't."

Strickland nodded slowly. He stared directly at her, with those eyes that she might have found charming if he was anyone other than who he was. "Yeah. I guess you're right. I wouldn't know what it was like to be emancipated at seventeen—"

"I was fifteen," Sara corrected.

"And I was seventeen. But you didn't know that about me, did you?"

She didn't. But she didn't give him the satisfaction of reacting.

"I joined the Army right away. A lot of states will let you do that. I had my first confirmed kill two days before my eighteenth birthday. Funny thing about the military. They don't call it 'murder' when you kill someone."

Sara bit her lip. She knew what it was like to kill someone. It had been a mercenary with the black ops team called The Division. He would have killed them, her and her sister, so Sara shot him in the neck. And though the nightmares still plagued her, she'd never once thought of it as murder.

"At one point I was on four different prescriptions," Strickland told her. "For PTSD. Anxiety. Depression. I abused them all. It was so much easier to be numb, to pretend that everything I did happened to someone else."

He smiled sadly. "And man, I was a good addict. No one knew. Or maybe no one cared as long as I was a good soldier. Eventually one of my Ranger pals found out. He started following me, keeping close tabs on me. It was so damned irritating. He even took me to see a therapist. It was really hard. It's so much harder to quit and deal with all your shit than to just take something. I still see a therapist, twice a week when I'm able."

Sara stared at a small stone on the sidewalk to avoid looking at his eyes. After everything her dad had put her through, Strickland could have been lying. This could have just been a story. But he told it with a lot of conviction. *Just like he was trained.*

"I know that you've experienced some awful things," he continued. "I know how hard it is to commiserate with normal people and listen to them whine about money or jobs or relationships when you've seen real, genuine horrors in the world. But don't stand there and lean on your crutch and tell me that I don't understand it. Because you're lying to yourself right now. You're heading down a path that's going to lead to addiction. Homelessness. Death. Is that what you want?"

"What I want..." Her voice cracked.

You will not cry. You don't do that anymore.

She cleared her throat and said as clearly as she could, "What I want is for you to leave me alone. I want to make my own choices and live with the consequences. I want to be free of any and all reminders that any of those things ever happened. That includes you."

He nodded, with a faraway look in his eyes that suggested defeat. "Okay, Sara. If that's what you want, I'll leave you alone. Be well." Without another word, he turned and strode back the way he'd come.

She stood there for a long moment. She was already late for work; another minute or two wouldn't matter much. She wished she'd hit Camilla up for a second bar. It was still morning and this day was already awful.

What else could possibly go wrong?

Chapter Six

Zero was lying on his back on the sofa, one leg up and the other on the floor. He had no idea what time it was or how long he'd been lying there in a daze, replaying the scene from the night prior over and over in his head like a recurring nightmare.

He knew that Sara wanted nothing to do with him—she'd told him as much directly—but he thought he still had a chance to make things right with Maya. Until last night, that is.

I don't ever want to see you again.

He didn't even hear the door open, but then she was there, standing over him, looking down piteously.

"Hey," Maria said gently. "You okay?"

He frowned. It couldn't possibly be late enough for her to be home. "What time is it?"

"It's about one o'clock. I took a half-day. Tried to call you a bunch of times."

"Phone's on silent. Sorry." He pulled himself up to a seated position. Maria sat beside him and took his hand in both of hers.

"I'm sorry that happened. It's not how any of us wanted it to go."

He shook his head. "You know, I keep playing it again in my head, as if I can change how things went if I think about it enough."

"Don't do that. You're just torturing yourself—"

"It was that damned kid," Zero continued. That was the obvious point at which everything had taken a turn for the worst, when Greg opened his mouth and called Maria "Mrs. Lawson." That was Maya's trigger. "If only he hadn't been there. If only she came alone, maybe we could have actually talked, worked it out..."

He trailed off as a realization hit him. He had been so nervous about seeing Maya, so anxious about how the night might go that he hadn't given it a second thought—but he did now.

"You knew." He looked Maria in the eye, but she looked away. "You knew he was coming. When they came to the door, as I was coming downstairs, you said, 'You must be Greg.' You knew, and you didn't tell me?"

"Yes," Maria admitted. "I knew. Maya asked me if she could bring him. I didn't tell you because I knew what you were hoping for out of this visit, and I didn't want to disappoint you."

"So instead you just let it happen," he accused.

"I didn't know he was going to say what he did!" Maria countered.

Zero pulled his hand from hers and stood, pacing the small living room. He had pins and needles in his legs from lying for so long, but he ignored them, treading the carpet quickly. "I don't believe this. That might have been my last chance to reconcile with her."

"I don't believe that," Maria said gently. "I think she just needs time, Kent."

A wave of unjustified anger washed over him. "I asked you not to call me that."

"You said while Maya was here—"

"Ever," he said firmly. "I'm not Kent Steele anymore. And while we're at it, you're not even Maria Johansson. Your name is Clara Barren. Or did you forget that?"

Maria closed her eyes and sighed. It was true; Maria Johansson was her CIA agent alias. But when she became deputy director, she'd continued to use it to distance herself from her father and his name, to avoid any accusations of nepotism. She'd even mentioned once or twice about legally changing it, though she hadn't gone through with it yet.

"Why does it matter what we call each other?" she asked. "We have history. We know each other as Kent and Maria."

"Kent and Maria aren't real," he said forcefully. He felt heat in his face and fire in his belly. It was the first time in weeks he'd really felt much of anything, but what he was feeling wasn't anything good. "Look at us. Using fake names. Playing house."

"Is that what you think we're doing?" Maria's arms folded over her chest as her eyes narrowed. "Why don't you tell me what's really on your mind?"

Don't say it. You're being irrational. You'll regret it later.

Zero cast his eyes downward to the carpet. "I don't want to have a baby with you."

He waited, expecting her to explode. To shout. To throw things. But it was worse than that. Maria simply nodded. "I know you don't. All you seem to want to do is lie on the couch and live in your head, in the past. But not me. I'm a deputy director now. I've got plans. I want to make this world a better place, and I want to bring a child into it. I know what I want. Do you?"

"No," he said honestly. "Maybe that's why we're still calling each other Kent and Maria. Maybe … maybe that *is* who we really are. I failed as a professor, and turns out I'm a shitty father. The only thing I was ever good at was torturing and killing."

Maria shook her head adamantly. "I don't believe that. You can start over—"

"You're not getting it. I don't *want* to start over. I don't want to forget the past. How can we?"

"It's not about forgetting. It's about forgiving yourself."

"It's not that easy," he insisted. "I can't look at my own hands without seeing the blood on them. And …" He sighed. "And sometimes, it's hard to look at your face and not see the things we've done. To not see what I did. To not see *her*."

Maria's shoulders slumped slightly as she stared at the floor and said nothing.

"I'm not trying to hurt you," he told her. "I'm telling you because we're not supposed to have secrets between us. But …" He chuckled sadly. "But we've never been very good at that either, have we?"

"No," she agreed, "we haven't." She was silent for a long moment before asking, "Do you remember when we had that talk? The one where you told me you didn't want to get married again ... didn't even want to put 'labels' on what we were ..."

"Wait a second," he said defensively. "You can't put all that on me. We both agreed—"

"Is that how you remember it? Because that's not what happened. *You* told me those things, and I agreed because I wanted to be with you. I should have said something. I should have told you how unfair it was that you had your shot at a family and I didn't. But I said nothing.

"And the next day, I left on an op. They didn't even need me; I just didn't want to be here with you. I was angry and hurt. We needed intel from an arms dealer, an Italian. So I went undercover. Gained his trust ..." She trailed off.

Zero could see the writing on the wall, but still he frowned deeply. "What are you trying to say?"

"I slept with someone." She refused to meet his gaze, her voice breathy as if it was actively resisting the words.

Zero blinked. His lips parted slightly. A thousand questions formed in his head, but he couldn't bring himself to ask any.

"It didn't mean anything," she told him. "It was mechanical. Part of the job, just like filing a report. At least that's what I told myself. Because ..." She finally looked up, and her gray eyes met his. "Because maybe you're right. Maybe we are just playing house. Maybe none of that other stuff is meant for us. Maybe it's all just a charade."

Zero stared back. It was strange; he would have expected such an admission to crush him, but instead he just felt cold. Detached. "I'm not hearing an apology in any of this."

"Because I'm not giving you one," she said succinctly. "I did what I felt was necessary for the preservation of international security. That's not an excuse. It's part of who I am. I won't apologize for doing whatever is necessary."

He didn't know what to say or do. He wanted nothing more than this conversation to end, but there was no going back to the life they'd had yesterday after everything they'd each just shared. "So," he said quietly. "Where do we go from here?"

"I'm not sure. But I think we need some time," Maria suggested. "Some space ... apart."

Zero nodded. "Yeah. I ... I think I'll go for a drive." He strode to the kitchen and retrieved his phone and his car keys. He patted his back pocket to make sure he had his wallet.

"Where will you go?"

He didn't answer, because he didn't know. He grabbed his jacket from the hook by the door, and then he was outside. It was a breezy afternoon, not cold but foreshadowing the weather to come.

"Kent?" she called to him from the open doorway. "Will you be okay?"

He didn't want to answer to that name anymore. But still he nodded vaguely before getting into the car. He didn't have a destination in mind—at least he didn't think he did, but as soon as he considered where he would go, the answer popped into his mind instantly.

He knew exactly where he had to go.

Not thirty minutes later Zero parked the car in the long-term lot at Dulles. He cut the engine, and then sat there behind the wheel in silence for several minutes.

"What the hell are you doing?" he murmured to himself.

He wanted to be angry with Maria. She'd been unfaithful and justified it in a bizarre fashion. But nothing that she said was untrue.

If he was being honest with himself, he was angrier at Kent Steele than he was her.

I should call Alan. He needed a familiar voice, a friend, someone with a bendable ear to whom he could vent his frustrations over a few drinks.

He could hear Alan's voice in his head now: *Wanna know what I think? Tough, I'm going to tell you anyway. Stop being an idiot. Cool down, go home, and talk to her. It's Maria, for Christ's sake. You'll apologize, she'll apologize. Then you'll have terrific makeup sex.*

He pulled out his phone and made the call.

"Zero?"

"Yeah, Todd. It's me."

"Wow. Been a while." Strickland sounded as confused as he did relieved. "It's good to hear from you."

"You too." Zero got out of the car and headed toward the terminal. "I need an address."

"For what?"

"You know what." Zero knew damn well that Strickland was still keeping tabs on both his girls. The young agent had made a promise, and he was the kind of guy who kept it. Not like Maria.

Not like Zero.

"I need to see her, Todd."

Strickland sighed. "Look, I'll give it to you straight, Zero. I just came from there. I'm on my way back to DC now. She's… she won't be happy."

"I know." *But I've alienated just about everyone else in my life.* He needed to know if it was truly too late. Perhaps enough time had passed that Sara, his youngest, his baby girl, would be willing to make amends with her dad.

Or maybe I'm just a glutton for punishment.

"I'm not so sure it's a good idea…" Strickland said cautiously.

"And I'm not asking you," Zero said harshly. "This isn't a request, Todd. Tell me where to find my daughter."

Chapter Seven

Three and a half hours later, Zero stood in front of a beige storefront in a small strip mall in what he would consider a rough neighborhood of the city. Its façade was chipped and worn, and the particular store in question was lacking a sign. Instead, two words were painted on the inside of the window in large white strokes: SWIFT THRIFT.

Strickland had given him both her home address and her workplace and let him know that she'd be done with her shift when the thrift shop closed at seven. It was about quarter after five, but Zero couldn't wait that long. Besides, he was aware she lived with several roommates. By the looks of the small store, he had a better chance of having a private moment there than he did at her home.

Her home. His heart broke anew with the thought, the realization that the place she called home was no longer the same place he did.

He took a breath, summoning his courage with it, and went inside.

There was no bell or chime on the door, but it squeaked a little on its hinges. An odor struck him immediately, reminiscent of his grandmother's closet from when he was a little boy. Mothballs, he realized. That's what the place smelled like. And something else beneath it—mildew, perhaps. Some kind of dampness in the air.

He navigated slowly around racks of clothing, shelves of used toys, assorted items that had been given away in lieu of being thrown out: old suitcases, board games with worn boxes, VCRs, questionable appliances. The cash register was near the back of the store, and someone was standing before it, an old woman stooped with age.

Opposite her, facing slightly away from Zero, was Sara.

Seeing her again made his breath catch in his throat. She looked… she looked so grown up. He hardly recognized her. Her hair was red, though her blonde roots were showing. She wore dark mascara on her eyelashes that made her blue eyes shine fiercely. She had gotten her ears pierced, with a little silver hoop in each. But her face… he would recognize that face anywhere, at any age. If Maya was looking more and more like her father each day, Sara was growing to become a spitting image of Kate.

"Thank you," she said to her elderly customer. "See you next week, Mrs. G."

The elderly woman turned away, and Sara's attention shifted toward him. Zero quickly spun, facing away from her, pretending to inspect a cracked blender.

This was a mistake. You shouldn't have come. You're not in the right state of mind to be doing this. The elderly woman shuffled past him on her way to the door.

"Can I help you with something?" Sara asked. She was right behind him. It was too late to do anything now except turn around and face her and hope for the best.

So he did.

"Hi, Sara." He was surprised at how meek his voice sounded.

Her smile evaporated instantly into a blank stare. Then the corners of her mouth drooped and, as if in a slow-motion replay, her eyes became narrow and hard, tiny creases showing at their corners. Her teeth clenched together like a snarling dog.

And he, Zero, who had faced terrorists and biochemical weapons and active warheads, he shrank under her glare.

"No." She shook her head as if trying to jar something loose. "No. Get out."

"Sara, please—"

"Get. Out!" she screeched.

"Two minutes," he said quickly. "Just let me talk for two minutes…"

"I'm calling the police." She strode quickly back to the counter and grabbed up a cell phone with a scuffed cover. She didn't dial anything, not yet, but made a show of holding it upright, her thumb poised over the screen. "You don't get to just walk back into my life whenever you feel like it! I told you I didn't want to see you."

Zero held up his hands, palms out, as if approaching a frightened animal. "Sara," he said cautiously, "I just want to talk to you. Can you give me that?"

She scoffed. "Did Todd put you up to this?"

He frowned. "No. Todd didn't even want to tell me where you were."

"Yeah. Right. Do you think I'm stupid? First Maya calls me, then Todd shows up to lecture me. Now you appear out of nowhere. And that's just supposed to be a coincidence? Let me guess; he told you about the drug thing. And you decided to run down here and play dad. Is that it?"

"What?" His throat felt tight. "Sara, what drugs? Are you…are you doing…?"

"Don't play dumb with me," she hissed. "It's your job to lie."

Drugs? He already felt like enough of an utter failure, standing here in a stinking thrift shop where his teenage high-school-dropout daughter worked—all because of him. But this…it was too much.

"Come home," he managed to say. "Please. I…I need you. Maybe you need me too—"

For the briefest of moments, it looked as if her hard expression faltered into something that resembled regret. Or doubt. But then Sara shook her head fiercely. "You don't get to say that to me."

She pressed a few buttons on the phone and showed it to him. She had dialed 9-1-1, but hadn't yet made the call. "Get out."

"What are you going to tell them? That you're being harassed by your father? That someone's trying to help you?"

She stared him down defiantly as she pressed the call button and put it on speaker.

"Nine-one-one, what's your emergency?" said a hasty female dispatcher.

"I'm at the Swift Thrift on Twenty-second Avenue," Sara said into the phone, still staring him in the eye. "The man who killed my mother is here, and he has me cornered."

She'd done it. She'd actually done it.

Zero walked briskly down the block with his hands in his pockets, his head bowed low, barely attentive of his surroundings. He had no idea where he was and didn't care. He knew he was heading generally east; the sun was dipping low in the sky behind him.

Sara had called the police on him. Worse, she'd called him a murderer. He had no choice; he got out of there quickly, before any authorities arrived. The last thing he needed was to have to make an awkward call to Maria from a Florida jail.

Even as he left the shop, Sara shouted after him. Reminding him that she didn't want to see him, now or ever. That if he came back there'd be a restraining order.

So he walked, sweating a little under his light jacket but feeling cold, not paying any attention to the passersby or where he was going. Twice he walked right into a street and a car screeched to a halt, the driver honking and shouting angrily while Zero just walked on, wondering why they'd even bothered to stop. Life would get a lot simpler very quickly if they'd just hit him.

He walked until he couldn't walk anymore. He'd reached the ocean, a thin stretch of public beach that was nearly vacant with the setting sun.

I could keep walking, he thought. *Walk out into the surf until it's over my head.*

Instead he walked parallel to the beach, following it for more than a mile until the sand turned to pebbles. A long breakwater of large, sharp rocks jutted about a hundred yards out to sea. He walked out on it, ignoring the signs that suggested he didn't and stepping carefully from wet stone to wet stone. The rocks were porous, brown, and craggy, some stuck fast with barnacles, small crabs skittering out of his way.

He'd never truly known what it was like to feel alone. Even in the most desperate moments of his past he always remembered he had his girls waiting for him at home. And then when he didn't, at least he had Maria. Who did he have now? There was Alan. He was a good friend—a great friend, even. But compared to Reidigger faking his own death and spending the last four years living incognito, Zero's problems of being a bad father and partner would seem paltry. Laughable.

His phone rang in his pocket. He ignored it.

Before he knew it he'd reached the end of the jetty. The sea roiled beyond the rocks, spraying cold white foam on his clothes and face. There was a sign there, the metal post of it stuck between two large rocks at an awkward angle. *Danger,* it said. *Peligro.* In English and Spanish, it warned of riptides and advised against swimming past the breakwater.

His phone rang again. He didn't reach for it.

Zero knew about riptides, currents so strong and fast that even the best Olympic swimmers couldn't contend with them. They would carry you miles out to sea in no time, if they didn't drown you first.

What if I took one more step?

What if I just let it carry me out and vanished forever?

He laughed bitterly at himself. He didn't have it in him to take the step. He dared his feet to move.

"Why?" he asked aloud. *Why am I thinking like this?* But he already knew the answer. His whole adult life, he'd been needed. He'd been needed by his wife. Needed by his children. Needed by his students. Needed by his country. Until recently he didn't know what it was like not to be needed, and he didn't know how to handle it.

"You need to be needed." He chuckled sourly again. "What a fucked-up codependency."

His phone rang a third time, shattering his introspective moment. For some reason a rage ignited inside him, swift and hot and aimed at the device. He yanked the phone out of his pocket and reared back to hurl it into the unforgiving ocean.

But before he could throw it, it chimed again—a text message.

He slowly lowered his arm and read it. He didn't recognize the number, and the message was only two words.

Zero. Please.

And then the phone rang again.

"Who is this?" he snapped as he answered.

"Hello, Zero." The voice was calm, smooth, female, and accented, though her English was flawless. Vaguely familiar too, though he couldn't quite place it. "I need your help."

"Who is this?" he demanded again.

"You would remember me as Emilia Sanders."

What the hell? Sanders was an agent of the FIS, Ukraine's intelligence agency. Eighteen months earlier, she had been posing as a White House aide and had helped him uncover the conspiring cabal within President Pierson's cabinet.

He knew that Emilia Sanders was not her real name, and that she was Ukrainian, but nothing else about her.

"What do you want?"

"You know of the private meeting between Presidents Harris and Kozlovsky?" she asked quickly.

"I have no idea what you're talking about."

"Have you not been watching the news, Agent Zero?" she asked with grim amusement.

Another flash of anger bubbled up within him. "I'm not 'agent' anything. And no, I've been pretty careful to avoid the news. The whole world can go to hell as far as I care. Goodbye, Sanders—"

"Wait," she insisted. "When I helped you before, I asked for nothing in return. Now I am asking you for one minute."

He swore under his breath. He didn't owe her anything. "Fine," he relented. "One minute."

Emilia Sanders spoke quickly. "Yesterday there was a meeting between the US president and the Russian president. Private, closed-door. It lasted for only a few minutes, and besides the two presidents there is only one person in the world who knows what they discussed. An interpreter. She is on the run. They want to kill her. She needs help. There is no one else to turn to. She needs you."

Zero was silent for a long moment.

"Hello?" Sanders said. "Zero?"

"It's been one minute. Goodbye." He ended the call. "That's not your life anymore," he reminded himself. Then he turned and headed back down the breakwater toward the rocky beach.

His phone chimed with a new message: *They will kill her for what she knows.*

"Not my problem," he told the phone.

He reached the beach and considered calling an Uber back to the airport when he got yet another text message from Sanders.

She is my sister.

"Don't care," he muttered. His thumb floated to the side button to power the phone off, but it lingered. "Don't," he told himself. But then the browser was open, and his thumbs were typing as if they had a mind of their own.

He searched for the term "president meeting," and it seemed that it was plenty to go on. Every media outlet in the country had been covering the Russian president's visit, and every pundit had a theory about the brief private meeting Sanders had mentioned.

Zero was confused. The new US president, Harris, was supposed to be one of the good guys. He didn't know much about Harris's politics, but he knew the man had been busy cleaning house and undoing damage since he took office. The people liked him.

Then he saw something else. A breaking news report from only a few hours earlier. An anonymous tipster told the media that the interpreter had recorded the secret meeting. The White House was denying it, claiming that any recording she had must be fake, and that the woman was trying to extort both sides for some personal gain.

They had released her identity. A Ukrainian-born woman named Karina Pavlo. And with it, a photo from some identification database. She resembled Sanders, at least in that she was slight-framed, brunette, with dark eyes and an angular chin. Zero couldn't help but think that she was quite attractive, in a foreign and mysterious kind of way.

Another text came through.

She needs you.

A cool sea breeze ruffled his hair as Zero recalled the events of eighteen months earlier, when he had tried to warn Pierson about the conspiracy. He too had recordings. In response, the White House had labeled him a criminal. A domestic terrorist. They had discredited him publicly. They tried to ruin his life and get him killed.

Maybe Sanders was lying, and this interpreter was actually extorting two presidents. But if she wasn't, then the people with the power were doing the same thing to her that they'd tried to do to him.

"Is she really your sister?" he asked when Sanders answered his call.

"Yes."

"What's your name? Your real name."

Silence. Then: "Veronika Pavlo. And my sister is—"

"Karina Pavlo. I saw. Is she FIS?"

"No. She really is an interpreter. She is afraid and will not trust anyone else but me. I have asked that she trust you."

"You know I'm not CIA anymore, right?"

"Yes. That is precisely why I'm willing to trust you. And only you."

You need to be needed.

Whatever Karina knew was enough for the presidents of both countries to be concerned.

She needs you.

"Where can I find her?"

Chapter Eight

Karina had never been so nervous in her life. Sitting in the dark, alone, she could hardly focus on the screen in front of her. Even in the meeting with the two conspiring presidents, or fleeing from the Secret Service, she had not been as anxious as she was then.

Veronika's plan had worked, at least to some degree. Both the authorities and the media believed she had fled to Richmond. Not only had their contact called in a tip, but since then several alleged sightings had been reported.

Still she was nervous, because the White House believed she had recorded the meeting. Regardless of whether or not it was true, it would make them that much more desperate to find her. She had traded being taken alive for a harder push to find her. It was a calculated risk that she was now wondering if they had miscalculated.

So Karina had followed Veronika's plan. She had, as instructed, gone to the movie theater and purchased a ticket for whatever was showing in auditorium 8. She sat alone in the back row as a horror movie played. It was fit for the season, with Halloween approaching, but she barely paid any attention to it. Even as the rest of the audience gasped or shrieked in fright with each jump-scare, Karina sat nervously, occasionally glancing around.

Every time someone stood to use the restroom or a man cleared their throat loudly, she wondered if it would be him. Yet no one came. No one sat beside her or whispered to her or anything.

Maybe he's waiting until the movie is over.

And then the movie *was* over. The credits rolled and patrons, smiling in embarrassment at their fright, filed out of the theater. Karina waited until everyone else had left, and then waited longer. Finally, as the theater employees came in to clean up before the next showing, she slowly rose from her seat and stepped out into the dim corridor.

Where do I go now? The digital marquee over the auditorium's entrance told her that the next showing was in thirty minutes. She had nowhere else to go. Veronika had told her to come here and stay put until this man, the man she called Zero, came for her.

So I will. There was a red plastic bench across from the auditorium entrance. She sat upon it, resolving to wait for the next show and sit again alone in the dark theater.

A group of teenage boys walked past her, chatting excitedly about some superhero film. A young mother held her daughter's hand as they entered the women's restroom across the hall. A man in jeans and a black shirt poked at a cell phone as he lingered near the bench.

Karina untied the silk scarf from over her dark hair and ran her fingers through it, letting it hang over her shoulders.

"Mind if I sit?"

She glanced up. The man in the black shirt was smiling down at her, gesturing toward the plastic bench seat.

"Not at all. Please." Her American accent was improving with use, she thought.

"Thanks." The man sat with a sigh and put his phone in his jeans pocket. "Just waiting for my wife in the bathroom."

"Ah." Karina glanced at him in her periphery. He looked to be in his late thirties, or a decent forty, in good shape, with dark hair just barely peppered with gray.

"What are you seeing?" he asked suddenly.

"Sorry?"

"What movie are you seeing?" He smiled again.

"Oh. Um, the horror one." She'd already forgotten the name of it. Or perhaps she hadn't been paying enough attention to know in the first place.

"Right, right. Something 'massacre' or other." He chuckled a little.

"And you?" she asked politely.

"We're going to see that, uh, new romantic comedy." He shrugged. "I'm not a big fan, but my wife loves them. It's always the same story though, isn't it? Overworked professional woman meets some laid-back cool guy. They couldn't be more different. Then they fall in love. Rinse and repeat."

"Yes." She forced a small chuckle of her own. "I suppose so."

The man sighed and checked his watch.

He's not wearing a wedding ring.

Her heartbeat sped up suddenly. Her fist tightened around the silk scarf in her hand.

"I think I'll use the restroom," she said, her voice tighter than she intended. She started to rise—

"No, Karina. Sit." The man's voice was not harsh or insistent; it was rather calm, and he gazed up at her with a light smile on his lips. "I was enjoying our chat."

They found me. Her throat ran dry as she slowly lowered herself to the bench again. *They found me. How?*

She looked the man over again, blatantly this time. He had no gun, at least not that she could discern. And he seemed to be alone. Would they not have sent more after her?

"There are a lot of people here," the man said. "I think it would be best if we go elsewhere to talk."

Realization struck her and she nearly sighed with relief. "Oh! You're him?" she said quietly. "The man I've been waiting for. The one called Zero."

The man looked left and right down the corridor. "Not here," he told her urgently. "They have eyes and ears everywhere. Look." He gestured to their right, toward the lobby.

Karina's breath caught in her throat. A thick-necked man in a suit stood just beyond the lobby, one hand at his right ear, his lips moving silently as he relayed a message into a radio. He stuck out like a sore thumb in the theater, but she knew right away that he was Secret Service.

He hadn't noticed her. At least not yet.

"How?" she said anxiously. "How did they find me?"

"We have to move," Zero whispered. "I need you to trust me." He stood then, and offered her the crook of his arm. "We'll be okay. Just do as I tell you."

She hesitated. But Veronika had seemed confident that this man could help her. She stood and took his arm with her left, her right hand still gripping the silk scarf.

He guided her directly toward the lobby and the agent. "Pretend we're a couple. We just got out of a movie." Then louder he said, "So. What'd you think?"

Karina swallowed the lump in her throat and tried to act natural. "Oh, it was okay. Honestly, I didn't think it was all that scary."

"Right?" Zero agreed. "They don't make 'em like they used to. Remember *The Exorcist*?"

She laughed as they walked right past the agent. He didn't even give them a second glance. "How can I forget? We watched it on our first date. *So* romantic." Then she let out a whooshing breath. "How did they find me?" she hissed.

"Facial recognition software," he whispered back. "They can tap into traffic cams, security cameras, even phones if necessary, and run it through a database until they get a hit."

"Dammit. I thought I was more careful than that."

"It's okay. I'm going to get you out." He pushed open the door and they exited into the night—and nearly ran right into another agent outside. The Secret Service man glared at them and narrowed his eyes.

Zero smiled at him. "Sorry, pal." He turned to Karina. "Hey, you hungry, babe?" He guided her away from the agent.

"I could eat," she said in her American accent. "And I could definitely use a drink." Out of earshot she whispered, "Christ, they're everywhere."

"My car's across the lot. Just keep walking and act natural."

She did so, her arm in his, trying to keep a smile on her face and the banter light.

"It's that SUV right up there," he whispered. And then: "Oh, shit."

She saw the SUV. She also saw that a sleek black sedan was parked right next to it, and two more agents were milling about behind it.

They both looked up at the approaching couple.

"Kiss me," Zero whispered urgently.

"What?"

He spun her around suddenly to face him and, before she knew it, his lips were pressed against hers. It was obvious, dispassionate, unconvincing. The agents would never fall for it, she knew.

Then she felt something cold on her wrist. Before she could pull away, a cuff clicked shut around it. She pulled back, or tried to, but the man before her held her tightly as he snapped a second cuff around her other wrist.

"You're under arrest." He grinned maliciously.

"You are not Zero," she said dumbly, the handcuffs biting into both her arms.

"No such luck, darlin'. Just didn't want to cause a big scene in public." He glanced over his shoulder as the two agents approached. "Radio the others, tell them we got her."

It was a ruse. And she had fallen right into it. *Stupid!* she scolded herself.

Zero, the real Zero, was not coming for her.

If she was going to get out of this, she'd have to do it on her own.

She looked down at the steel cuffs on her hands. She opened her fist, and the silk scarf she'd been holding fluttered to the ground.

Karina bent over to pick it up.

"Hey, stand up!" the man barked.

She clasped her hands together tightly. Then she twisted her body at the hips and drove the club of both fists into his midsection.

"*Oomph!*" The man doubled over, and Karina swung again, upward, right into his face. The shock of impact ran up both her arms as the man's head jerked back, blood from his nose arcing into the air. He fell flat on his back on the asphalt.

"Stop!" one of the agents commanded. They both reached for their guns.

Karina ran, ducking low behind cars and pumping her legs as fast as she could. Adrenaline coursed through her. She'd never struck anyone like that before, and now she was running for her life.

"She's on the move!" one of them shouted behind her.

A gunshot rang out, impossibly loud and too close. A car window shattered. An alarm whooped. People screamed. Karina's legs nearly failed her, almost turning to jelly beneath her at the thunderous crack of the gun.

They're shooting at me. I'm going to be shot.

Still she kept moving forward, ducking low as possible. She weaved between the cars, no idea where she was headed or where she might be able to run to. Her only instinct was to get away, to stay out of their hands…

She rounded the rear bumper of a Jeep and an arm came out of nowhere, straight and strong and unyielding. The arm caught her at the collarbone. Her legs flew out from beneath her. For a moment she was weightless, and then she hit the ground hard enough to knock the breath from her lungs.

Karina gasped desperately, even as several strong arms lifted her to her feet. There were four of them; she was surrounded. There was a gun in her face. Her breath came shallow and labored. She felt dizzy and vaguely aware of pain in her skull.

"Fucking bitch." The man she thought was Zero stalked up to her, holding one hand to his nose, blood eking between his fingers.

"Is it broke?" asked one of the suited agents.

"No, just hurts like hell." He sneered at her. "Get her in the car. Keep a gun on her. And call HQ. We might have a problem."

"What problem?" asked an agent. They all looked the same to her: black suits, white shirts, thick necks, combed hair. Her vision was fuzzy. She likely had a concussion.

"She thought I was Zero."

"Zero?" One of the agents laughed. "Come on. Guy's a ghost story."

"No," said the man in the black shirt. "He's real, all right. He's just been out of the game a while." He leaned close to her, dropping his hand away from his bleeding, swelling nose. "For some reason, she thought he was coming to get her. But don't worry. We're going to find out why."

Chapter Nine

"Ten-HUT!"

The cadets snapped to attention, arms at their sides, spines straight, eyes forward in two parallel lines facing each other. Between them, on the floor of West Point's south-wing gymnasium, lay a thick green mat. Sergeant Castle paced over it between the two rows of cadets. He was a short man, five-six at best, but every inch of him was bulky, heavily muscled, except the shaved top of his head. He wore the same uniform that the cadets wore, a simple gray T-shirt and matching shorts.

Maya kept her eyes forward as Castle moved to the other end of the mat. She didn't dare look at the boy in the opposite row at the edge of her periphery. Greg.

"At ease," Castle ordered.

Maya shifted her hands behind her back and widened her stance, though she still didn't look over at him. They hadn't spoken since she'd left him behind at her dad's house. Somehow he'd made it back to New York. The rumor mill around school was charged with whispers of what she'd done and a thousand different reasons why, ranging from a practical joke gone wrong to him pressuring her to have sex with him, and not one of them the truth.

The most important thing was that no disciplinary action had been taken against her. Greg hadn't gone to the administration, and it seemed he hadn't even run off to his rich parents to have something done about it. It was a small comfort. She didn't give a damn about her reputation with the other students, but he could have potentially hurt her academic career.

"Tonight I want to see your proficiency in locks and throws," Castle ordered. Despite his rugged exterior, his day job was teaching mathematics at the academy. But three nights a week, Castle taught judo as an extracurricular. "And to add insult to potential injury, we're going to start with someone who can set the bar for all you tough guys." He looked right at her. "Lawson, front and center."

Maya stepped forward without hesitation. "Sir!"

"Show these fellas how to fight like a girl, cadet."

To say that she was the best in the class might have been braggadocio, which only made it fortunate that she didn't have to say it. They knew it. Maya enjoyed judo; it taught someone like her, someone shorter and lighter than a lot of the boys, how to use her body to fight off someone bigger. It evened the playing field. And, as she had discussed after class with Castle one afternoon, it was basically math; as long as you remembered your angles, your weight distribution, and your balance, you could do anything, take down almost anyone.

"And with her, let's see ..." Castle scanned the cadets.

Please no. Please no. Please no.

"Calloway! Get up here."

Dammit! She didn't dare show a physical reaction, but inside she was cursing as Greg stepped forward to face her on the green mat.

She looked at his face. Met his gaze. He stared back at her, expressionless.

Part of her wanted to apologize right then and there, to say she was sorry, but she didn't. She wouldn't, because she wasn't sorry.

"Anyone want to take a bet on this?" Castle asked casually, eliciting a few small laughs.

"I'll put twenty on Lawson!" one of the cadets shouted.

"Trick question, Gilbert. There is no gambling in this academy. Now give me fifty."

More laughter as the sharp-nosed cadet groaned and dropped into pushup position.

"Any time you're ready," Castle told them.

She had no choice. She squared up across from Greg, a slight bend in her knees as they took the starting stance—one hand on the opponent's shoulder and the other cradling just below their opposite elbow. Typically in a practice position like this, Castle would have them alternate, one executing a move while the other practiced technique of going with the throw and to the ground safely.

Typically.

"Ladies first," Greg said.

Maya nodded. She kept her eyes on him as she began to shift her weight. In the instant just before she started to take his balance, she saw the flash of a smirk cross his face.

Then he stepped forward suddenly, pushing her backward hard, forcing her to briefly go on one foot to keep from falling over. She wasn't at all prepared for it. He swung out his left leg and, with a swift kick to her calf, swept the foot from beneath her.

She fell flat onto her back on the mat. It didn't hurt, though it knocked the wind from her and her calf would no doubt be bruised.

A few snickers arose from the gathered cadets. Castle frowned, but said nothing. It wasn't a move he had taught them; it was a cheap shot.

Maya got to her feet. She said nothing and showed no emotion. Instead she simply got back into position. Greg did too, though she could tell he was trying not to smile.

She started to push him back again, adjusting her weight, but this time he went completely rigid, every muscle going taut, and shoved her sideways. As she lost her balance, he snaked one arm low, in her groin, and the other hand clamped on her shoulder.

Then he lifted her clear off the mat. For a moment she was in the air, legs over her head. Then Greg twisted around and threw her to the ground in a body slam.

It hurt that time, even with the mat. The impact rattled her whole body. A few of the cadets actually groaned aloud, and one of them said, "Looks like Gilbert's gonna be out twenty bucks."

"Calloway!" Castle barked. "This ain't the WWE."

"Sorry, sir." But with his back to Castle, Greg grinned down at her. "Bet that hurt," he said quietly.

Okay. She rose once again. *If that's how it's going to be.*

Maya squared up once more, but this time she looked past him, to Castle. The sergeant gave her a furtive, almost imperceptible nod.

She grabbed onto Greg's shoulder and opposite elbow, and he did the same.

"Go ahead," he whispered harshly, scowling at her. "Try something. See what hap—"

Maya yanked his elbow down, bending her knees and dropping her body weight with it. Greg's body jerked to one side, dangerously off-kilter. She swung one leg up, high, high enough to get over his head, and hooked his neck with her calf. She kept going, using her momentum and Greg's downward motion to spin him and get her leg fully around his neck, twisting her spine and arcing her leg in a way that none of these boys could ever hope to. Then she leaned backward as she yanked one of his arms up, and she leaned back, pulling her weight and Greg's body with her as she sat on her butt.

As she hit the mat, Greg's neck was pinched tightly between her legs, one arm awkwardly stuck in there with it. She quickly brought her other leg around and locked her ankles.

Then she squeezed.

Greg made a choking sound as the crook of her knee cut off his air. A few of the cadets cheered; one of them whistled loudly.

"What's the matter?" she whispered under the din. "Can't breathe?"

His free arm reached for the mat to tap out. *No.* She twisted her hips and kept his arm from reaching the ground.

Her calf, the one right in Greg's face, had thin white scars running its length. Though they had long since healed, they would never fully fade. The letters *R-E-D.* A number, *23.* And then more letters: *P-O-L-A.*

"See those?" she whispered to Greg. He let out another choke. "You never asked me where they came from. What they meant." It was the message she had carved into herself to let her dad know what train the human traffickers had put her sister on. But in Greg's ear, close enough that only he could hear it she hissed, "I see them every day. That's my constant reminder that people far worse than you couldn't get the best of me. You're nobody. Don't forget that."

"All right, Lawson," said Castle casually. "Let him up before he turns blue."

She released him and rolled away. Greg sucked in a breath, his face nearly purple, blotchy and ugly, eyes bloodshot and moist.

A few of the cadets chuckled.

Greg scrambled to his feet and spun on the group angrily. "You think that's funny?!" he shouted hoarsely. He spun on Maya. "You're just a whore!"

"That's enough, cadet!" Castle barked sternly. He stepped forward and put one hand flat on Greg's chest. The boy wilted immediately, despite being several inches taller than the sergeant. "If I hear that word again, I'll let her choke you out. You understand me?"

"Yes, sir," Greg said meekly.

"Now get the hell out of my gym. Go."

Greg shot one more glare at her and then sulked away. She'd pay for that in some way, she was sure, but for now it was worth it to see him humiliated in front of his peers. She couldn't believe she'd nearly let herself fall for him; now she could see him for what he really was.

"You okay, Lawson?" the sergeant asked.

"Yes, sir."

"Good." Castle paused before saying, "I didn't teach you that move. Where'd you learn it?"

Maya hadn't even given it a second thought, but the sergeant was right. He hadn't taught her that.

"My dad," she murmured. "He taught it to me." She remembered the day well, more than a year and a half ago now. Her dad had discovered that she was secretly taking a self-defense course after classes at Georgetown. He had insisted that if she wanted to learn, she would learn from him. They practiced in the basement of their house in Alexandria with a few thin foam mats on the floor.

I can't, she had told him when he showed her the takedown. *I can't do that.*

You can't? His smile. She remembered his smile. How long had it been since she'd seen it? Then he had asked her: *What's the square root of five hundred twenty-nine?*

Twenty-three. She knew it without skipping a beat.

Uh-huh. And who ruled England during the Hundred Years' War?

The House of Plantagenet. Then she'd scoffed. She knew what he was doing.

Still he smiled and asked, *How did you know that?*

I learned.

Right. You learned, and you memorized, and you practiced until it was just instinct. Why is this any different?

"Lawson." She snapped out of her own head as Castle raised an eyebrow toward her. "You with us?"

"Yeah. I mean, yes sir."

"Why don't you take five?"

She didn't want to take five. She wanted to tell him that she didn't need to take five. She didn't need his sympathy or his help. She didn't need *anyone's* help. But she couldn't say any of that.

Instead she said, "If it's all the same to you, sir, I'd like to actually get some practice in."

Castle stared at her pointedly for a moment, and then nodded. "All right then. Who's up next?" He turned to the gathered cadets at the edge of the mat.

But suddenly they all seemed very interested in the floor.

Chapter Ten

It was just a little after nine-thirty at night by the time Zero got to the movie theater, where Sanders told him he would liaise with the interpreter. But he didn't need to go into auditorium 8 to know that she wasn't there.

The parking lot was crawling with police cruisers, lights flashing as they evacuated the cineplex and tried to get people to go home. But a small crowd had formed of disgruntled patrons whose movies had been interrupted. Some were demanding refunds while others were clamoring to find out what was going on.

Zero edged closer, around the crowd, catching brief snippets of conversation as he did.

"... heard someone got shot in the parking lot..."

"... those were gunshots? I thought it was thunder..."

"... kids say they saw a woman get kidnapped..."

Near the box office, two officers were setting up sawhorses to keep the crowd away from the doors while another pair of uniformed cops was talking to a teenage boy with two friends behind him.

"You asked me what I saw, and I'm telling you!" the kid insisted. "Some guys in suits took a lady away. They had her cuffed and they had a gun on her and everything."

"I think you've been watching too many action movies, kid," said one of the cops. "Every other eyewitness is saying it was shots fired from a moving car."

"Most likely gang-related," said the other officer. "An initiation or something like it. No one was hit." He leaned toward the teen and added, "No one was taken. You hear me?"

The teenager scoffed and walked away, followed by his two friends. Zero pushed through the crowd and followed them out to the dark parking lot. He knew exactly what was happening; the authorities were already covering it up, gaslighting anyone who claimed to have seen what they saw. He'd used the tactic himself a few times.

"Total bullshit," he heard the kid saying. "I know what I saw…"

"Hey." He trotted up to them. "I believe you."

The three kids stopped and glanced at each other. The one who had been talking to the police, a skinny kid with spiked hair, spoke up. "You a cop?"

"No. I'm a friend of the woman who was taken. I need to find her."

The teenager eyed him suspiciously. "If that's true, why don't *you* go talk to the cops? Maybe they'll believe you."

Zero shook his head. "Can't do that." He wasn't CIA anymore; there was no need to be discreet. "They're trying to cover it up so no one thinks anyone was kidnapped. The guys in suits are in on it. So are the police. Others too."

"For real?"

"For real. So I need you to tell me what you saw. Every detail you remember."

The teen looked to his two friends. One of them shrugged. The other one nodded. "Yeah. All right. We were coming out of the movies, and we saw—"

"From where?"

The kid pointed. "Those doors. Walking towards Ben's car. This is Ben." He nodded towards his friend. "He's parked over there. Anyways, we were walking, and we heard the shots—"

"How many shots?"

"One," said the kid.

"Two," said Ben.

"Two," confirmed the third friend. "There were two shots."

"Was she hit?"

"Nah. She was running. Staying low." The kid told him about her coming around the corner, being handcuffed, getting knocked down, and then dragged away by four men in suits. "And one other guy. He was in a black shirt and his nose was all bloody."

He had them describe what Karina was wearing, and which direction she'd been running from. Then he slipped them a fifty-dollar bill. "Don't tell anyone what you've told me," he said gravely. "It could put you and your families in danger." And then before the kid could ask he added, "For real."

Across the parking lot he examined the asphalt, hoping to find something, anything that might lend a clue to what had happened to Karina or where she had been taken. He knew what kinds of places people were put when they had information they didn't want to give up. There was nothing pleasant about them.

The lot began to empty as the cops slowly won their battle with the crowd, sending people home and assuring them that the movie theater would reverse transactions for the interrupted showings. A few people passed him here and there, but no one paid him any attention, even as he scrutinized the ground around him like someone who had dropped their wallet.

Then he spotted it.

Headlights blared and a car horn honked as he nearly stepped right out in front of someone trying to leave. *Watch yourself,* he warned. It seemed his instincts were not as keen as they once were.

He stooped and picked up the silk scarf, turning it in his hands. He sniffed it; it smelled like shampoo. Someone had been wearing it over their hair. He used the flashlight on his cell phone to inspect the ground around it and saw a line of spattered blood only a few feet away.

Those kids mentioned a man with a bloody nose. The picture was coming together. Karina was jumped here. She struggled as they cuffed her. She dropped her scarf. Struck one of them in the face. Ran for it. Got caught.

"But why did you come out here in the first place?" he murmured aloud. Sanders said the interpreter would be in the theater waiting for him. Did they find her and force her to follow them out to the parking lot? Wouldn't she have struggled and caused a scene, rather than go willingly?

It didn't matter much now. Karina had been taken, and he had no idea to where. He had no way to find her. He felt a deep pang of guilt; he'd been too late. If he had arrived just a little earlier, he could have helped her. She needed him, and he failed before he even began.

He was about to make the difficult call to Sanders and tell her so when footsteps caught his attention. He looked up to see a man in a dark suit approaching, a thin smile on his face. Zero knew the look; the guy was an agent, either FBI or Secret Service.

Zero looked around. Most of the cars had gone, and even some of the cops. The few who lingered were inside the movie theater lobby, visible through the glass doors, but they might as well have been a mile away for all the good they could (or would) do him.

"Hi, Zero," the suited agent said as he drew near.

"Who?" he asked, feigning innocence.

It didn't work. The Secret Service agent smiled wider. "What are you doing here?"

"Well, I was trying to watch *Mountain Cabin Massacre,*" he said casually. "But then the cops evacuated, so I'm just heading home."

"Sure. What's in your hand there?"

Zero opened his fist and showed him the silk scarf. "Don't know. Just saw it here on the ground."

"Uh-huh." The agent shook his head a little, still smiling. "I thought they taught you to lie better than that."

Zero tensed as the agent paced near him. If he was in for a fight, he wasn't entirely certain how he would fare. It had been a long time, and the agent was not only younger but in much better shape.

"You don't remember me," the young agent said. "Why would you? But I was there, on the bridge that day. A year and a half ago, when you rescued President Pierson. I was one of the agents that thought you were a renegade. I even took a few shots at you." The agent shrugged one shoulder. "Sorry about that."

If he was telling the truth and still had a job, it meant the agent was clean, not a part of the conspiracy. *Then why do I still feel like something is about to go down?*

"Don't worry about it. Water under the bridge." Zero faked a smile of his own. "No pun intended."

"Clever." The agent ceased his pacing. "You know, that woman asked for you. By name. And now here you are. Strange, right? So you want to tell me again what you're doing here?"

"All right, you got me." He'd have to try a different lie. "The CIA had a contact to the interpreter, a Russian who knew how to reach her. We set up a meeting here with the promise that we'd protect her in exchange for information. Take her to a safe house. Of course that was just a setup to get to her. But your boys seem to have gotten here first."

"We sure did. Just one thing." He narrowed his eyes. "We didn't call the CIA in on this. And even if we did, I happen to know you're not with them anymore."

Zero scoffed at him. "You know 'covert' means secret, right? If you knew about it, then I wouldn't be very good at my job. You can clear all this with my deputy director. She'll tell you." He regretted it as soon as he said it. Despite what was going on in their personal life, he knew Maria would go to bat for him—though he was blatantly jeopardizing her position.

"Yeah," the agent agreed. "Let's do that. Come on, we're going for a ride."

Headlights suddenly flicked on behind the agent, high beams, bright and blinding. Zero shielded his eyes with a hand as he cursed under his breath. He had walked right by that car and hadn't noticed anyone in it.

I'm getting rusty in my old age.

"I drove here," he told the agent. "I'll follow you."

"I'm not asking, Zero. I'm telling you to get in the car. Don't make me use force."

He weighed his options. He had no idea if he could take on the one agent by himself, let alone however many others were in the car. "Fine," he said at last. "Lead the way."

The agent directed him to the backseat of the black sedan, and then went around and sat beside him. In the front seat were two other men; the driver looked like Secret Service as well, but the passenger looked like some kind of mobster. His black hair was slicked back on his head, and he had a thick mustache over a frowning mouth and stubbled jaw. He wore an all-black suit with no tie.

"Let's go," said the young agent. The driver nodded and pulled the car out of the lot.

The sinking feeling hadn't left Zero's gut. *Relax*, he told himself. *You haven't done anything wrong. You'll be able to talk your way out of this. Maria will be furious, but she'll help.*

He felt a twinge of guilt at his inability to help the interpreter. But not only could he not help her now, he'd landed in hot water himself. There was nothing he could do for her.

She needs you…

No. No one needs me. It was foolish of him to think otherwise.

The rough-looking fellow in the passenger seat put a cell phone to his ear. "We've got him," he said gruffly.

But he wasn't speaking English. He spoke in Russian, though Zero understood every word. He glanced casually out the window and tried to pretend he hadn't. *Glad to see my language skills are up to snuff at least.*

It was silent enough in the car for him to hear the voice through the phone. "Bring him to the compound. Kozlovsky wants to know how he knows the woman."

"She is not talking?"

"Not yet. Either she will, or he will when he sees what we do to her."

"Fifteen minutes. *Do svidaniya.*" The Russian ended the call and nodded once to the driver.

What compound? Zero wondered. *And why does it feel like the Russian president is running the show here?* His mind went immediately to the events of eighteen months prior. Whatever was said in that meeting was important enough for them to not only want the interpreter, but to want to bring him in as well.

"So," he asked, trying to sound cavalier, "where we headed?"

"Like you said," the young agent told him, "we're going to see your boss."

"Uh-huh. So to Langley then?" *At almost ten o'clock at night?* Not likely.

"Right. To Langley."

Zero's heartbeat sped up, but he didn't show it. He weighed his options: stay put and let these men bring him to wherever they were going to bring him and improvise from there, or do what he could here and now.

Sure. It's one against three. You're unarmed. That wasn't entirely true; he still had the silk scarf in his hand. He almost laughed at himself. It wasn't exactly a formidable weapon.

The driver pulled the car off the main street and onto a back road winding its way out of downtown proper. Zero knew this area; in just a couple minutes there would be fewer homes and businesses as they gave way to larger, sprawling properties in a wealthy neighborhood. *A compound,* he thought. *Is it someone's home?*

His window in which to act was closing quickly, but his trepidation was keeping his muscles taut and unwilling to move. He stretched his elbows up.

The young agent beside him reacted instantly, hand reaching for the gun at his shoulder holster but not drawing.

Zero chuckled at him. "Relax. I'm just stretching. Joints get stiff, you know?"

The agent simpered and his hand fell away from his jacket. "Getting old, Zero?"

"Happens to us all." *Relax,* he told himself. He'd have to relax for what he was about to do. *This is crazy.* He reached over his shoulder and tugged the seatbelt down across his body. "Forgot my seatbelt."

The agent behind the wheel laughed lightly. "If half the stories about you are true, I'd imagine a seatbelt is the last thing you'd be worried about."

"Safety first."

He said it in Russian.

The *Bratva*-looking guy in the passenger seat whipped his head around, his eyes wide in surprise. At the same time, Zero threw out his right arm, his hand flat and rigid, and struck the young agent in the windpipe.

"*Ack!*" Both hands flew to his flattened trachea.

Zero's other fist loosened and the silk scarf fluttered free. He leaned forward and whipped it around the driver's face, and then yanked back with both hands.

The car veered to the right as the Russian reached for his gun. The tires left the road, the driver blinded by the scarf, and they bounced violently over furrows in the grass as they careened down an embankment. Zero jostled left and right, but kept his grip on the scarf even as the caroming Russian managed to free a pistol from his jacket.

The car's front end plummeted into a deep rut at forty-five miles an hour and the bumper struck earth, stopping them instantly. The Russian's head smacked the window hard enough to crack it as the back end of the car shot upward. The young agent tumbled into the front seat.

For a moment the car stayed upright, front end in the narrow ditch and rear bumper reaching for the sky. The seatbelt dug painfully into Zero's chest but kept him in place. Then, with a deterministic groan of metal, the car fell forward and crashed down onto its roof hard enough for the windows to burst.

Zero was upside down. He winced as he pushed himself up from the roof, unclipped the seatbelt, and carefully climbed out of the broken window. A quick wiggle of limbs, fingers, and toes told him nothing had broken. Then he checked the damage.

The young agent who had been in the backseat with him was in a crumpled heap resting on the roof of the car. His eyes were closed, but he had a pulse. The driver was tangled in him. His eyes were open wide, staring back at Zero as he took rapid breaths through clenched teeth. One of his incisors was missing, a bloody gap where it had been only moments earlier. His left arm was pinned beneath his cohort; his right was clearly broken, evident by the lump of bone jutting just below the elbow.

"You," he hissed. "You ... you ..."

"Shh. Don't move. Don't try to talk." Zero quickly relieved them both of radios, phones, and guns. Each carried a compact black Glock, his own personal preference in small arms. He hefted the weight of the gun, felt the smooth grip, the action. It felt good in his hand. "I'll call you an ambulance soon. Just hang in there." These two had just been following orders. They were likely good agents and decent men who had been misled.

The *Batva*, the Russian gangster, moaned as he opened his eyes. He was mostly upside down, shoulder and half his body resting on the car's roof. Zero quickly rounded the car, reached into the broken window, and dragged the man out by his black jacket. The Russian yelped and tried to strike him, tried to flail, but he was weak and disoriented.

Zero found his cell phone and stuck it in his own pocket. "Where were you taking me?" he asked in Russian. "Where is the compound?"

The man looked up at him, his eyes glazed and unfocused. "Go. To. Hell," he said in heavily accented English.

"Kind of figured you'd say something like that." Zero checked the cell phone. He opened the GPS app and took a look at his recent history against their current location. Earlier that same evening the Russian had entered an address a mile and a half away. "Never mind. I got it."

He reached into the broken window again to tug the keys out of the ignition and turn the headlights off. It would be unlikely that anyone could see the overturned car from the road at night, down the steep embankment as it was, but he didn't want to risk it before he could get to his destination. As he climbed back out he noticed something resting on the floor—or rather, the roof—of the car. The Russian's pistol, a Sig Sauer with a suppressor on its tip.

"Must be my lucky day," Zero murmured to himself. He carefully climbed back out of the wreckage, noting that his lower back ached in protest.

A flash of movement in his periphery. As he spun, the Russian tugged a small revolver from a holster at his ankle and brought it up. Before Zero could react, he fired. It missed him by inches, whizzing past his ear. Zero fired once in response, a single silenced shot that entered the Russian's right cheek and exited the back of his skull.

He frowned. His reflexes were slow, and his aim was a bit off. He flexed the fingers of his right hand. He'd sustained a pretty heinous injury when the hand had been crushed with a steel anchor by a member of the Brotherhood. Three surgeries and a lot of physical therapy later, he thought he'd regained use of it, but now he realized he hadn't fired a gun since it healed.

He'd have to remember that. There would likely be more shooting.

It almost didn't seem real. On the one hand, he suddenly felt more like himself than he had in months, maybe longer. On the other, he fully realized that in less than two minutes he'd grievously injured two Secret Service agents and killed a man who was presumably a member of President Kozlovsky's attaché. In typical Zero fashion, he'd made a quick decision to not become a victim and simply acted. It wouldn't be long before the car was found, and the two agents that were still breathing would sing. He couldn't bring himself to kill them. Besides, the Russian had already radioed that they had Zero in custody.

There was only one thing to do. With the two Glocks tucked in his pants, the Sig Sauer in his jacket, and the Russian's phone in his hand, Zero jogged up the embankment to the road and followed the GPS route to his destination.

She needs you.

He was out of breath by the time his feet touched asphalt. His back hurt. His whole body hurt. He'd likely have a nice long bruise across his chest where the seatbelt had dug in.

As he jogged down the dark road, he thought of Danny Glover, the actor who played Roger Murtaugh in one of his favorite action movies, a real classic. *Lethal Weapon.*

He murmured the line to himself as he jogged.

"I'm getting too old for this shit."

Chapter Eleven

He was more than halfway there, following the GPS route on the Russian's phone, when his own cell chimed from inside his pocket. He'd almost forgotten he had it, which could have spelled trouble if it went off when he was trying to sneak around.

Zero pulled his phone out and saw a text from Maria.

Where are you? Are you okay?

Right. He'd nearly forgotten about that too. In fact, the fight with Maria, if it could be called that, felt like days ago now even though it had only been earlier that afternoon—before he impulsively flew to Jacksonville, briefly visited his irate daughter, and then (equally impulsively) accepted a death wish of an assignment from a woman he barely knew to save another woman who might have been dead already.

He thought about replying with a lie or an excuse, or simply saying that he needed time before they spoke again, but ultimately he opted not to say anything. It wouldn't be the truth. Maria could have just used CIA resources to track his phone and find out where he was, but she hadn't invaded his privacy.

So instead he opened the back of his phone, tore out the battery, snapped the SIM card in half, and tossed each piece into the tall grass to the right of the road as he continued his brisk pace toward his destination. The people at this "compound" were expecting him to arrive any moment, and Maria was far from the only one capable of tracking a cell phone.

According to the Russian's map, he was to make the next left onto a narrow road and follow that as it wound its way to the compound. He tossed the Russian phone into the grass on the side of the road, no longer having a need for it, and continued on his way until he found the access. It was one lane, the asphalt pristine in the moonlight, suggesting it wasn't driven on often. It seemed as if it was simply a long driveway to the compound.

There were headlights behind him, and Zero turned away from the road as the car approached and silently hoped that it wasn't there for him. Thankfully the vehicle didn't slow as it passed, and soon the brake lights vanished around the next bend. Still he didn't move from his position at the mouth of the narrow road.

Wait. Think about what you're doing before you go down this road.

Yesterday he had spent half his day lying on the sofa, feeling sorry for himself. Now he was about to storm some compound and—what? Kill more Russians? Save this woman, this interpreter, who for all he knew could be a lie by Sanders to get one of her FIS agents out of a tight spot?

But he knew he'd already come too far. Attacking the Secret Service agents, killing the Russian... Maria couldn't get him out of that, and there would be no more presidential pardons for him. He wasn't an agent anymore—he wasn't *anything* anymore, he reminded himself again—which meant that what he had just done was assault and murder.

There was only one thing to do. Get to this interpreter, find out what she knew, and hope that the information was valuable enough to strike a deal with the powers-that-be. Involve Maria and the CIA with clear evidence so that he could justify his actions and be granted immunity.

Besides...

She needs you.

He started his way up the dark road as it sloped upward along a gentle hill. There were small trees on both sides, planted a near-perfect twenty feet apart and about five feet in front the driveway's edge. This wasn't a compound, he realized, as much as it was a stately home, fit for the area.

The narrow road made one last gentle bend before the structure was in view. Zero stepped off the road and into the darkness of the stout trees. Ahead he saw a black iron gate as wide as the pavement, most likely electronic, lit by a pair of floodlights behind it. There were silhouettes behind the gate, little more than two dark shapes pacing. Waiting, no doubt, for their Russian friend to deliver Zero.

On either side of the iron gate was a stone wall, about eight or nine feet tall and extending for a few dozen yards before making an abrupt turn. Zero stole through the trees and followed the wall, away from the floodlights and around to the eastern side of the property. Then with a slight groan he grabbed the top of the wall and pulled himself up, peering over the stone.

The wall enclosed about an acre and a half of perfectly manicured lawn and beautifully appointed landscaping, stout cherry blossom trees dotting the yard from small mounds of dark black mulch. In the center was a house, if it could be called that, a contemporary design of glass and sharp angles, well lit from the inside. The home was only one story but sprawling. A short distance behind it he saw a dark guest house and a small maintenance shed.

Zero knew what this was. He'd heard of places like this, properties owned by the government that were away from the city proper, isolated and quiet. They were kept on reserve for diplomats and invited guests and visiting dignitaries who traveled with families or otherwise preferred it over the downtown penthouses or White House guest suites.

But it seemed as though the Russians were using it as a hideaway.

He pulled himself over the wall and dropped to the soft grass with a slight grunt. The place wasn't exactly a fortress and security seemed lax; so far he had only noticed the two guards at the gate. Clearly they weren't expecting any trouble, though he wasn't about to assume that they weren't prepared for it.

Zero stayed low and crouched behind the nearest tree, the trunk of it barely wide enough to conceal him.

Okay, what's your plan here?

Get in. Get the woman. Get out.

Sure. Piece of cake. But you might want to come up with something better than that.

The two Russians at the gate could pose a problem getting out, and he needed to know if they were armed. He'd have to neutralize them first.

And try not to kill anyone else, he reminded himself.

He stayed low as he crept closer to the gate, keeping mindful of the bright floodlights. The two men wore black, one in a suit and the other in a leather jacket. The guy in the jacket had a submachine gun slung over his shoulder by a strap. The other one didn't have a gun in hand, but Zero could see the pistol holster at his hip. They paced the width of the driveway as they muttered to each other in Russian.

"They should be here by now. Try him again."

"I just did. No answer."

"Something is wrong. We should tell Kozlovsky."

Kozlovsky? Zero hadn't actually expected the Russian president to be there in person. *What are you going to do, stick a gun in a president's face?*

"Don't bother him. Just get a car," said the one with the compact SMG. "We'll go and—"

The sound of wailing sirens cut him off. Both Russians ceased their pacing and looked out beyond the gate.

Someone must have found the wreck and called it in, Zero reasoned. As the pair of men stared off into the distance, the floodlights suddenly clicked off. In the darkness, the Russians were mere silhouettes.

"Do you think they ran into trouble?" one of them said.

"Get a car. We'll go take a look for ourselves."

Now! Zero rushed forward to take them by surprise. He took two steps, and suddenly the powerful floodlights clicked on again, practically blinding him. Motion sensors.

The two Russians spun and they too froze for a moment in shock. The three of them stared at each other.

"Hey!" The Russian reached for the submachine gun hanging from his strap. The other snaked a hand into his jacket.

Zero sprang forward, instincts kicking in. He stuck out a hand and pushed against the suited Russian's elbow, keeping him from pulling his gun. He mule-kicked backward into the second Russian's gut, doubling him over. A solid hook to the one in front of him crumpled the man. Then he spun, grabbed hold of the submachine gun, and twisted it around his own shoulder. The strap went taut against the Russian's armpit and neck and his feet left the ground. Zero turned his body ninety degrees as he dropped to one knee. The Russian flailed, careening ass-over-teakettle and landing on the asphalt with a thud that rattled Zero's own teeth.

He stayed like that for a moment, on one knee and breathing hard, listening to the sirens of several emergency vehicles in the distance. The floodlights clicked off and he sat there in the darkness. If either of the Secret Service men in the car were conscious and could talk, he might be expecting unwanted guests in minutes. He had to move.

He got to his feet and the lights clicked on again. Zero winced. The Russian he'd thrown stared up at him wide-eyed and not breathing, his neck bent at an odd angle. It must have broken when he hit the driveway.

So much for not killing anyone, he thought dourly. He grabbed up the SMG and turned to head toward the house.

Then he froze.

Over his head, where the iron gate met the stone wall, was a camera angled downward, staring directly at him like an unblinking eye.

"Dammit," he muttered.

If anyone was watching the feed from inside, they already knew he was there. He couldn't assume they *hadn't* seen him; sneaking in could mean walking into a trap. And with the authorities at the scene of the car wreck, he couldn't imagine he had much time before there were visitors.

Well, he thought to himself. *It's been a while since I've made a big entrance.*

Chapter Twelve

Karina was seated on the center cushion of a large, comfortable sofa wrapped in soft brown leather, her slight figure sinking deep into it. The home around her was elegant yet cozy, unpretentious. Above the flat-screen television was a ship in a bottle, and art on the walls, and a fireplace nestled along the southeast of the large living room. It looked as if the place had been staged by a professional decorator to make guests feel invited—which was made all the more bizarre by the fact that she was flanked on either side of the sofa by Secret Service agents with pistols in their laps.

The handcuffs had been taken off, but that was of little comfort considering that across from her, seated in a recliner that matched the sofa, was Aleksandr Kozlovsky. Behind him stood a thick-necked Russian with his hands clasped in front of him. He was not carrying a gun, but an AK-47 leaned against the wall within reach.

Kozlovsky grinned as he noticed her glancing around at the décor. "Do you like it?" he asked in Russian. "The US government owns this place. People like me can opt to stay here if we wish. To be frank, I prefer it... after all those meetings and press conferences, forcing myself to smile. To shake hands. To play nice. It is a relief to return to a place like this and not have to pretend I enjoy being here."

Karina scowled at the Russian president, saying nothing.

"The truth is," Kozlovsky continued, "all of those public appearances were carefully scripted and staged, just to afford me the few minutes alone that I needed with him."

"What do you think these two would say," Karina gestured to the Secret Service agents on either side of her as she spoke in Russian, "if they knew the truth?"

Kozlovsky laughed. "By all means, tell them. They are good men, loyal to their leader and their country—which is their error. They believe what they were told, that you are a traitor, an enemy of the state. They would not listen to a word you said." He leaned forward in the recliner and folded his hands. "Now. I do not believe that you had the means to record that meeting. But still you have caused a great deal of trouble. Simply being alive threatens everything we've done here. Rest assured, we are going to kill you. How fast that happens depends entirely on you."

Karina's hands trembled slightly. She shoved them in her lap, clasping them together to hide it.

"I am going to ask you four questions," said Kozlovsky. "And I expect complete honesty. Did you record that meeting? If so, where is the recording? Did you send it or share it with anyone? And why?"

Karina again said nothing. She wouldn't, no matter what they did.

Kozlovsky sighed. "I assumed as much. You will tell me, eventually. We have all night. No one is coming for you. No one knows we are here but our own people. And Vasily here," he gestured to the Russian standing over his shoulder, "is soon going to start carving your face."

Karina swallowed the lump in her throat. She didn't care that her voice sounded tremulous as she said, "Well? What is he waiting for?"

Kozlovsky grinned wide, baring his teeth. "I like you. You are bold. Or at least you think you are. We are waiting for a friend of yours, who should be arriving any moment."

She frowned. *Friend? What friend?* The closest contact she had was Veronika's FIS liaison in Richmond, and she didn't even know his name.

Kozlovsky looked over his shoulder at Vasily. "Where are they? They should be here by now."

The big Russian reached for a remote control on the oak coffee table in front of them. He clicked a button to check the feed from outside, but the television's screen remained dark. Karina squinted; she could just barely make out the outline of the driveway and lawn just beyond the entrance of the gate.

"Lights are off," Vasily muttered in Russian. "Where are those two—?"

Suddenly the screen flickered with light as the motion-sensing flood lamps clicked on. Karina sucked in a breath. Vasily took a step back. The two Secret Service agents leapt to their feet, one of them hissing, "What the hell?!"

On the screen, one of the Russian sat up in the driveway, rubbing his jaw. The other was lying on his back, eyes open, unmoving.

"They're down!" Vasily shouted. He lurched for the AK-47, but before he got there a window shattered loudly. Karina jumped at the sound, coming from the front of the house. The Secret Service agents bolted for the hall.

Vasily started to follow, but Kozlovsky grabbed his shoulder. "Stay with me!" he ordered. The big Russian brought the rifle to his shoulder and waited. "You!" Kozlovsky glared down at her. "Do not move!"

"Watch your six!" Karina heard one of the agents shout.

"There!"

Two gunshots rang out in quick succession. Someone grunted loudly. Then a yelp of pain. Another window shattered.

Then, silence.

Vasily glanced over his shoulder nervously at Kozlovsky. The Russian president nodded tightly, and then reached into his jacket for a phone.

The big Russian whipped around the corner, aiming the AK down the hall. But it was evident by his expression that he saw nothing.

More glass shattered, this time behind him, coming from the rear of the house. A large stone, big as two fists, sailed through and smacked the floor, cracking a tile. Vasily spun, but not fast enough.

Thwip! She heard the suppressed shot at the same time as Vasily's knee exploded. He shrieked in pain as he crumpled.

A man stepped through the broken glass door at the rear, a silenced pistol in his hand. He kicked at the AK, sending the rifle spinning across the floor and into the kitchen. Vasily grabbed for him, but the man kicked again, this time into the big Russian's chin.

Then he turned his gun on Kozlovsky.

"Put down the phone," he ordered in Russian.

A slow grin spread on Kozlovsky's face as he lowered the phone to the coffee table. "You must be Zero. I've heard much about you."

Zero? Karina looked the man up and down. *He can't be.* He certainly didn't look like the man Veronika had described. He looked rather … ordinary. His dark hair was too long, creeping down his neck and over his ears, going gray at the temples. His eyes were sharp, but the rest of his face appeared tired, and he had a slight paunch pushing just over his belt buckle.

This is my would-be savior? She was beginning to think that maybe her sister had actually lost her mind.

"Tell me," Kozlovsky said calmly. "Do you think it is wise to point a gun at a sitting president?"

"Not really," the man replied in Russian. "But if you've heard about me, you know I'm not particularly well known for thinking things through." He reached behind him and pulled a black pistol from his waistband. Without taking his eyes off of Kozlovsky, he held it out to Karina. "You know how to use this?" he asked in English.

"I do." She did not particularly like guns, but Veronika had insisted that she learn how to shoot. Karina took it, racked the slide to put a round in the chamber, and pointed the gun at the man that called himself Zero.

"Um …" His confused gaze flitted between the president and the gun pointed at him. "I think you misunderstand what's happening here. This is a rescue."

"And I have been tricked before," she said curtly. It was how she got here, after all. The real Zero would not have known how to find her. For all she knew, this was another ploy by the Russians; this "attack" could have been staged to gain her trust, and as soon as she told him what she knew, he would kill her. "If you are Zero, then prove it."

"Sorry? Prove it?" He scoffed. "Prove it how, exactly?"

Kozlovsky laughed, even as his bodyguard Vasily writhed and whimpered on the floor mere feet away. "This is rich," he said in Russian. "She does not trust you, does she?"

Karina heard rapid footfalls behind them. She spun toward the sound. Zero did too, but as he turned he dropped to the floor, practically falling to his back with the gun aimed. At nearly the same time, the man in the black shirt rounded from the hall, a gun in his hand and a bandage over his nose.

The man skidded to a stop as he found his gun leveled at President Kozlovsky. Zero fired once from the floor, striking the man in the sternum. The gun fell from his hands as both pressed over his wound and he fell to his knees.

"Zero," he hissed painfully.

The alleged Zero turned to face her. "Your choices are stay here, or come with me," he said quickly. "Any minute now, we're going to have more guests. Now can we *please* get out of here?"

"He's here!" Kozlovsky barked in Russian. "Zero is here!"

They both spun again. The Russian president had grabbed the phone and was shouting into it. Karina acted without thinking; she aimed the black pistol and fired once. The shot came within two inches of hitting Kozlovsky in the head—but instead it struck the phone, sending it spinning out of the president's hand.

Along with two of his fingers.

Kozlovsky stared at his trembling, bleeding, three-fingered hand for a long moment. Then the screaming began.

Karina nearly dropped the weapon, simultaneously shocked and mortified by what she'd done. She'd never fired at anything living before; this was clearly a day of many firsts.

"Time to go." Zero grabbed her arm and pulled her to the kitchen. "Garage?"

"Um ... that way!" Karina shook herself from her stupor and pointed down the hall, past the bathroom, where she had been brought into the house. "Wait, keys!" She grabbed the ring from the granite countertop and tossed them to Zero.

They pushed out into the three-car garage, occupied by two SUVs and a town car. Zero pressed the fob and the lights of an SUV flashed. He reached for the large white button on the wall to open the garage bay when Karina pointed the gun at him once more.

"Come on," he groaned, "not this again."

"How did you find me here?" She needed to know she could trust him before she got in a car with him.

Zero grunted irritably. Then he took a deep breath and spouted, rapid-fire: "Your sister contacted me. I knew her as Sanders when we worked together a while back. Her name is Veronika. Yours is Karina. At least those are the names she gave me. I went to the theater to find you, but you were already gone. Friends of theirs picked me up to bring me here. Their car is crashed about a mile and a half from here, but only one of them is dead. The cavalry is coming, so we need to leave *right fucking now*. Okay? Is that good enough for you?"

She nodded once. "Yes. Let's go." She rounded the SUV and got in the passenger side. Zero smacked the button and the garage door began to roll up slowly. He slid in behind the wheel, pushed the key in the ignition—and then winced at the sudden bright lights that nearly blinded them.

"We're too late," Karina murmured. The headlights of at least four vehicles, maybe more, raced up the driveway toward them. She'd waited too long, delayed them unnecessarily.

"Not yet we're not." Zero twisted the key and the engine roared to life. "Put your seatbelt on."

Chapter Thirteen

Zero smashed down on the accelerator and the SUV lurched forward, the RPMs leaping nearly to six thousand as they took off from the garage bay like a shot. The interpreter frantically pulled her seatbelt across her chest.

We could have been clear of here if she'd just listened to me, he thought irritably. He clicked on the high beams as he played chicken with the oncoming cars.

"What are you doing?!" Karina shrieked beside him.

"Hang on." The oncoming vehicles weren't as reckless as he was; they veered to the right to avoid hitting them. Zero jerked the wheel to the left and drove onto the lawn, the tires tearing up the manicured grass. He swerved left and right to avoid the cherry blossom trees dotting the landscape.

"Wall!" Karina pointed ahead of them. "Wall!"

"Yeah, I see it!" He spun the wheel again, the back end of the SUV scraping against stone as they turned and raced parallel to the wall, toward the rear of the property.

"Where are we going?" she cried.

"Finding another way out. There must be a second gate, another exit."

"And if there's not?" she asked.

"Well, that's just poor planning on their part..."

Shots rang out behind them as the cars pursued them. Bullets smacked into their bumper. The rear windshield splintered, but held. *Bullet-resistant glass. Good to know.* Zero spun the wheel again, flying past the guest house, but he didn't see another gate. "Dammit."

He shifted his weight to try to pull the SMG out from beneath him, but the strap around his shoulder and neck was tangled in his seat belt. "Get the gun, the machine gun."

Karina reached over the center console as Zero spun the wheel again, circling back around toward the front of the house. The pursuers were still behind them, but if he could get out of the gate, he might have a chance to elude them. The interpreter tugged on the gun, which pulled on the strap, which pulled Zero's neck to an awkward angle.

"Jeez, careful! Just unclip it from the strap!"

"Oh. Right." Karina unfastened the gun and handed it to him.

"Thanks." The SUV spun around to the front of the house and back toward the driveway. Two of the vehicles were waiting for them. "Get down!"

Karina ducked low as bullets pounded the grille, the windshield, the door. Zero winced with each impact, but the glass held.

"Hold onto something!" He straightened the car and pushed the pedal to the floor as they hurtled toward the iron gate.

"Wait, don't—"

The SUV hit the iron gate at fifty-five miles an hour. The front end crumpled; the rear end came off the ground for a moment, and then crashed back down. Both Zero and Karina keeled forward violently as the airbags exploded in their faces.

The gate barely budged.

A slight moan escaped Zero's lips as he pushed himself upright in the seat again. His vision was blurry, his head pounded, and there was a ringing in his ears. He glanced over at Karina, slumped over the dashboard with blood eking from one nostril and white powder from the deflated airbag all over her face.

"Hey," he said weakly. "You okay?"

She winced as she looked over at him. "Why… in the *hell*… did you think that would work?"

He didn't really have an answer for that—well, he did, but the moment was not the right time to say *because I'm Zero, and things like that usually work out for me.* He glanced in the rearview mirror. Four cars surrounded them in a semicircle not ten yards behind the SUV, engines idling, doors open, the silhouettes of suited men taking cover behind them.

"There's nowhere to go!" a male voice shouted. "Come out with your hands on your head!"

"What are we going to do?" the interpreter screeched.

"For starters, we're going to stop shouting in my ear." Zero glanced around. The SMG had tumbled to the floor between his feet when they'd hit the gate. He reached for it. "Secondly, we're going to stay as still and silent as possible."

She gaped at him. "They're federal agents, not snakes…"

"Just please stay still and silent." He pressed the button to roll down the window. Thankfully, it still worked, or at least got about halfway before the bent door frame stopped it. "Still and silent."

Karina gulped, but did as he asked. Behind them, the agents continued shouting the usual rhetoric: "Come out with your hands on your head!" "You're surrounded!" "There's nowhere to go!" "Get out of the car, now!"

They know we're armed. There was no other reason for the agents to act so cautiously, for them to be taking cover, biding their time. But eventually they'd make a move and come for them. *Just don't move.*

"Do you have a plan?" Karina whispered.

"Yes," he whispered back. "I mean, sort of. When I say go, make a run for the wall and jump it."

"That's your plan?!"

"Stay still!"

"'Make a run for it'? You have got to be the most inept, useless, ineffectual—"

Click! The floodlights went out and Karina fell silent as they were thrust into darkness. Even the agents behind them ceased their shouting, unsure of what to do now that they couldn't see a thing.

Come on. Come get us.

He watched in the rearview mirror, taking care not to move his head and activate the lights again, and saw several silhouettes creeping forward, pistols at the ready.

Just a little further.

"They're coming," Karina whispered hoarsely.

"No kidding. Stay still."

One of the agents came around the rear of the SUV, walking heel to toe, gun aloft—

Click! The floodlights suddenly came to life again with the agent's movement, bright and powerful and near-blinding. In the same instant, Zero leaned out of the driver's side window and pulled the trigger on the SMG.

Karina let out a small shriek as a fusillade of bullets sprayed out like a thousand snare drum rolls. Zero waved the gun back and forth, hitting cars and asphalt and, by the yelps and shouts, a few people.

"Go!" he hissed to her.

She shoved the door open and tumbled out. Zero pushed his door open as well as he fired another burst. The banana clip in the SMG was a higher yield than usual, but he'd be out soon.

The agents ducked, ran, and leapt for cover as he fired recklessly. Then he tossed the SMG over the wall and scrambled up over it himself. Return fire pounded the stones as he vaulted feet over head and landed with a jolt on the other side. An electric pain sizzled up his spine and neck; crashing the gate had given him whiplash. He'd definitely be paying for that later.

He grabbed up the SMG again and fired the last of the rounds over his shoulder. Then he pulled the second Glock from his pants and started firing that back at the wall, even as he ran. A head appeared at the top, and then dropped back out of sight just as quickly as the bullets chipped stone.

Then Karina was beside him, keeping pace as they ran through grass adjacent to the narrow road. There were headlights coming up around the bend. "The trees!" He pointed, and the two of them sprinted toward the stout, thick-limbed trees lining both side of the road.

Zero reared back and hurled the empty SMG about fifteen yards out into the grass.

"Up!" he whispered.

Karina stared at him blankly. "Up? Up what? The tree?"

"Yes, the tree!" He could hear the voices shouting behind him, the Secret Service agents up the hill vaulting the wall and rushing down after them. Zero laced his fingers together and held them at knee level to give her a boost.

He was well aware of how ludicrous it sounded, hiding up in a tree like a squirrel, but they had no other choice. They couldn't outrun them on foot. They couldn't hide. They couldn't fight them off.

Karina seemed to come to the same conclusion. She stepped into his hands and he pushed her up high enough to reach the lowest limbs. As she pulled herself up, Zero ran past her, to the next nearest tree, and he jumped up and grabbed hold of a sturdy bough.

Pain shot through his back once again as he struggled and pulled himself up. *Yup, getting too old for this…*

The vehicle that had been coming up the winding road screeched to a halt mere yards from them. At nearly the same time, four agents ran over to meet it. Zero peered through the leaves as best he could.

It was a SWAT van. *Thank god we got out of there when we did.*

The SWAT captain got out, in full body armor and helmet, and nodded to the agent that approached him. "Sir."

"We've got two suspects on foot," the lead agent said quickly, "a thirty-four-year-old Russian woman and a man in his mid-forties."

Mid-forties? Zero almost scoffed aloud. *Screw you, pal.*

"They should be considered armed and extremely dangerous," the agent continued. "They can't have gotten very far. They'll most likely try to find a place to hide or steal a vehicle—"

"Sir!" one of the agents called out as he picked the SMG up from the grass. "Looks like he dropped this. They must have gone this way."

"All right," said the agent in charge. "You four, head that way on foot. Look for any trail, footprints, evidence of where they went." He turned to the SWAT member. "Captain, I want your guys canvassing every house in the vicinity. There aren't many. Look for tripped alarm systems, cameras feeds, and check for missing vehicles. You." He turned to the agent beside him. "Head back up to the house and help the others secure the Russian president. Emergency services are en route. Check on whoever might still be alive up there. Then call local PD and have them set up roadblocks a mile in each direction. Any car that comes by gets searched. Even if it's one of our own."

The SWAT van backed up, pulling a K-turn on the narrow road as they headed back down the way they came. For a brief moment, Zero's tree was awash in their headlights and he held his breath, fearing being spotted, but the van rumbled back down the long drive. The agents headed out on foot, their vehicles inaccessible until emergency services could clear the wreckage he'd caused by crashing into it.

Even after they'd all left, Zero remained in the tree for another thirty seconds or so, waiting and listening to the silence. It felt like much longer. Eventually he clambered down, noting the ache in his limbs, and then helped Karina down.

"Now what?" she whispered.

In response, he took her by the hand and led her down the winding road, sticking to the darkness of the tree line until they reached the crossroad. Zero dared to peer out and looked both ways. He saw no movement, no headlights. The last thing the agents would have expected them to do was stick around; they assumed the two were running for their lives at the moment.

"Come on." They crossed the road and stepped down the gentle slope on the other side, and then followed the road the same way Zero had originally come. If they followed it long enough, they'd reach the wreckage he'd left behind, but they wouldn't need to go that far.

"Is this wise?" Karina asked nervously. "Following the road?"

"Ordinarily, no. But we need a phone. I don't have one, and I doubt you do."

She shook her head.

"I found this place using one of the Russians' phones. But I tossed it. Now we need to find it." He scanned the grass in the darkness, trying to ascertain how far along he had been when he threw it. It hadn't been all that far from the mouth of the winding drive that led to the house.

"Can't they track it?" she asked. "The Russian's phone?"

Zero crouched, squinting down at the grass near his feet. "They can, but I don't think they will. Whatever's going on here, whatever dirt you've got on them, I think it's a good bet it's limited to the two presidents."

"What makes you say that?"

"Those Secret Service agents are loyal men. They attacked us because they were told we're the enemy." *The Russians learned their lesson last time. They're keeping this small, personal.*

"You realize you might have killed a couple of those 'loyal men'?"

"Yeah," he said quietly. "I realize." Then louder, "It should be right around here. Help me look."

Karina crouched low, scanning the dark, tall grass for any sign of the phone. "For what it's worth, I'm sorry. For calling you inept and useless."

"And ineffectual," he reminded her.

"Yes. And ineffectual. Your methods might be a little ... uncouth, but at least we got out of—"

Zero grabbed her arm and pulled her down to the grass as he scrambled to lie flat beside her. A vehicle rumbled by slowly up on the road, a mounted spotlight on the passenger side scanning the small hillside slowly. The light shined over their heads and passed.

Zero glanced up as the car moved on. As he pushed himself up from the wet grass, he grinned—the phone was lying two feet from his head. "Bingo." He grabbed it up and helped Karina to her feet. "We're not out of the woods yet," he reminded her. "Save your sorry until we're actually clear. Come on."

Chapter Fourteen

They hiked for another two miles, through a wide field and across a couple of back roads, barely talking, staying as silent and alert as they could. Zero spotted one of the roadblocks in the distance, two cop cars with their lights flashing and sawhorses set up across the asphalt. Hardly subtle and easy enough to avoid. They came to a gas station but skirted around it; there was a police cruiser parked in the small lot, the officer visible through the window chatting with the clerk. Looking for them.

Beyond the gas station was a stretch of trees. He knew where they were; if they crossed through the woods they'd come out in the DC suburbs, and the city beyond that.

In the relative safety and darkness of the trees, Zero paused. "I just need to know one thing. Did you actually record that meeting?"

Karina didn't reply. Instead she stared at her shoes.

"It's okay," he told her. "I understand. The only reason you're still alive is because they thought you might have." *Though this whole thing would be much easier if you had.* "So we need them to keep thinking that, but it paints a much bigger target on both our backs. Sanders—or rather, Veronika—wants me to get you to Kiev, but we'll have to take what we can get."

"But how will we get out of the country? They'll be watching every airport, every highway, every port…"

"I know. That's why I'm going to call in a favor." He punched the number into the Russian's phone and waited as it rang three times. Just when he thought it was going to go to voicemail, the line clicked and a gruff voice said, "Yes?"

"Alan. It's Zero."

"Zero! Whose number is this? Why are you calling so late? Are you okay?"

"Not really," he admitted. "I'm in a bit of a bind. I could use some help."

"Of course, anything you need."

"Great." Zero took a breath and said, "I need safe passage overseas for me and one other, as close to Kiev as we can get. Noncommercial, under the radar. I need aliases; IDs and passports. I'll need some cash too. A couple grand, ideally. Whatever you can spare."

Silence on the other end of the line.

"Alan?"

"When I said *anything*, I meant I'd help you move a sofa or something like that…"

"Alan, please."

"Christ, Zero. What did you get yourself into?"

"Long story. Too long to tell right now. Can you help?"

Reidigger blew out a sigh. "My contacts aren't quite what they used to be, but I can help. Where are you?"

"On foot. Eluding the cops."

"Of course you are," he muttered. "I'll come get you."

"Meet us at Walker Mill Road, near the little park, in twenty-five minutes."

"You got it."

"Thanks, Alan." Zero ended the call, but he hesitated with his thumb on the phone's screen. "I have to make one more call," he told Karina. *And it's not one I want to make.*

"We shouldn't linger," Karina said nervously.

"I know. It'll just be a minute." He dialed the number before he could think twice, and as he put the phone to his ear he meandered a short distance from the interpreter for some measure of privacy.

"Johansson," she answered. It sounded like she was driving.

"Hi, Maria."

"Kent! What the *hell* have you done?!" She sounded furious. He assumed she would have heard by now, but he thought she'd be more worried than angry. He was wrong. "One minute I'm sitting in bed, wondering where you are and if you're going to come home, the next I'm getting a call that you *attacked* the Russian president?"

"It's not what it seems like—"

"He was shot!" she shouted. "And a Russian diplomat was found dead on the road..."

Diplomat? He scoffed. The gangster he'd shot was a glorified thug, hardly a diplomat.

"Several Secret Service agents are hospitalized, two in critical condition—"

"I know," he said quickly, "but there's more to it than—"

"All this for an extortionist?"

"She is *not* an extortionist," he said forcefully, feeling anger rising in his face. "Maria, she knows what went down in that secret meeting, and it's nothing good. It's happening again, but they're being smarter about it this time—"

"And you know that how?" Maria interrupted. "Did she tell you what was said?"

"Well... no."

"Jesus, Kent." Maria scoffed. "Why are you doing this?"

"Because..."

"Is it because of what happened? Between us?"

"No!" he said sharply. "It has nothing to do with that."

"Then why, Kent?"

"Because..."

She needs me.

"Because I was asked to," he said. "Because I can't turn a blind eye to something like this. You know that."

"This isn't who you are anymore," Maria insisted.

"It's who I always was. I just forgot that for a while." He ran a hand through his hair, pushing it back off his forehead. "Look, I called you to tell you the truth. I'm not asking for your help."

"Good," said Maria. "Because I don't think I can help you now, Kent. I'm on my way to Langley for an emergency meeting to determine what the agency is going to do about you." She lowered her voice. "I can't believe I'm saying this, but the best thing you could do right now is cut her loose. Let her go her own way, and turn yourself in. Given your track record, we can vie for some leniency. Maybe tell them you were lied to, that you didn't know who Kozlovsky was..."

"You know I'm not going to do that."

"I care about you, Kent. But you have no ties to the agency anymore, no protection. If you keep going, this ends with you being locked up or dead. And I'm going to be obligated to do what I can about it. About you."

"Yeah," he muttered. "I know. It's your job, right? You'd better get to your meeting, Deputy Director. Be seeing you."

"Kent, wait—"

He ended the call. Before she could call back, he tore the battery from the phone and stomped it to pieces, out of practicality and catharsis in equal measure. That hadn't gone at all how he'd hoped.

But what were you hoping? That she'd offer help? Amnesty?

There was a time when Maria would have dropped what she was doing and destroyed anything and anyone that got between her and him. How many times had she told him that it was the two of them against the world? Against radical factions that threatened entire countries. Against assassins hell-bent on ending their lives. Even against the CIA and people they'd once called friends.

But not anymore. Maria had changed. The mysterious, dangerous beauty he'd found holed up in an Italian safe house was gone, replaced by a career woman and would-be mother playing the game of politics while wanting him to be the stay-at-home dad.

Zero almost laughed at himself as the realization hit him. That was the problem, wasn't it? There was no more mystery or intrigue between them. His memory had been restored. He knew who she was, and she knew him. They'd traded guile and covert operations for a domestic partnership and quiet dinners at home, but that wasn't what either of them really craved. At least not him. The love might still be there, but their spark, the lust, the fire they'd both once felt, was rooted in mistrust and deception.

Am I really that broken? he wondered.

He felt a hand on his shoulder. "Zero," Karina said gently. "We should go."

"Right." He had to get his head together. They were on the lam from every law enforcement agency in the land now, including the CIA. *Which means they know we'll try to leave the country.* Maria was plenty smart enough to know that he'd turn to Alan. He could only hope that she wouldn't give Reidigger up—or at the very least, give them a head-start.

"My contact is going to meet us. Let's go." He led the way, picking his way carefully through the meager woods.

"That second call," Karina said in a whisper behind him, "it didn't seem to go well. Was that someone you care about? A wife? Or girlfriend?"

He glanced over his shoulder at her. In the dim moonlight filtered through the trees, Karina's features were shadowy, dark, except for her brown eyes, which appeared to shine brighter than they should have been able.

Zero shook his head. "No," he said simply. "Former partner." He started again through the trees. "Come on. We have to move fast."

Chapter Fifteen

Maya rubbed sleep from her eyes as she followed the officer down the corridor, her bare feet padding softly against the tiled floor. She ran a hand through her hair and tried to look awake. Not five minutes earlier, she'd been shaken from sleep in the barracks by the MP, who had leaned over and harshly whispered, "Cadet Lawson. Come with me. *Now.*"

The man hadn't said another word. He hadn't even given her time to pull shoes on; he simply led the way out of the barracks and toward the administrative wing of the academy. Maya was in a T-shirt and shorts and bare feet, feeling rather stark as she followed the uniformed MP, fairly certain she knew their destination.

This is it, she thought glumly. *Greg reported me for leaving him behind in Virginia last weekend. Or maybe for kicking his ass in judo class.* Then a worse thought struck her: if the administration deemed Greg's complaint as assault, Maya could get booted from West Point. Attacking another cadet was a grievous offense, and Greg's parents had pull.

As she suspected, the MP led her straight to the closed door of the dean's office. Her heart sank as the officer positioned himself beside the door and without even looking at her said, "Go on in, cadet."

Maya swallowed the lump in her throat as she turned the knob and pushed the door open.

It was after eleven o'clock at night, yet the dean was still in full dress uniform, seated behind her desk in the spacious but admittedly austere office. Brigadier General Joanne Hunt was the first female USMA Dean in history, a 1984 graduate of the Point herself, and an accomplished and decorated officer. Maya had met her personally on two brief occasions before, as Dean Hunt liked to make time for short meetings with each cadet every year. Their interactions had been little more than a checking-in, but still she'd found the dean to be personable, even likable.

Tonight, however, Dean Hunt had her hands on the desk, fingers tented pensively, and a tight, if not stern expression on her face.

And she was not alone.

Maya closed the door behind her and stood at attention. "Ma'am."

"At ease, Ms. Lawson." Dean Hunt gestured to one of the two green guest chairs in front of her desk. "Please, have a seat."

"Thank you, ma'am." Maya lowered herself into the chair, trying not to look directly at the man standing beside BG Hunt's desk. He was older, early sixties perhaps, in a crisp blue suit. Between the dean and this stranger, Maya felt practically naked in her gray shorts and shirt.

"Do you know who this is?" Hunt asked, gesturing toward the man beside her.

"No, ma'am, I do not."

"I wouldn't expect you to, young lady." The man in the suit smiled. She didn't like his smile; it looked forced and insincere. "My name is David Barren. I'm the Director of National Intelligence." He held out a hand.

Maya shook his hand, though a nervous tingle ran up and down her spine. She was keenly aware that this was not at all about Greg. In fact, there was only one person this could possibly be about. *What has he done?*

"Ms. Lawson," said Dean Hunt, "there's no denying you are an asset to this academy. Judging by your success here so far, I am certain you'll go on to do great things. And you should know that very few people here know who you really are. Rather, who certain family members might be." Hunt paused for effect, but Maya simply sat there and did not allow herself to react.

But internally she was thinking, *They knew? All this time?*

"Of course I know about it," said Hunt, "as does Director Barren here."

Maya's stomach tightened. She didn't want the dean to keep talking; she didn't want to discover that she'd been admitted on the merit of being Agent Zero's daughter, like part of some twisted covert legacy. She wanted to keep believing she'd done it all on her own.

"We just want to ask you a few questions," said DNI Barren. "We understand you visited home this past weekend."

Maya nodded. "I did, sir. Though it was a very brief visit."

"During this visit," said the DNI, "did anything seem particularly amiss? Did your father mention any upcoming... trips? Anything he might have had planned?"

What are they fishing for? Maya wondered. They were being irritatingly pleasant, almost sycophantic. As if they were speaking to a child.

"No sir," she said honestly. "He didn't. In fact, he barely said anything. To be frank, our relationship has been strained for some time. The visit over the weekend was a halfhearted attempt at reconciliation. It was, in hindsight, a bad idea. I haven't seen or spoken to him since, and I have no desire to anytime soon. Sir."

Barren's smile faltered. "I see. May I ask the nature of this falling out?"

"No, sir, you may not." The words spilled from her mouth like a leaky faucet. Her heart skipped a beat; she was dangerously close to mouthing off to a very high-ranking government official in front of the dean. "With all due respect," she added quickly, "it's quite personal."

Dean Hunt and the DNI exchanged a glance. Some kind of an understanding seemed to pass between them, though Maya couldn't tell just what it was.

"You're obviously a very intelligent young woman," said Barren. "So I think we should just drop the pretense and get right down to brass tacks."

"Agreed, sir."

Barren sat on the edge of Hunt's desk and looked Maya right in the eye. "Earlier this evening, at approximately twenty-two hundred hours, a former CIA operative—your father—stormed a government property, injured several people, including the Russian president, and absconded with an interpreter who was extorting both the US and Russian leaders. Both she and your father are currently missing. The interpreter is a Ukrainian-born woman who may have extremely sensitive information."

Maya couldn't hide her reaction this time. Her eyes widened in surprise and her lips parted slightly as she gaped at the DNI. *What? Why would he do that?* She had just seen her father a couple of days ago, and he seemed—well, he had seemed so subdued. Defeated, even.

To her surprise, she found herself worrying for him, hoping that he was all right. It was a perfectly natural reaction, she reasoned. Still, it made her think twice about the way they had left things.

But then an even more alarming thought struck her. The dean hadn't just called her in here to tell her about this. They had woken her, dragged her out of bed, and brought her there because they thought she might have information on her father's whereabouts.

And just a moment later, David Barren confirmed it. "Naturally, Ms. Lawson, you have to imagine that your recent visit there, and being his next of kin, has led us to believe you might know something about all this."

"To be clear, cadet," Dean Hunt cut in, "you're not in any sort of trouble. Yet. You have an opportunity, here and now, to be on the right side of things. To tell us anything you might know, or anything he might have mentioned. We need you to really think."

"Because if we discover later that you knew something, and you withheld it," Barren said sternly, "there would be a steep price to pay, and it would come out of your future."

Son of a bitch. She had tried, tried so hard to extricate herself from her father's image, his influence, his deceit. Yet here he was again, threatening her goals without even being present in the room. It was astounding how difficult it was to separate herself from Agent Zero.

And still, she found herself hoping that he was okay.

"Sir. Ma'am," Maya said carefully. "I am telling you with complete honesty and candor that I don't have any information for you. I don't know why he's done this. I don't know where he would have gone. If he has a plan, I don't know what it is. I understand that my visit to him so recently might look suspicious, but I have witnesses that will tell you that the visit ended with me telling him that I never wanted to see him again and storming out of his home."

She looked directly at the Director of National Intelligence as she said, "You want to know what caused the rift between me and my father, sir? Lies and deception are more than just his livelihood. They're his addiction. And like any good addict, he would deny it to be the case, but I don't think he knows who he is without it. I've come to believe that his life as a professor and a husband and a father was, to him, just a cover. His identity as a CIA agent was his truth. His reality. I can't tell you what you want to know because I don't understand him. I don't believe I actually know him anymore ... if I ever really did."

The dean's office was silent for a long moment after, though Maya held the DNI's gaze so that he understood she was being genuine. He blinked and glanced over at Dean Hunt, who nodded slightly.

"Thank you, cadet," she said. "You may return to the barracks. I hope you understand that you'll be monitored until this situation is resolved."

Maya nodded. "I have nothing to hide, ma'am."

"And if he attempts to contact you in any way," said DNI Barren, "you'll do the right thing."

It didn't sound like a question as much as it did a demand. Still, Maya nodded again. "Yes, sir."

"Thank you for your time, Ms. Lawson." Barren shook her hand once more, and again he flashed his forced, insincere smile.

Maya pushed the door open and stepped into the corridor. The waiting MP, as if on cue, turned on a heel and began leading the way back to the dorm. Maya followed dutifully, though her mind was racing a mile a minute. She knew she'd get little sleep that night.

Why would he do that? she wondered again. Her father was a lot of things, but stupid wasn't among them. He had to have a reason. But he wasn't CIA anymore—which meant this wasn't part of an assignment. Had he done this on his own? Did he discover something himself? How, when he spent his days alone in that small house?

More importantly, did he not stop long enough to realize how this might reflect on her? That he could, once again, be screwing up her life, her future, and her plans?

In all her confusion and indignation she hadn't realized what was potentially the biggest problem of all—and when it dawned on her, she nearly stopped in her tracks.

She had lied, not only to Dean Hunt but also to the Director of National Intelligence. She had outright lied when she said, "*I don't know where he would have gone.*"

She knew that in a time of crisis like this one, her father would turn to the only man he could trust: his best friend and fellow former agent, Alan Reidigger. Maya knew that, and she had said nothing. A small part of her actually thought about turning around and marching right back into the office, but she kept going, following the MP.

Alan had saved her life. Sara's too. Maya knew he'd been living almost four years incognito under the guise of a mechanic named Mitch. She was one of only a handful of people in the entire world who knew the truth, and she couldn't turn on him like that. Whatever reasons he had for keeping up the charade were his own; it was not her place to out him.

She could only hope that Alan would do the right thing, and turn her father in.

Chapter Sixteen

The plane jostled with turbulence and Karina gasped in the darkness of their cramped quarters.

"Tell me," she said wryly, "do all CIA agents travel in such luxury?"

The two of them were sitting with their backs against opposite walls of a five-foot-by-five-foot crate of sturdy, industrial plastic. The narrow door to Zero's left was locked from the outside, and the crate was situated atop a wooden pallet which was in the cargo hold of a small plane which was flying over the Atlantic Ocean en route to Europe.

"I'm not a CIA agent anymore," he reminded her. He imagined that she only knew that because of her sister, if they were really sisters, Emilia Sanders or Veronika or whatever her real name was. "How much did she tell you about me?"

"Not much," Karina admitted. "Only that you worked with her when FIS discovered the Russian plot to seize the Ukrainian assets in the Baltic. You saved the president's life. And you jumped off a bridge or something foolish like that—which, after what I've seen of your work so far, I fully believe."

He grinned in the darkness, though Karina couldn't see it. In their cramped space, her left leg was pressed against his, their feet nearly reaching the crate's opposite wall. Aside from a thin blanket on the floor for padding, they had a few bottles of water and a wad of cash and nothing else.

They'd met with Reidigger at the appointed spot, and he'd taken them straight to a small airstrip in southern Maryland. He knew a pilot there that specialized in transporting live animals overseas, to zoos and nature preserves and occasionally to be reintroduced into the wild. With a greased palm and a debt called even, the pilot was more than happy to transport a crate to his destination, which was Dusseldorf, Germany. It was still quite a distance from Kiev, but it was the closest that Alan could get them on such impossibly short notice. Zero knew he couldn't ask for more; it was a small miracle that they were able to even get that.

Alan's instructions to the pilot were simple: do not look inside the crate, unload it at the freight depot in Germany, and unlock the door before he left.

From there, Karina and Zero would have to stay under the radar while they met with another of Alan's contacts, a forger from Cologne who already had their photos and would have American identifications and passports ready for them. They were to meet him at the train station adjacent to the airport. And then they would be able to travel freely to Kiev, where they would liaise with Veronika and her FIS team.

Zero couldn't help but wonder just what in the world Alan had done in the two years he'd been MIA to have garnered all of these contacts and owed favors. But he wasn't sure he really wanted to know.

"I'm starving," Karina grumbled. "I can't remember the last time I've eaten."

Neither could he. He hadn't been thinking about it until she'd said something, but his stomach roiled with hunger. "We'll get something as soon as we're able. Just another…" He sighed. "Five hours or so, I guess."

"I would try to get some sleep, but our situation is far from comfortable."

"Oh. Well, let's try to resituate here." He shifted to the side, noting the cramping in his back, the protest of pain in his shoulders and spine. *What I wouldn't do for a couple of aspirin.* He'd taken off his jacket since it was warm inside their crate; he rolled it in his hands and held it out. "Here, use this as a pillow."

She reached out in the darkness, her fingers brushing his and, if he wasn't mistaken, lingering a moment too long. He was probably mistaken. She took it and shifted herself to one side, her back against his legs now and her feet curled up beneath her own legs.

"Thank you."

"No problem."

"I mean …" She hesitated. "For helping me. For doing all of this. I would be dead now otherwise."

"It's sort of what I do," he said casually. "Or what I used to do." He thought for a moment before saying, "But there is a way you could at least start to repay me. I want to know what you know. Why they're so bent on getting to you. What was said in that meeting."

Silence reigned in the crate, the only sound the loud humming of the plane's engines that had become little more than background noise after the hours they'd already spent in there.

"No," she said quietly.

"No?" Zero blinked. "It might have sounded like a question, but I wasn't exactly asking. I've risked my life to save yours, and now I'm risking it to help you. I think I deserve to know."

"Telling you would endanger you further," she said, her soft voice implying that she was facing the side of the crate with her head on his jacket, even though he could barely see her.

"It's a little late for that, you realize," he said flatly.

"If you knew what I know, they would want to capture you as well—"

"Right, instead of just killing me outright, which they're willing to do now—"

"So they could torture you for what you knew, all because I told you—"

"You think they'd be the first to torture me for information?" He scoffed, his voice getting heated. This woman was getting pretty presumptuous about who he was and what he should or shouldn't know. "Worst people have tried."

"Mr. Zero," she said harshly, "this is not a competition about who is most adept at torture. If my being unwilling to tell you what

I know bruises your fragile secret-agent ego, perhaps you should keep in mind you are far from the only person to risk life and limb in the interest of their country and its people."

Despite himself, Zero snorted and let out a small laugh. "Did you just call me 'Mr. Zero'?"

"Well...yes. You've made it clear that you're not an agent anymore."

He chuckled again. *Mr. Zero.* He almost wished Alan was there to hear it. "It's just Zero." The amusement of the moment faded quickly, and he found himself once again thinking about her refusal to tell him how the secret meeting shook out. "It's self-preservation, isn't it?"

"I'm sorry?"

"The reason you won't tell me. The people after you want to know what you know. If you told someone else, like me, then you'd be less valuable. They might kill you and take your confidant instead. Keeping the information to yourself is how you think you'll stay alive."

He didn't intend for it to come out as harsh or demeaning, though once he'd said it he understood how it could be taken that way. But he didn't apologize for it, and Karina fell silent for a long moment.

At last she said, "If that was the case, would you still help me?"

"Yeah. I would."

Silence stretched between them, the plane's engine thrumming beneath their crate. At last Karina said, "President Harris is in the Russians' pocket. I don't know what he did to get there, but I have reason to believe they helped him attain the presidency. In the meeting, Kozlovsky asked two things of Harris, both of which threaten not only my country, Ukraine, but potentially the world at large." She lowered her voice and added, "That is all I'm willing to say right now."

Zero nodded, though she couldn't see him in the darkness. She kept her word and said nothing further, and soon he felt her breathing grow deeper and rhythmic, her back shifting slightly against his calf. She'd fallen asleep.

He leaned his head back against the hard plastic wall of the crate. It wasn't comfortable, but he was exhausted. As he closed his eyes he wondered what his daughters would believe if he was killed while helping Karina. No matter what might be said publicly, would they know in their hearts that he had tried to do the right thing? Or would they think it was just one more fool's errand in a long and storied history, the swan song of a has-been attempting to relive some past glory?

The thought was hardly a comforting one, but it was the only one he had as the plane's steady engines lulled him to sleep.

Zero was trapped, confined to a tiny space. He couldn't stand, he could hardly move—but the walls were no longer thick plastic. They were made of packed dirt. The air smelled of earth and moisture and rank body odor. An iron grate was over his head, the only exit, locked tight with a padlock the size of a fist.

He'd seen holes like this one before, though he'd never been in one. It was where people were put when the world wanted to forget about them, people who weren't worth the effort to kill, people who deserved the worst sort of slow death that this vicious oubliette could offer.

There was a sound above him, a clang, and then boots on the iron grate. The padlock was removed, the grate raised, and then hands were reaching for him, pulling him from the hole. He tried to resist, but his limbs were weak. His voice did not seem to work.

His captor pulled him up out of the hole as if he weighed nothing, and then tossed him to the ground. He was in a small dome-like structure, practically a tent, with the iron grate set in the ground in the center and a single bare bulb overhead.

Zero's fears were confirmed. This was H-6, the Moroccan black site where the CIA and other government agencies left the worst of the worst to die. The place they jokingly called Hell-Six.

His captor brushed the hair from her forehead as she reached for her back pocket.

Zero could not believe his eyes. He wanted to shout to her, but again his vocal cords failed him.

Maya!

She pulled something from her pocket, something shiny, metallic, small—a pair of pliers.

No…

He tried to scramble away, but she dropped a knee on his chest. There was no escape. This was her job now. But she didn't want to know what he knew; he could feel it in her intense glare. She just wanted to hurt him.

Maya grabbed his chin and forced his head still, even as he gasped for breath and tried to strain against her grip. She was strong. Stronger than him.

Maya, please…

Don't!

There was nothing he could do as she forced the pliers into his mouth.

Chapter Seventeen

Zero awoke with a start as the plane dropped in altitude, the pressure change making his ears pop. It was a dream—no, a nightmare. He was still inside the gray plastic crate on a cargo plane bound for Germany, and by the sensation in his gut telling him they were descending rapidly, it seemed as if they'd arrived. He groaned as he sat up against the crate's wall; his neck was not only sore, but now stiff as well. He stretched it left and right as he said, "Karina?"

"Mm." She let out a soft groan as she pushed herself up from the crate floor.

"I think we're landing—"

The wheels hit the tarmac with a *whump* that had them both sucking in a startled breath. Karina's hand shot out to steady herself and latched onto Zero's knee. She laughed nervously at herself.

"Finally," she murmured in Polish. "Thank god."

He smiled in the darkness of the hold and the crate. "You really are an interpreter, aren't you?"

"Yes. Did you not believe me?"

"In my line of work, I tend to have a lot of doubts." As the plane taxied on a runway he asked, "And Sanders—rather, Veronika. Is she really your sister?"

Karina stretched her arms as best she could in their narrow confines. "Half-sister, if you want to be technical. Her father passed away when she was only an infant. Our mother remarried and had me two years later. But that hardly matters; to me, she is my sister, the only one I've ever known."

Zero didn't press any further, because he was pretty sure he knew how the story went from there. Sanders/Veronika became an agent of the Ukrainian FIS, and her little sister became an interpreter. When Karina needed help, she turned to the only person she believed she could trust.

The plane slowed and taxied to a stop. The ensuing several minutes were spent in darkness and silence, each of them waiting and listening until the plane's engines powered down and the electronic hatch at the rear whirred, lowering against the tarmac.

"What time is it here?" Karina whispered.

"Not sure." Zero had no phone or watch. "Assuming the flight took about ten to eleven hours, plus accounting for the time difference, I'd guess it's close to seven p.m. local time."

Karina sighed. "We lost almost an entire day."

Zero heard a rumbling outside the crate, wheels against the metal floor of the cargo plane. Then a rumbling beneath them as a pallet jack was pushed under the crate. They bounced slightly as someone—presumably the pilot—pumped the jack, lifting the pallet and crate a few inches, and then pulling it down the ramp and off the plane.

Zero braced his arms against the walls of the crate as they rumbled over tarmac for a short distance before finally coming to a stop. The pallet jack hissed slightly as it lowered the crate, and Zero heard the lock slide open from the other side.

Still he didn't move or dare to open the door yet. "Let's just stay put for a bit," he whispered softly to Karina.

Zero listened intently near the door for another several minutes before he dared to push it open an inch. He saw a sliver of purple skyline; the sun had set, but night hadn't fully descended yet. He saw no movement, so he pushed the door open the rest of the way and climbed out, at last able to stand to full height—which was both a blessing and a curse, evident by his aching lumbar region.

"Clear," he said over his shoulder, and Karina climbed out after him. She handed him his jacket and he pulled it on, then making sure the silenced Sig Sauer was still tucked in his pants.

They were standing on a runway, not far from a stout building that was likely a freight depot, with a few inert planes parked behind it. Their crate was in line with several other containers and pallets of goods that were waiting to be moved to one place or another. There were lights on inside the building, which likely meant people, which to Zero meant they should go the opposite way.

Karina stretched, shook out her dark hair, and then gingerly sniffed her shirt, making a face. "I can't remember the last time I've needed a shower so badly."

He nodded his agreement. "Identities first, shower later. This way."

The runway on which they'd landed was part of the larger complex that was the Dusseldorf International Airport, but the commercial terminals were far from where they'd been dropped off. Zero kept his head up and made no attempt to hide himself or sneak around, and instructed Karina to do the same; no one was looking for them in Germany, so as long as they looked like they belonged they could get by without much issue. Or so he hoped.

"Can I ask you something?" he said as they walked around the perimeter of the runway, toward an access road that would lead them toward the airport's main terminals. "I understand having distrust; believe me, no one has more trust issues than me. But why not take what you know to the media, or to the FBI?"

Karina chewed her bottom lip for a moment. "A couple of years ago," she began, "I was interpreting for a German diplomat who lost his temper in a meeting and said some very untoward things. Afterward, he tried to rescind his statement by blaming me for skewing his words. Despite my best efforts to set the record straight, I was reported as having been the cause of the relations breaking down. This diplomat was not only quite wealthy, but had significant investments in the German media. I was publicly ridiculed; no one would listen to me. I am fortunate it didn't destroy my career. I haven't set foot in this country since."

"I'm sorry," Zero told her quietly. He knew all too well what it was like for those in positions of power to stifle a voice, especially one that wasn't supposed to be heard in the first place.

"It taught me a valuable lesson about the influence of politics and wealth." One hand absently touched the pearl stud in her left ear. "The truth does not have to be what actually happened; sometimes it is just what the most prominent voices declare it to be."

He nodded his agreement. "I can relate." There was something about her eyes in the moonlight that made them look no longer brown, but an amber color, as if there was a light behind them shining out into the night. In fact, he hadn't noticed it before, what with all the fleeing and shooting and escaping, but she was quite beautiful—

Stop, he told himself. This was just another mysterious and potentially dangerous woman. *Don't do that to yourself again.*

Karina raised an eyebrow, as if reading his mind or maybe just wondering what he was thinking. But she didn't ask.

"Once we rendezvous with your sister," he continued, "what do you plan to do with this information?"

"Simple," she said. "With Veronika at my side, we will bring it to the Ukrainian government. They might not take my word for it alone, but they will listen to her and FIS. And I will let them decide what course of action will be best. After all that I've been through, I don't trust anyone else to learn what I know first." Then she turned and continued toward the airport as she said, "You must have an interesting view of the world, Zero."

"How's that?"

"You clearly believe that the information in my head is worthwhile—and you are correct—but I'm curious to know what your plan will be after we liaise with Veronika."

"Sorry?"

"You admitted yourself that you killed a Russian. You injured several more. You threatened a president at gunpoint. You rescued me—which I'm sure could be construed as kidnapping or aiding and abetting or perhaps all of the above. Do you think that revealing the knowledge of the presidents' meeting will nullify all of that?"

"I..." He was about to say that yes, he did think that, but again the stark insight flashed through his mind that he didn't have the protective aegis of the CIA anymore. Maria had made it clear that she could not help him. Previously everything that he did while on an op—which often including killing, injuring, sometimes torturing, destruction of property, stealing vehicles, all manner of things that would be deemed felonies to ordinary citizens—was done in the name of national and international security.

Karina was most likely right. No matter how dire the circumstances of the secret meeting, he would still eventually have to face the music. He was reminded of the old and hackneyed saying: *Two wrongs don't make a right.*

It just hadn't ever been applicable to him before.

"How about we just take this one step at a time?" he said finally.

"Agreed."

They reached the airport and made their way toward Terminal C, and from there took an escalator down to the lower floor. They would not be getting on any planes, of course, since they lacked identification; in fact, that was the whole reason they were there.

Beneath Terminal C was the Dusseldorf *Hauptbanhof,* or Central Station, where they would meet Alan's forger contact and procure their IDs. From there they could hop on a speedy white train and take it east, over the border toward Ukraine.

The train station was not all that dissimilar to those in the United States, a large building that was primarily one enormous chamber, high-ceilinged and echoing, with various offshoots and stairs that led to different platforms. The two of them headed across the wide floor, skirting around passengers either arriving or departing as they made their way toward a café at the farthest end of the station. It was there that Reidigger said they would meet the forger.

They entered the café and got in line behind two other people at the counter. Zero glanced around casually; Alan had been adamant that neither the forger nor Zero would know the other's identity, but he had told him to look for a man in his late forties with dirty-blond hair and eyeglasses who would be wearing a brown jacket.

He didn't see anyone who fit the description. There was a clock on the wall that told him the local time was seven thirty-five in the evening; the forger was supposed to have arrived at seven thirty and waited one hour until Zero and Karina could get there.

Karina cleared her throat loudly (and somewhat obviously) as a man got in line behind them. Zero resisted the urge to shush her and instead pretended to examine the menu board overhead, though he was actually checking the man out in his periphery.

He looked the right age, and had sandy hair, and the brown jacket—though he wasn't wearing eyeglasses.

To his surprise, as he was deliberating whether or not to address him, the man spoke first. "What is it you are looking for?"

Zero turned to face him. The man needed a shave, and his eyelids had deep creases that suggested he spent a lot of time squinting. Though he spoke English, his accent was clearly French, not German—though, he realized, Alan had never explicitly said that the man was native German. He'd only said that the forger was coming from Cologne.

Still, it didn't feel right to him.

"Just getting a cup of coffee," Zero replied. He turned back around and said to Karina, "What looks good to you?"

She frowned at him, clearly wondering why they were not addressing the man behind them. "Leaving here on a train would be nice," she said quietly. Before he could stop her, she turned around to the man and asked, "Are you meeting someone?"

"Indeed I am," the Frenchman said. "Two people, in fact. Americans." He gestured toward a round table nearby. "Shall we?" He left the line, and Karina followed.

Zero hesitated. He had a bad feeling about this. If the man they were supposed to meet in Germany was French, Alan would have told him that. Wouldn't he? It wasn't likely a detail he'd overlook … but at the same time, they had been in a rush. All of this had been hastily organized.

The barista behind the counter cleared her throat. Zero was next in line and holding up those behind him. "Oh, um, changed my mind. Thanks." He stepped out of line and joined Karina and the Frenchman at the table.

"Let's be quick," the Frenchman said. "I do not want to linger." He reached into his brown jacket, but Zero held up a hand.

"Wait. Just one question. The name of the man who sent you. Our mutual acquaintance."

"Certainly," the man said. "Just as soon as you tell me precisely why you are here."

Zero raised an eyebrow. The persistent feeling that something was amiss was growing stronger by the second. "Come on," he said to Karina. "We're leaving." He stood, and she did too.

But while he took two steps away from the café table, Karina remained, glaring down at the alleged forger. "You don't know what we've done to get here," she told him quietly, venom in her tone. "You've been paid. You've made the trip here. Either you have what we want or you don't."

The man glanced up at her, a thin smirk on his face. He reached into his jacket again, this time pulling out a small document case of black leather, not much wider than his palm. He set it on the table's surface and pushed it toward her.

Karina glanced over at Zero for a moment, and then reached for the case. He looked over her shoulder as she opened it.

It did not have two passports inside.

Instead Zero looked down at a small silver shield—a badge. And opposite it, an ID card with the word "INTERPOL" in large capital blue letters.

Zero was right.

This man was not the forger. He was an Interpol agent.

"My name is Inspector Ives," he told them. "And you are both under arrest."

Chapter Eighteen

Zero's instincts kicked in immediately and he spun, ready to sprint out of the café. But two more men in plainclothes appeared suddenly at the coffee shop's entrance. One had a hand on his hip, the holster obscured by the hem of a coat, and the other inside a jacket.

A thousand questions sped through his mind, chief among them: *How?* Reidigger certainly hadn't sold them out. It must have been the forger, the real forger. But he didn't even know who they were. All Alan had told him was that two Americans needed identification…

They don't know who we are, he realized. This was a sting operation to catch the recipients of the forged documents. Interpol didn't know who Zero and Karina were—because if they did, they would have brought an army.

The man who'd posed as the forger, Inspector Ives, tucked his badge back into his jacket as he stood. "I assure you, you are very much surrounded. We do not want to cause a big scene, so please put your hands on your head and face the wall."

Zero nodded to Karina once and slowly raised his hands to his head.

But she did not do the same. Instead she glanced at him with panic in her eyes. "We cannot…" she said in Russian.

"Just do as he says," Zero told her, instinctively responding in the same language.

"What is that you said?" Ives demanded as he stepped over to Karina, handcuffs already out. The other two agents approached from the entrance, hands resting on holsters.

"We cannot let them take us in," Karina argued, her gaze flitting between Zero and the cautious Ives. "We must get to Veronika!"

"I have a friend in Interpol," Zero said quickly, still speaking in Russian so that the inspector would not understand. It had been quite a long time, more than a year, since he'd even thought of his friend Vicente Baraf, let alone actually spoke to him. "We'll contact him and tell him what's going on. He'll believe me—us. He'll believe us. He can help."

"Enough!" Ives barked at Karina in English. "Hands on your head, and turn around!"

Karina scowled deeply at him, but she slowly began to raise her hands to her skull. Ives held the cuffs up, ready to secure them around her wrist—but then she shot out a hand, pushing the flat of her palm right into his face. Ives's head jerked back, and in that moment of imbalance Karina launched herself at him and tackled the Interpol agent to the ground.

"Karina, stop!" Zero shouted, but at the same time he saw the other two agents making a move toward them. His instincts kicked in; the Sig Sauer was already in his hand and aimed before he realized he'd grabbed for it. "Stop!" he demanded. "Hands up!"

The barista behind the counter shrieked. The few other patrons in the coffee shop scattered at the sight of the gun, dashing for the exit. The two agents complied, putting empty hands over their heads. Neither of them wished to be shot in what they likely presumed would be a simple operation.

Behind him, Inspector Ives shoved Karina off of him with a grunt—but the interpreter rolled away with something in her hands. It was his sidearm, a black Beretta 92FS yanked free from his jacket.

She scrambled to her feet and aimed it at Ives, breathing hard.

She's good with her hands, Zero noted dourly. *Too bad she wasn't using her head.*

"Karina," he said lowly. "What are we doing?"

"I will *not* turn myself in to anyone other than my sister," she said, teeth clenched.

Zero could see no other choice but to get out of there as quickly as possible. There was no way this would end amiably now. He relieved the two agents of their pistols and deposited them in the nearest silver trash bin. "Over there. Sit. If you follow us, we'll start shooting people."

Ives chuckled hoarsely as he slowly rose from on the floor.

"Don't move!" Karina grunted at him, aiming the Beretta at his head.

Still he climbed to his feet, seemingly unafraid of her. "You do not actually believe you are going to make it out of here, do you?"

In response, Karina delivered a solid crack to the top of his head with the butt of the pistol. The Interpol inspector folded like an empty sack.

"Karina!" Zero scolded in disbelief. He grabbed her arm and yanked her toward the exit. "Come on, time to go." They ran, Zero shoving the Sig Sauer into his jacket and Karina hiding the Beretta in the back of her pants. But as they left the café and rushed out onto the main station floor, they saw more than half a dozen white-uniformed security guards hurrying toward them, pushing past and around fleeing travelers.

Zero skidded to a stop. *Now what?* He really didn't want to fight his way out; it would just give Interpol more time to intervene.

But Karina seemed to be one step ahead. She shrieked loudly, clutching at Zero's shoulder and her expression contorting to horror. "*Gewehr!*" she shouted at the security officers as she pointed toward the café. "*Gewehr!*"

Gun!

The bewildered guards pulled revolvers of their own as they entered the café, or attempted to, because at the same time the two Interpol agents that Zero had disarmed were trying to exit, and they ran smack into each other with shouts and threats of stopping and putting hands up and proving identification.

Zero grabbed Karina's hand and pulled her along behind him as they hurried toward the terminal's row of glass doors that led outside. "Nicely done," he murmured.

"Thanks," she replied breathlessly.

"That was sarcasm. Why in the hell did you attack that agent?"

"As I told you," she hissed, "I will not turn myself in to anyone but FIS. We cannot afford to get caught now. We've come too far. As you said before, we're still in the woods."

"Not out of the woods yet," he corrected under his breath. If they stopped moving for even a moment, it wouldn't take long for the Interpol agents to catch up to them, to call for backup, or to convince the security team that it was them they should be after—

"Whoa!" Zero backpedaled suddenly, one hand on a glass door's crossbar. Through it he saw three German police cruisers parked right outside and five uniformed officers rushing toward the entrance. "This way!"

He and Karina ran back the other direction. There was another exit on the other side of the station that emerged onto a parallel street, but there would likely be cops there too. To their left was an escalator heading down to a sublevel train platform. He headed for it with Karina in tow.

"There!" a voice shouted to the right of them. The two Interpol agents were on the station floor, surrounded by the white-uniformed security guards, pointing right at Zero. "Those two, there!"

"Down!" Zero instructed as he pulled her toward the escalator. He let go of her hand and reached for the small of her back, tugging the Beretta from the waistband of her jeans. "Just gonna borrow this real quick." He tucked the gun under his armpit, concealing it as best he could, and fired twice from the crook of his shoulder.

The shots were impossibly loud, echoing in the vast station. Both struck a narrow advertising kiosk. Glass exploded and people screamed, scattering, having no idea what direction the shooting was coming from. Zero ducked his head amid the frothing sea of fleeing station-goers as the two of them reached the escalator and hurried down.

"We can't exactly get on a train!" Karina followed closely behind him as he elbowed people out of the way.

"Sure we can," he replied. He stopped abruptly when they reached the bottom of the escalator; two more security guards were hurrying toward the stairs.

Karina grabbed one of them by the shoulder. "Up there," she said quickly in German. "Two men are shooting! They are posing as police! Hurry!"

The guards thanked her and rushed up the escalator, one of them drawing a revolver while the other radioed what she'd said. Zero was impressed; though he didn't have time to say it in the moment, it seemed that she was quite good at sowing confusion.

They jumped the turnstile and hurried toward the nearest platform just in time to see a sleek white metro train pulling into the station. The disembarking passengers had no idea what was going on, and didn't even seem to notice that the platform was empty besides the two of them. Anyone who had been waiting for the train had fled at the sound of the gunshots.

"Zero, what are we doing?" Karina protested as they stepped onto the train.

"Act casual," he told her, hiding the Beretta in his jacket. A few passengers seated on the three-quarters full train glanced up at them, but then looked away just as quickly in disinterest.

"We have nowhere to go!" she hissed quietly.

Come on, he thought impatiently, waiting for the doors to close. *Come on, come on…*

Through the window of the train, he saw the two Interpol agents, several security guards, and a handful of police dashing onto the platform.

The doors still hadn't closed.

One of the agents spotted Karina through the train's window. He pointed, shouting something that Zero couldn't hear but didn't need to.

Shit! He had to think fast—which, he already knew, usually meant he was about to do something reckless and impulsive.

He raised the Beretta over his head, barrel at an angle toward the ceiling, and fired once. The blast was deafening and sparks showered from the broken lights. The reaction was instant; passengers leapt or even fell out of their seats, dozens of heads snapping in the direction of the gun, as if it was an animate object and not being held by a man.

"Off the train!" he bellowed.

Karina picked up the command in German. "*Steigt euch dem Zug aus!*"

Given the choice between remaining on the train with a gun-wielding madman or following the order, the people on the train unanimously seemed to come to the same conclusion. They rushed the doors so quickly that several people were knocked down, some crying out as four or five people at a time jammed the doors and squeezed through.

The agents and officers trying to get to the train were suddenly swept up in the flood of passengers hurtling the other way. Zero saw at least one security guard vanish beneath the crowd, and one of the Interpol agents was shoved roughly against a concrete column.

Zero strode to the front of the train car, threw open the door, and fired another shot. "Off! Off the train!" More than half of the next car had already emptied, having heard the gunshot. "Come on!" he called to Karina as they continued onward toward the front.

The train emptied quickly, some people leaving behind their bags and personal items as Zero pushed through another car. Finally, mercifully, the doors hissed closed and the train began to roll forward, a recorded female voice announcing the next three stops in both German and English.

Automated, Zero thought with a sigh of relief. The train system was automated—which meant that it knew to leave the station, but could likely be stopped remotely as soon as it was confirmed that they were aboard. They didn't have much time.

Through the window of the car, he saw one of the Interpol agents from the café reach the train and smack the glass angrily as they pulled away from the platform.

He let himself relax then, at least a little, the tension leaving his shoulders and taking what felt like the first breath since the inspector had revealed himself in the café.

He felt a hand on his waist as Karina stepped toward him, her hands under his jacket as if she was going to hug him. For a moment, he was terribly confused—but then she stepped back, and the silenced Sig Sauer was in her hand.

She aimed just past his left arm and fired once, behind him. As Zero spun, he heard a yelp. A German officer had snuck onto the train with them and reached their car. The bullet hit him in the thigh; he dropped his pistol as his leg buckled, both hands pressing over the bleeding wound.

"Thanks," he murmured.

"Mm-hmm. Trade?" She offered him back the Sig in return for the Beretta, and then she retrieved the cop's gun from the floor as he groaned. Karina leaned over him and said, "Hang in there. They'll stop us soon." Then she looked up at Zero as if the message was meant for more than just the officer.

He nodded. There was no way they would let the train get as far as its next stop. "They'll gather whoever they can and try to cut us off somewhere in the open, somewhere they can surround the train and minimize potential casualties." But he didn't know Dusseldorf well enough to assume where that might be, let alone the train's route.

In the window he saw his own translucent reflection, and beyond it the darkness of the night and the road that ran parallel to the tracks. He saw the blue flashing lights of several police cruisers as they sped along, past the train, toward whatever destination they would inevitably stop. Then the tracks curved downward, staying at ground level while the road rose in an overpass.

"Ideas?" Karina asked.

"Just one." He raised the Sig Sauer and fired twice at the oblong window. The safety glass splintered into a spider-web pattern but held in the frame. Zero stood on a bench seat, lifted a foot, and kicked at the window. The first two kicks warped the window in its frame; on the third kick the glass gave and fell away in one piece, tumbling into the darkness.

The idea had sounded like a much better one in his head before he saw the landscape speeding by below him. Even so, he turned to Karina and said, "We're going to jump."

Chapter Nineteen

"You must be kidding," Karina said flatly.

"This is a commuter train." Zero glanced out the window as cool air whipped by. "We can't be going more than ... fifty, maybe fifty-five miles an hour." And there was grass along the train tracks on the stretch of rails between the airport and the city proper, which was preferable to concrete.

Karina muttered a slew of curses in both Polish and Ukrainian, weaving in and out of the two languages in such a way that Zero only got the gist of her rant, which seemed to vaguely amount to "*I honestly have no idea how I'm still alive after following this man*," but despite her protests she got up on the bench seat and swung a leg over the window frame, clutching the top of it from the inside with one arm.

"Listen," he told her, "when you hit the ground, bend your knees and let yourself roll into it, or else you might break your legs."

"Great," she said flatly. She looked dubiously down at the darkness rushing by below, hesitating to make the leap.

Suddenly the brakes on the train let out a protesting squeal. They were being slowed. "We have to go now!" he said urgently.

Karina didn't hesitate further. She swung her other leg out so that she was momentarily perched on the narrow window frame, and then she pushed herself out. Zero saw her hit the ground, saw her tuck into a roll, but then she vanished quickly as the train barreled onward.

He clambered out of the window himself, ready to jump. But the wheels of the train locked suddenly. The entire car lurched, and before he knew what was happening he was tumbling over the side. There couldn't have been more than a single second elapsed between the time he fell and the time he struck the ground, but in that briefest of brief moments he thought of Sara, his young daughter—not the way she was now, sixteen and red-haired and angry, but the way she had been, innocent and young and sweet. If he tried to pinpoint the precise moment that the innocence of her youth had been stolen from her, he would guess it was a moment just like this one, when she had thrown herself from a moving train to flee from traffickers and rapists. She'd broken her arm in the process. But if he had to speculate, he would say that her spirit had broken in that fall as well.

Then he hit the ground hard. Luckily he hit feet-first, but his angle was off and he pitched forward, instinctively throwing out both arms to stop himself. Pain rocketed up his hands, wrists, elbows, to the shoulders as he struck the grass, and then he was tumbling end over end, two full rotations before coming to an abrupt stop on his back.

He was seeing stars—both the literal stars in the night sky overhead and the swimming sort that came with a knock to the head. Everything hurt, and even though the brakes continued to squeal on the train as it hurtled past him, all he wanted was to lie there for a while.

But then Karina's face filled his field of vision, her dark hair hanging around it as she looked down at him pitiably. "That was a terrible jump."

"I fell."

"Uh-huh. Come on, we have to move." She held out a hand to help him up. He took it, but even the slightest of tugs from her sent searing pain through his left shoulder.

He grimaced and let go of her. "Shoulder," he said through clenched teeth. "Must have dislocated it in the fall." He climbed to his feet without her help, noting that his shoulder was far from the only part of him in pain. But the train was slowing, and in the darkness little more than a quarter mile ahead he saw the flashing lights of police and other German emergency vehicles as they brought the train to a stop. It would not take long for them to discover that the two of them were not on it.

"We've got to find a place to lay low." He started away from the tracks, across a stretch of grass and some dark structures ahead. To his right he could see the multitude of lights from the airport and train station; in the distance to his left was the city of Dusseldorf. This span between them appeared to be largely rural and open—which did not work in their favor.

"We have bigger problems," Karina said as she followed. "Your friend obviously sold us out."

"No," Zero said adamantly. "This wasn't Alan's doing. He wouldn't do that."

"Anyone can be bought," Karina insisted. "With the right leverage, anyone can be threatened—"

"Not him."

"How can you be so sure?"

He spun on her irritably. How could he explain it to her? It wasn't enough to say that Alan was a friend, a confidant, a man in which Zero had put his own life numerous times. He couldn't tell her how Alan had given up his own shot at a normal life for his sake. He couldn't very well just put in words how Alan had put Zero's family over his own well-being on more than one occasion.

"I just am," he said finally. "I'm certain. It must have been the forger. He was probably on Interpol's radar and tried to exchange his most recent clients for leniency." He was limping slightly; his right ankle was aching. "Those Interpol agents, that inspector, they didn't know who we were. If they did, they wouldn't have approached us with only three men."

"Which means that both the Americans and Russians will soon know we are here," Karina added somberly.

"If they don't already." Zero looked toward the police blockade of the train tracks in the distance. "And as soon as they realize we're not on that train, they're going to backtrack all the way to the airport. We can't be anywhere near here when they do."

"So we should go to the last place they would expect us to go," Karina said simply.

Zero nodded. As insane as it sounded, heading back to the airport would be their safest option, "safe" being a very loosely applicable term. The authorities would expect them to flee, not turn around.

"I don't like it much," he admitted, "but you're right. We'll make it work." His body hurt all over and his dislocated shoulder throbbed. "But no more attacking Interpol agents. No more shooting cops. Okay?"

"I'm sorry," she murmured. "I panicked."

"Well..." He looked into her eyes, those soft brown eyes that appeared amber in the starlight.

Don't, he told himself. He didn't know her. She was just another mysterious and potentially dangerous woman in his life.

"We need to move," he said finally.

"Of course." Her grip tightened on his hand. Before he knew what was happening, Karina tugged his arm upward, perpendicular to his torso, and gave it a solid yank.

The breath caught in his throat as his shoulder popped back into socket. He pulled away from her instinctively, pain searing through his arm and radiating into his chest.

She grinned. "Now we can go."

He followed along behind her, rubbing his sore joint and glaring. "You could have warned me first."

He didn't say it in the moment, but one thing was clear. Though Karina had proven herself resourceful in their escape from the train station, she was obviously not going to stop for anyone or anything until she made it to her sister. Whatever was in her head was valuable enough for her to risk her life again and again to get it into safe hands. Zero would get to the bottom of it, just as soon as they found a place to rest easy for a short while—assuming they weren't caught first.

Chapter Twenty

Maria sat behind the desk in her office at the George Bush Center for Intelligence, the CIA's headquarters in Langley, Virginia, and rubbed her tired eyes. On the desk before her was a hard copy of the photo, a black-and-white printout of the digital still image that Interpol had sent not twenty minutes earlier.

She hadn't slept at all the night before, and the day had been a long one of meetings and phone calls and conferences. The higher-ups, among them the new CIA director (Maria's direct boss) and the new Director of National Intelligence (Maria's own father), were very concerned about what they called "this Zero situation." They were worried about what might happen if a top former operative with a head full of national secrets turned on them. They were nervous that he'd joined forces with a renegade Russian interpreter with national secrets of her own. They were troubled that Zero had become paranoid and assumed that these new administrations must be hiding something, must be just as bad as the ones they had replaced. Their unease and perturbation were such that David Barren, both the DNI and Dad to her, was inspired to hop a flight to New York and pay a visit to Maya Lawson, apparently not entirely trusting Maria's word when she said that the young woman had nothing to do with Zero's sudden disappearance and actions over the past forty-eight hours.

They weren't showing it, but the superiors in the CIA were panicked. Maria, on the other hand, was more concerned about what would happen to him and why he had done this in the first place.

Last night and that same morning she had done all she could to delay the agency from taking action—but then the photo came.

Interpol had caught up with a known forger who had ties to domestic terrorism in France. He'd been apprehended leaving Cologne, Germany, and after questioning, gave up his destination and that he was meeting two Americans. What should have been a routine sting dissolved into an outright mess involving shots fired in a busy train station, several injuries, and an entire train being hijacked. Interpol sent the photo from the station's security cameras, the clearest image they could get, and the CIA tagged it immediately.

Maria forced herself to spread her fingers over her face and looked down at the grainy black-and-white photo. If she squinted, it hardly looked like him. But there was no mistaking it. The photo showed Kent, mid-stride across the station's floor, his head turned slightly as he looked over his shoulder and his face in full view of the camera's lens. He had the woman by the hand, pulling her along.

It was that last part that really stabbed at Maria. That personal edge to it. She knew all too well herself how such a gesture would be meaningless and miles from romantic when fleeing from Interpol agents and eluding police. But now she understood all too well how hurt Kent must have been by her admission about the Italian arms dealer. To her it had been a cold, mechanical thing to do, a part of her job. But now, looking down at the photo and feeling like her heart was being squeezed in her chest, she understood.

It had happened in Dusseldorf, which meant that she could no longer delay CIA involvement. If it hadn't been before, this was now definitively an international matter. She'd already dispatched a team of three agents to find him.

She hadn't sent Strickland. For one, she didn't think he would actually act against Kent. And secondly, if anyone could find him, it was Todd... and if she was being honest with herself, she didn't want him to be found that easily.

Besides, she had another task for Todd. Kent had gotten the interpreter out of the country without anyone knowing, and while the CIA and FBI were scrambling to discover how, Maria knew all too well.

She looked down at the photo again and heaved a heavy sigh. At any point in the past it would have been her at his side, not this interpreter. Maria would have marched through hell itself for him. *What changed?* she asked herself.

She knew the answer. *You did.*

There was a knock at her office door, and then Strickland peered in. "You wanted to see me, ma'am?"

"Don't call me 'ma'am.' It's weird. Just come in. Close the door."

He did so, and then stood in front of her desk at halfhearted attention. He was a good guy, a great agent, and had been a terrific friend to both her and Kent—but he was also Army trained, which meant that despite their friendship it was difficult for him not to view her as a superior.

"Have they found him yet?" Strickland asked.

"Interpol? No. But our people are en route to Germany."

Todd raised an eyebrow. "I think we both know that by the time they get there, he won't be in Germany." His gaze lowered to the photo sitting blatantly on her desk, and when he looked at her again, his expression had changed.

Don't look at me like that, she wanted to say. It resembled something near pity, and she was feeling enough of that for herself already.

"You know," he offered, "if you sent me, I could find him."

"I know you could," was all she said by way of reply. Strickland had cut his teeth tracking Al Qaeda operatives through the desert for years with the Rangers. "I have something else I want you to do for me. There's a place called Third Street Garage in Alexandria. A mechanic works there by the name of Mitch. He's a bigger guy, beard, usually in a trucker's cap. I want you to bring him here." Kent getting out of the country completely under the radar had Alan Reidigger's name all over it—at least it did to her.

Strickland frowned. "I remember the place. That's where we planned the op to rescue Pierson, right?"

"That's right." Maria had forgotten that Strickland had been there before, but not while Reidigger was also there. At the time, Alan had been in a Nebraska safe house, keeping watch over Kent's daughters.

"Who's the mechanic?" Todd asked.

"He's ... an asset," Maria told him. It wasn't totally a lie. "But he's completely off the books. More of a personal asset than an agency one. So don't hurt him."

"Don't hurt him?" Todd repeated. "Should I expect this guy to be combative?"

"No," she said quickly. Then just as quickly she added, "Not necessarily. But maybe." She wished she could go in person, but her absence in a time of crisis might look suspicious, and she certainly didn't want anyone following her to Alan. But if she sent him a text or called him to say, "Hey, just so you know, I'm sending an agent to pick you up," Reidigger would be gone in an instant.

"Just be careful," she told Todd. "Tell him I want to see him personally, and that he's not in any trouble. And don't hurt him. Please."

Strickland was obviously uncertain, but he nodded. "Yes ma'am—sorry. You got it, Maria." He started for the door, but then paused. "Oh, I almost forgot. You know President Kozlovsky left today, right?"

Maria nodded as she checked her watch. "I heard the doctors cleared him for flying." Apparently the altercation with Kent and the interpreter had taken two of Kozlovsky's fingers right off his hand. "He would have gotten on a plane, what, about an hour ago?"

"Right. But I was grabbing a coffee and one of the techs from downstairs told me that Kozlovsky's flight plan got changed last-minute. Like *very* last-minute."

"So?" Maria asked pointedly. It wasn't that uncommon for flight plans to change when it came to heads of state, or for entirely fake flight plans to be registered.

"So, it could be nothing, but his new flight plan has a layover in Germany. Specifically, Frankfurt."

"Hm." Now *that* was a bit strange. Layovers in general were quite atypical for someone like Kozlovsky, and if it was necessary at all it would be at Zurich or Charles de Gaulle. Stranger still was that Frankfurt was barely a hundred miles from Dusseldorf. "What are you thinking?"

"I just think it's strange is all," Todd said. He wasn't about to say anything that might resemble an accusation about a sitting president, even a Russian one—at least not inside the walls of Langley. "Maybe something to keep an eye on."

"Yeah," Maria murmured. "Thanks. Now go pick up Alan, would you?"

Todd frowned. "Thought you said his name was Mitch."

Shit! "Yes. Mitch. Sorry, I'm exhausted and I was thinking about something else. The mechanic's name is Mitch. Thanks, Todd."

He nodded and left the office. Maria rubbed her face and groaned. She wasn't thinking clearly in her worried, sleep-deprived state. She genuinely hoped that little slip-up wouldn't come back to bite her later.

More curious was Kozlovsky's little side trip to Germany. She was certain that his plane would land, refuel, and then head on to Moscow—but who would still be on it? Or who might they be hoping to gain?

What if this interpreter is right, and it's happening again? Maria glanced down at the photo once more, but instead of Kent, she scrutinized the dark-haired woman whose hand he gripped tightly. She was pretty, and in this photo she looked anxious but not scared.

Who the hell are you? What do you know? Whatever it was, it was enough for Kent to agree to all of this in the first place.

Maria picked up her phone and dialed a number.

"Fisher," answered the agent. He was lead on the op to track Kent, along with two others were on a Learjet hurtling toward Europe at that very moment.

"It's Johansson," she told him. She was still accustomed to addressing agents that way, often forgetting to include her title of deputy director. "Listen, there's something else I want you to look in on in Germany. Keep it quiet, but I have intel that President Kozlovsky and his attaché are landing in Frankfurt."

"Ma'am?" Fisher sounded confused. "Are you asking us to … to track Kozlovsky's movements?"

"No," she said quickly. "Not him specifically. But his people … just keep your eyes open. I don't think I need to tell you that we're far from the only ones looking for these two."

But we need to be the ones that get to them first.

Chapter Twenty One

After the leap from the moving train, Zero and Karina backtracked to Dusseldorf International Airport as quickly as they could under the cover of darkness. They kept their heads down and their eyes open, though the police presence seemed to have waned there.

"The authorities must think we fled the train and are hiding out in the countryside," Zero noted. "That'll make it easier."

"Make what easier?" Karina asked as they circumvented the central terminal.

"Stealing a car." He led her to the airport's long-term parking lot as casually as if they belonged. Zero chose an older model, a gray sedan with no alarm system, and after making sure the coast was clear, broke out a back window with an elbow. They rolled down the other windows to make it less suspicious, paid the man at the gate, and drove away without incident.

As they headed away from the airport, Zero realized that he knew these roads. It was still a strange sensation; despite having his memories back, there were still some things that he couldn't recall until he thought about them, much in the same way that any ordinary brain would not evoke specific memories unless triggered by a stimulus. He took Route 44 to the southwest, the autobahn carrying them past small cities like Grevenbroich and Eschweiler, and finally to Aachen.

Karina catnapped as he drove, slipping in and out of semiconsciousness as if she were afraid to fully let her guard down. She did not fully wake until he pulled into the far corner of a fast-food restaurant's parking lot a stone's throw from the border.

"Where are we?" she asked as she rubbed her eyes. "Near Poland?"

"No. Near the Netherlands." He braced himself for the reaction he expected to come.

Karina frowned deeply, her lips parting in disbelief. "We've gone completely the wrong direction!"

"We're not going to Kiev," he told her simply. "Interpol knows that it was us in Dusseldorf, which means that the CIA does too, and likely the Russians. Anyone who's anyone is going to guess we'd head to Ukraine. I'd bet anything they're waiting to cut us off at the German/Polish border. So instead, we're going the opposite way. We're going to Belgium."

"But Veronika—"

"No one knows about Veronika," Zero said firmly. "She can travel freely; we can't. I don't really want to hang around in Germany while they're looking for us, and I don't think they'll be looking for us in Belgium. As soon as we're across, we'll contact Veronika and have FIS come to us."

Karina shook her head. Clearly she did not like it, but as she mulled it over, she seemed to come around. "Fine," she acquiesced at last. "Then what do we do now? How do we get across into Belgium?"

"We ditch the car here. Pull the license plate so it's more difficult to track as stolen from Dusseldorf. And then we find a mark."

Karina blinked. "A what?"

"Someone who looks gullible enough to take us across the border."

They left the car behind, hiked across the street to a petrol station, and took a seat on a bench outside the station, but they did not have to wait long. About fifteen minutes later a man pulled in towing a horse trailer and parked at a pump.

Karina raised an eyebrow. "I believe I've spotted a mark." She stood first. "Follow my lead."

"Oh, I'm following you now?" Zero smirked, but did as she asked as they approached the bald man with the horse trailer.

"Hello!" Karina said brightly. She was not using her fake American accent but rather her natural Ukrainian voice, which to an untrained ear sounded quite a bit like a Russian accent. "Can you help, please?"

The man raised an eyebrow. "Help with what?" He was Dutch, but replied in English.

"My husband and me," she gestured to Zero, "we are tourists here, from Russia, and we have lost our passports."

Zero had to hold back a grin. She was exaggerating her accent, pretending her English was not as good as it was, in the hopes of inspiring some amount of pity. And to her credit, it worked; Karina sweet-talked the man into believing that they needed to get to Brussels and the embassy there, which was much closer than Berlin but required crossing the border.

Whether or not the Belgian man believed it didn't matter; he accepted the lie and the two hundred US dollars they offered him for his troubles and he agreed to take them as far as his destination of Liège. They rode in the trailer, sitting on the floor of it between two snorting horses with the scent of manure in their nostrils.

Security at the European land borders tended to be lax; the officers between Germany and the Netherlands checked the driver's ID, asked where he was going, and shined a flashlight into the trailer at eye level until the beam fell upon the face of a horse, while Zero and Karina lay flat beneath the two beasts. They were granted passage without incident, and the truck rumbled onward through the southernmost tip of the Netherlands, a span of only a few miles that stretched down like a spike between Belgium and Germany.

"I feel as if I should once again comment on the glamorous nature of our travel accommodations," Karina noted wryly at one point during their brief journey.

"Only the best for international fugitives," Zero said with a chuckle, or an attempt at one, since the scent of the trailer nearly gagged him.

Less than twenty minutes later the truck stopped again, and the Dutch man opened the rear of the trailer and let them out just outside the city of Liège on the Meuse River. They thanked him and he continued on his way, with Zero hoping that he and his horses would forget they ever saw the two alleged Russian tourists with no passports.

"Wow," Karina said quietly as she marveled at the sight of the riverside hub, the lights sparkling against the night sky. "It's quite pretty."

"It sure is," Zero agreed, though he had some difficulty fully appreciating the view. They had arrived in Belgium, but they were still forty-something miles from Brussels (and therefore, the nearest airport) with no vehicle, no identification, and almost no plan. The entire trip from airport to Liège had taken barely more than an hour and a half, but it was getting late. Local time was after nine p.m. They were both exhausted, aching, and smelled of livestock.

A minor saving grace was that no one was looking for them in Liège, so they could walk about freely. The first order of business was a phone with which to contact Veronika to let her know about the change of plan. It did not take long to find a department store with a sign in the wide front windows that stated "We Accept Dollars," not an uncommon occurrence in cultural hubs and places where American tourists might shop.

"Let's see if they have burners," Zero suggested.

"I'm not familiar with that term," Karina admitted.

"Oh. It's just a cheap phone that you prepay with minutes," Zero explained. "Something you can use to make calls without being traced, and throw away afterwards."

Karina smiled. "Marks, burners... it feels like you're teaching me another language."

Zero laughed lightly as they headed inside. A woman passed by them as they entered, making no attempt to hide her wrinkled nose in their direction. He leaned close to Karina. "I think we might smell like horses."

They lingered in the department store for just a bit longer than was necessary—or perhaps precisely as long as was necessary, considering that this was a brief reprieve in what had been and would likely continue to be a harrowing experience. There they purchased a change of clothes, a few toiletries, and two burner phones. With the exorbitant twenty percent exchange tax, the total was more than two hundred dollars; their cash supply was dwindling fast, but Zero didn't think twice about it. It might not matter soon anyhow, he reasoned, if they were arrested or found before they could rendezvous with FIS.

As soon as they were out of the store, Zero peeled one of the burners out of its blister pack and powered it on. It held a small charge, enough to make a phone call with. Then he gave it to Karina to make her call.

"Veronika," she said into the phone. "It's me." She spoke in English, and Zero wondered if it was for his sake. Even if it wasn't, he appreciated being privy to at least one side of the talk. "Yes, I am safe. *We* are safe. Zero is with me. We cannot go east to Ukraine; Interpol is aware of us. They will be watching the borders. Instead we went west, to Belgium."

Karina told her sister about Liège, and asked how soon she could get there. Zero waited patiently as Karina murmured a series of yes and no answers, and then said a quick "I love you" in Ukrainian before ending the call.

"Veronika will secure a jet," Karina told him. "She and her FIS team will fly to Brussels, and from there they will come for us. She asked that we remain here and lay low. It may be six to eight hours before she can arrive. Then we will both be taken back with her to Kiev."

Zero nodded. He didn't like the idea of waiting around, but there were far worse places than Liège to do so in.

"It would seem," Karina said with a half-smile, "that your part in this is nearly over, Zero."

"I guess it is." He didn't want to think about what would happen after all of this was said and done. There would come a time to answer for the things he had done—it was either that, or stay on the lam forever.

Karina motioned toward the shopping bag in her hand. "I suppose six to eight hours is plenty of time to find a place with hot water and comfortable beds?"

He smiled. "I suppose you're right."

Walking around Liège with a pair of shopping bags almost made them forget that they were international criminals on the lam from every major law enforcement agency in the world. The city was a stunning blend of history and modern culture, remnants of medieval era architecture alongside contemporary design. They were in no rush; they walked leisurely as if they were simply a couple of people on vacation.

While they walked, Karina slipped her arm in the crook of his. Her cheeks flushed pink as she said, "For appearances' sake."

"Sure," he murmured. "Good idea." He cleared his throat, trying to think of something interesting to say. "Um… Did you know that Liège has been the setting for several insurgencies and battles over the centuries?"

Karina looked at him as if he had suddenly started speaking Latin. "Is that so?"

"Uh, yes. And it was once the home of Christina the Astonishing. She was a Christian holy woman, in the late twelfth century, who later became canonized as the patron saint of people suffering from mental health disorders."

She laughed then, and it took Zero a moment to realize that she wasn't laughing at him, but rather laughing at the moment. "How in the *world* do you know that? Are you some sort of history buff?"

"Professor, actually." Then he quickly corrected himself and said, "I mean, I was. I used to be. That was my… alter ego, I guess you could say."

"Professor Zero," Karina chided gently. "Forgive me, but it's difficult to imagine."

"Well, anyone who knew me then would say the same about being a CIA agent."

"I know exactly what you mean," she said with a sigh. "A week ago I spent my life in quiet meetings and conferences wearing heels and blazers. If you had told that woman she would be jumping from moving trains and being shot at, she would have laughed at you in four languages."

"Isn't laughing the same in every language?"

"Of course not! Haven't you ever heard a Frenchman laugh?" And then she let out a soft laugh of her own, lilting and pleasant to his ears.

As they walked along the lit boulevards, among the people, Zero found himself more at ease than he had been in a long time—months, certainly. Maybe more. Eventually they found an inn, a discreet place that looked like an oversized cottage not far from St. Paul's Cathedral. The clerk was more than happy to accept double the going rate for a night in exchange for accepting American dollars and no questions asked.

Their room was tidy and inviting, with just a touch of foreign influence. Karina said a brief prayer of thanks in Ukrainian at the very sight of a bathtub. "I am going to take what is likely going to be the longest shower of my life," she announced. "You should probably make yourself comfortable."

Zero chuckled at that. "Knock yourself out." But as soon as the door was closed behind her, the smile fell away from his lips.

He couldn't stop thinking about what she had said earlier. *It would seem that your part in this is nearly over, Zero.* But it wasn't. Even after FIS came, even after the intel that Karina had was safely with the Ukrainian leaders and she was with her sister, he would still have to confront the things he had done to get here. FIS had not made any guarantees about his own safety, and he couldn't be sure that they even would. Veronika might owe him her gratitude, but he had no idea who she was, not really—and vice versa, for that matter. He had no safety net with her.

Beyond the closed door to his right he heard the shower running, imagined that Karina was happy to finally wash off the dirt and blood and general muck and mire of everything they'd been through so far.

But when he looked down at his own hands, all he saw was the blood on them.

Chapter Twenty Two

Strickland switched off the headlights and parked the unmarked car a half a block away and across the street from the Third Street Garage. He cut the engine and sat there for a few minutes, watching the dark building. The layout was as he remembered it; beige, one story, with a flat rooftop, three garage bays, and an adjoined office. Behind the garage bays, he knew, was a small apartment, attached but only accessible from the outside. Judging by the fact that there were no lights on, he guessed that would be the best place to find the mechanic.

He wasn't happy about being used for this glorified errand. He wished he'd been sent to Europe—the notion that Fisher and his team would find and apprehend Zero was laughable—but he also knew that Maria had a soft spot for him. In fact, though he'd never say it aloud, he suspected that she was attempting some minor sabotage by sending Fisher instead of him, giving Zero more time to get to wherever he was going.

But where is he going? That was the question. Todd couldn't even imagine what had sent Zero off on something like this in the first place. He could imagine the sort of conspiratorial dirt that the alleged interpreter may or may not have, but why Zero? What had inspired him to suddenly come out of retirement after a year and a half and do all he'd done?

He really hoped it wasn't Sara. When last Strickland and Zero had talked, it had been to tell him where to find his younger daughter. Strickland hadn't followed up to see if Zero had actually gone or not, but if he had, Sara would not have had anything pleasant to say to him.

I wonder if that was his tipping point.

He wondered if the former Agent Zero had finally cracked.

Todd pushed the thoughts out of his head and got out of the car, approaching the garage casually as if he was just a passerby. He peered into the dark windows of the office and garage bays but saw and heard nothing. So he circled around to the back and the door of the small apartment.

He had his hand on the holster of his Glock when he stopped and reminded himself that this man was an asset, not an insurgent. He could have laughed at himself; he had become so used to doing things a certain way, in the Middle East with the Rangers and elsewhere with the CIA, that his natural inclination was to kick down the door with gun in hand and tear the man from his bed.

There were no lights on through the apartment either. He pounded on the door solidly three times with the back of his fist and said loudly, "Mitch ...?"

It was only then that he realized that Maria hadn't given him a last name. At the time it hadn't seemed odd, but suddenly Strickland was keenly aware that "Mitch" was likely an alias.

Not to mention that she accidentally called him "Alan." Maria was a lot of things, but scatterbrained wasn't one of them. Fatigue and stress were old friends of hers.

"Mitch," he said again loudly. "This is Agent Strickland with the CIA."

No answer. Todd gently tried the doorknob. Naturally it was locked.

It looked as if he was going to have to do this the old-fashioned way. He reminded himself again to keep the gun where it was as he reared back and, with one swift kick just below the knob, cracked the doorjamb. It splintered and flew open, and he stepped inside.

"Mitch," he said immediately to the darkness of a small kitchen. "Don't be alarmed. I'm with the CIA, and I'm here to—"

Suddenly there was a flash of light, so intensely bright it was as if he was staring directly at the sun. All he could see was white as every photoreceptor in his eyes were activated all at once. The flash was accompanied by an explosion, a single bang as loud as an entire Fourth of July display going off only a few feet away. The blast was so loud and instant that he didn't hear it as much as he felt it, rattling his teeth and actually cracking two windows.

Todd's knees gave out immediately, his equilibrium thrown by the instant imbalance of fluid in his ears. He couldn't see. He couldn't hear anything but a high-pitched whine. The logical part of his brain knew that it was a stun grenade—also known as a flash-bang. He'd used them before and had them used on him.

The other part of his brain, however, instantly plucked a memory from the recesses of his mind. An operation to rescue hostages in Bahrain. He and his unit had gone in dark, or so they thought. The enemy had assaulted them with stun grenades as they entered a compound and then opened fire.

As that memory surged through his head, automatic guns chugging and fellow soldiers screaming, Todd reached for his Glock. Before he could gather his senses he had it up in front of him, unable to see anything, unable to hear the real world but having the sounds of the harrowing recollection roaring through his head. He fired three times from a one-knee position, indiscriminately into the apartment. Glass shattered somewhere.

Stop!

He struggled to gather his wits, first shoving the gun back into its holster and then rising shakily to his feet. His vision was returning, but there was a bright afterimage every time he blinked. The ringing in his ears slowly subsided.

There was no one there, at least not that he could see. *This place was booby-trapped. Just who was this guy expecting a visit from?*

As soon as he thought it, he heard a stomping footfall. A large shape rushed at him from the darkness beyond the kitchen. He got his hands up in time, but they weren't enough to stop the charging bull of a man. His assailant knocked into him full-force, knocking the air from Todd's lungs as his feet left the ground and the rest of him sailed backward through the broken front door. He landed with a jarring crunch on the gravel outside, whatever air remaining in him abruptly forced out.

His assailant hurtled over him and kept going, boots pounding the gravel as he ran around the corner of the building.

"Hey," Todd tried to say hoarsely, but he had no wind. He scrambled to his feet, stumbling and nearly falling over, and then half-jogged after the man. "Mitch!"

Whoever this guy was, he'd been inside when Todd announced that he was CIA, but he was still in a hurry to get out of there. This time he drew his gun. As he rounded the corner after him he heard an engine roll over.

In the garage. He's trying to get away.

Todd shoved open the office door, which was thankfully unlocked, and took a breath before pushing into the garage with the three bays. Two of them contained vehicles, and one of them was idling, the headlights on but unmoving. The bay door wasn't even open. *Strange.*

Todd approached it carefully, gun aimed. It was nothing much to look at, a boxy old brown sedan that looked like it had driven right out of an early nineties movie. But he could hear the throaty engine under the hood and tell that it had a V8 turbocharged engine. It was a getaway car, and he had little doubt that it could leave his unmarked town car in the dust.

The windows were tinted dark, too dark to see inside. He pointed the Glock at the driver's side window as he shouted, "Get out of the vehicle, now!"

There was no movement. If the bay door started to roll up, or the engine shifted gears, he'd have to shoot. Or else this guy would be long gone in an instant.

"Get out, now!" Todd reached for the door handle.

As he did, he saw a flash of movement in the window's reflection. *Behind you!* He ducked out of the way a half-second before the steel head of a two-foot-long monkey wrench smashed into the glass, shattering the window.

The burly mechanic reared back immediately for another swing.

"Hey, wait—" Todd managed before he threw his body to the right, evading a swing at his ribs.

The mechanic was broad-shouldered and hefty, but he moved with a speed and grace that indicated he'd had combat training, and plenty of it. As he missed his swing he moved with the momentum of it, bringing the wrench up and then straight down as if it were an axe.

Strickland twisted his body and the deadly tool whizzed right past his ear, very nearly clipping his shoulder. In close quarters, he wrapped an arm around both of the mechanic's thick wrists and trapped them tightly in the crook of his elbow.

"Stop!" he said hoarsely. "I don't want to fight you!"

The corners of the mechanic's beard curled up in a grin. "Bet your ass you don't." His head shot forward and the trucker's cap flew away as the top of his skull smacked into Strickland's forehead. His neck jerked back and stars swam in his vision. His grip on the mechanic's arms slipped away, as did his Glock. It was all he could do to backpedal, but his hip struck the rear fender of the other car in the garage and he spun as he fell to the concrete floor.

"Wait." He was woozy, his vision blurred, still disoriented from the flash-bang let alone the blow to the head. "I'm CIA…"

"Yeah? How many did you bring with you?" the mechanic grunted as he advanced with the wrench. "Your boys got this place surrounded?"

"I'm alone," Todd insisted. "Johansson sent me."

Mitch paused, but glared dubiously down at him. "You shot at me."

"I didn't mean to. I have… it's PTSD. The flash-bang triggered me. I'm sorry."

The larger man considered this for a long moment, and then stooped to pick up his oil-stained hat. He brushed it off and set it back over his matted hair. "What's your name?"

"Strickland. Todd Strickland."

The mechanic's expression softened. He seemed to have heard the name before. "And you say Maria sent you?"

"Yes." Todd pulled himself to his feet and rubbed his forehead. "She said you were a 'personal asset,' whatever that means. But I know you helped Kent's kids before, at a safe house in Nebraska. I don't know what your ties to them are, but I think it's safe to say we're on the same side." He paused and said, "I'm going to pick up my gun now and holster it. Okay?"

Mitch nodded, but he kept an eagle-eye on him as Strickland slowly picked up the Glock and put it away. "Johansson wants me to bring you to Langley. She wants to talk to you."

"Mm-mm." The mechanic shook his head. "She should know better than most that I'd never willingly step foot in that place again. You go back and tell her that if she wants to talk, she knows where to find me."

"She's not going to like that answer."

"She's not going to like any answers I have for her," the mechanic grunted. "Tell her all the same. And sorry about the bump to the noggin."

Bump? Strickland couldn't remember the last time he'd been hit that hard.

"Sorry I broke your door," he offered in response. He'd call Maria as soon as he was back at the car and see how she wanted him to proceed. "Be seeing you, Mitch. Or Alan. Whatever your name is."

As he started toward the door to the office he heard the mechanic growl behind him, "What did you just say?"

"Nothing," Strickland replied. "It was just something Johansson—"

His breath was suddenly cut off as a thick arm snaked around his neck in a three-point chokehold, the muscles flexing and pinching off the blood supply to his head. He tried to tuck his chin, but the mechanic was strong, stronger than him. He tried to go limp, but the bigger man had no problem holding him up. He tried to pinch the nerve in the hand, a hidden point between the thumb and forefinger that weakened the arm, but nothing happened.

"Nerve's been dead for years," the mechanic hissed in his ear. "Did she sell me out? Did she tell them who I am?"

Strickland could only respond with a choking rasp.

"I'm not going to kill you because I know you're one of the good ones. But I need you to tell Maria not to forget where my loyalties lie. I've always been on his side, and always will be."

The edges of Strickland's vision grew fuzzy. But before he lost consciousness, he heard the mechanic whisper, "And if she's not standing with us, then she's against us."

Todd awoke on the cold concrete floor of the garage with an intense pounding in his head and bruising around his neck. But the middle garage bay door was open and the car was gone; not the brown one with the shattered window, but the other one, the details of which Todd had barely noticed in his zeal to run down the mechanic.

He pulled out his phone. He'd only been unconscious for a few minutes, but he knew the chances of catching up to or even finding the man were close to nil. He called Maria's cell.

"I'm going to guess it didn't go well," she said by way of greeting.

"You could have warned me. Jesus, he's like a paranoid ox."

"What happened, Todd?"

"I…" Rather than go through the whole ordeal, he simply fessed up to the important part. "I heard you call him Alan earlier. We both know that wasn't just a slip of the tongue. I might have called him that too."

"Shit," Maria sighed. "He's gone."

"He's gone," Strickland confirmed, "and we're not likely to catch up to him."

"At least not stateside," Maria said. "But I know where he'll go."

He thought about what Mitch, or whoever he was, had said just before choking him out. *I've always been on his side, and always will be.* The mechanic would go to Kent. "I can track him," Strickland offered quickly.

"No need," Maria said casually. "With a little luck, we'll soon know where Kent is ... roundabout, at least."

"How?"

"Seems that Kozlovsky's people landed in Frankfurt, just as you said. And their plane is still there. A friend of mine in Interpol confirmed that some Russians that identified themselves as intelligence agents were sniffing around Dusseldorf," Maria explained. "I'm heading down to Bixby right now to see if he can hack the phones of any of Kozlovsky's known people and track their location."

Strickland blinked. "You're going to have him perform an illegal hack on Russian diplomats' phones to find a wanted fugitive without the agency knowing?"

"When you put it like that, it sounds bad." Maria's tone softened. "Look, Todd, this could make the difference between Kent coming back in cuffs and him coming back in a body bag. Just get back here as soon as you can."

Chapter Twenty Three

Karina exited the bathroom as Zero flicked idly through television channels. He had the TV on mute, but he found its glow somehow comforting. As if their time at the inn was just a perfectly normal thing.

"My," she said dreamily. "The things we take for granted."

He barely glanced up as she stepped around the bed to retrieve the shopping bag with the fresh change of clothes in it—and then he did a double take. Karina stared in a mirror affixed to the wall as she reinserted the pearl earrings she'd been wearing. Her dark hair hung damp and straight over the edge of the fluffy blue towel she had wrapped around her, tucked in the front between her breasts. The wet towel clung to her hips, her curves, stopping just midway down her thighs, showing off the contour of smooth muscle.

He felt a shiver run through him and forced himself to look away, but not fast enough. Karina shot him a smile with half her mouth as she said, "What?"

"Nothing." Then he admitted, "I was just thinking about what's going to happen when all of this is over."

Karina nodded as if she understood, but he knew she couldn't. He'd been thinking about it the whole time that she was in the shower, and he had determined that he would have to contact Maria directly. He could stay in Kiev for a while; as long as he needed to, if he was hidden. They had no extradition treaty with the US. But even so, what kind of life would that be? What chance would he have of ever seeing his daughters again?

He was about to lay all of that out for Karina and get her thoughts when she suddenly murmured, "*Bozhe moy.*" My god.

He followed her blank gaze to the television screen. It was a Belgian newscast, in French but on mute. Zero was proficient enough in the language to read the ticker that scrolled across the bottom of the screen, which translated to: US ANNOUNCES PLAN TO TEMPORARILY WITHDRAW FROM NATO, PENDING INVESTIGATION.

Zero frowned deeply. "What the hell? Why would we do that?"

"It's already starting," Karina said quietly.

He looked over at her sharply. "This? Was this part of it, the meeting between Harris and Kozlovsky?"

She slowly nodded.

The Russians were running the show. That's what he had thought back in the stately compound just outside of DC. And Karina had mentioned that Kozlovsky had asked two things of President Harris. Now the picture was coming together: Kozlovsky played nice with Harris in public, but behind closed doors told him to withdraw from NATO. A withdrawal would mean that the US was not part of the mutual defense network that NATO stood for, which could only mean that someone was making plans, which could be anything from a seizure of assets like Russia had tried before to a full-on incursion.

"They are already starting," she said softly. "I thought I had more time, that the threat of a recording would delay them …"

"Karina, they know by now that you don't have a recording," Zero told her flatly. "If you did, the smartest move would have been to take it to the media for immediate release and let them decide whether or not it was fake."

She chuckled derisively. "Do you believe I would trust such a thing to the American media? What, so that pundits could poke holes in it? So that bloated suburbanites could argue about its validity on Facebook? So that twelve hours later some school shooting swallows it whole and no one gives it a second thought?"

Anger flared in him for a moment, but not because of her derision toward the US. "Fine, let me rephrase. *I* know you don't have a recording." To her questioning glare he said, "I looked through your clothes while you were in the shower. So unless you're hiding a listening device under that towel, there is no recording. Is there?"

Karina stared at the carpet, neither confirming nor denying it.

Zero pressed his fingers against his closed eyes, irritated at the lack of response from her.

A memory flashed through his head; his small bungalow back home, his sofa, his classic movies, a woman in the kitchen stirring a pot of Polish stew. But it was not Maria he saw in the kitchen. It was Karina, her dark hair and dark eyes and devilish smile.

"I don't even know who you are," he murmured aloud.

"I've told you who I am," she insisted.

He conjured another memory. The safe house in Rome, the apartment just beyond the courtyard that held the famous Turtle Fountain, where he first reunited with Maria back before his memories returned. He'd found her there, a mysterious and dangerous beauty who knew him even though he didn't know her…

But once again, it wasn't Maria standing in the doorway, astonished to see a dead man come back to life. It was Karina.

Fantasies and suspicions. Just like the Swiss neurologist, Dr. Guyer, had said might happen. They were manifesting in his head, messing with his memories. He could hardly picture Maria's face anymore. When he tried, Karina appeared.

Just another dangerous, mysterious woman to lead you down a deadly path.

"Veronika will come for us soon," Karina insisted. "And I don't believe that you have any intention of turning yourself in. We will figure this out. I promise you that. I won't abandon you, Zero."

You and me against the world.

She needs you.

"I can't just run forever."

"We will find a way," she said with a smile. "Together." She opened the shopping bag. "Turn, please."

"Right." Zero shifted himself on the bed, turning so that he was facing the open bathroom. He heard the soft sound of the towel dropping to the floor, but then only silence.

He felt her hand on his back, soft and cautious, fingers running up his spine until they came to rest on his shoulder. An electric tingle ran through him as he felt her lips on his ear.

"Maybe," she whispered, "none of that matters inside this room."

He closed his eyes as she kissed his neck gently.

"Maybe right now, we just live."

He turned to face her. She stood naked at the foot of the bed, as stunning and vulnerable as she was strong and confident. Mysterious and dangerous and beautiful. Scarred and flawed in all the perfect ways.

She knelt on the bed, putting a leg on either side of him, straddling his lap, and then his face was in her hands as she kissed him deeply.

Out in the world, governments schemed and agencies hunted them. Somewhere, bombs were falling and bullets were tearing into flesh and blood spilled onto sand, but none of that mattered. Suddenly nothing existed outside their tiny quilted island. He felt himself sinking deeply into the ocean of her dark eyes, let himself carnally acknowledge who he was, what he wanted, and what he should feel.

He needed her too. And nothing else mattered.

Chapter Twenty Four

Sara stared at the two blue pills in her palm. Camilla had left her purse on the nightstand that stood between their beds and gone to the bathroom, and Sara had quickly dug into it and found the orange prescription bottle.

She knew that Camilla would gladly give her one if she asked for it—but one wasn't enough anymore, and if her roommate knew that she needed two, she'd want to talk about it. At best, she'd be concerned about Sara's habit. At worst, she'd want to start charging her for them. Xanax weren't cheap.

She hoped that Camilla wasn't counting her pills. Yesterday she'd given Sara one and then she'd swiped a second. They got her through the day at the thrift store, or at least most of it. Then last night she'd done a bump of coke to pick herself up after work. Just a little one. But then it wasn't just one, it was two and three, and then she lost count, and then it was four o'clock in the morning and she had dragged herself to bed and slept for five hours before she had to be up again for another shift.

Sara knew that if she took these now, the cycle would repeat. Then two wouldn't be enough. She'd start experimenting with other things, more potent stuff.

I don't need them. She reached for Camilla's purse to put them back when the doorknob rattled. She quickly stuffed the pills into the pocket of her jeans as the door to the bedroom swung open and then Camilla was standing there, a frown etched in her face.

"What?" It came out more defensively than Sara intended.

"Baby girl, you in some kind of trouble?" the older girl asked. "There are two dudes in black suits at the front door asking for you."

"In suits…?" Sara winced as a suspicion crept up on her. It couldn't just be coincidence that she'd had a very unwelcome visitor less than two days earlier, and now two "dudes in black suits" were at the door.

Is that why he came to see me? Was he running from something? Or someone? She groaned. This was not at all what she needed right now.

"If you need to get out the window, I'll distract them," Camilla offered.

"No, it's fine. I'll talk to them." She huffed as she crossed the bedroom and headed downstairs, her roommate on her heels. Downstairs she noted with chagrin that Tommy and Jo were crowding the doorway to the kitchen as if some show was about to start. Sara shot them a glare as she crossed the living room to the front door.

Sure enough, two men were standing on the co-op's porch, on the other side of the closed screen door. One of them was tall and white and wore sunglasses; the other was shorter, broader-shouldered, with dark skin and a crew cut.

Sara opened the screen door, but did not cross the threshold. "Yeah?"

The one in the sunglasses smiled at her. "Sara Lawson?"

"Uh-huh."

"My name is Agent Ferguson, and this is Agent Rodriguez—"

"Those are some nice generic names you've got there, 'agents,'" Sara mused.

His smile waned. "We're with the FBI." The shorter one, apparently Rodriguez, flashed a badge at her. "We'd just like to ask you a few questions about—"

"I don't know where he is," she said sharply.

"Hmm." The agent named Ferguson took off his sunglasses so she could see his look of suspicion. "That's a pretty direct answer to a question I didn't ask yet."

"Yeah, well, let's not pretend we don't know why you're here," Sara said, her tone snarky. "Yes, he came to see me. It was a very short visit and I don't know where he went from here. I don't have any information for you."

"Are you aware that he's missing?" asked Agent Rodriguez.

"Nope," said Sara.

"And that he's absconded with an interpreter who has highly classified information?" said the other one, Ferguson.

"Nope," Sara said again, "and I don't care."

The two agents glanced at each other. "Can you describe the nature of his visit?" asked Ferguson.

"Sure. He came to my work. I told him to get out. He asked me to come home. I called the cops. The end."

The two agents appeared dubious. "Ms. Lawson," said the one named Rodriguez, "this would be better for everyone if you cooperated—"

"God, for an intelligence agency, you guys are clueless." She scoffed. "Do I need to spell it out for you? I'm a sixteen-year-old emancipated minor living with five roommates and working in a crappy thrift store. You think this is some kind of cover? You think he sent me here to live like this so I'd be safe? No. I left. So did my sister. We don't know anything about him anymore… if we ever actually did. Okay? We done here?"

"Ms. Lawson," said Ferguson, "we just want to know if he said anything, anything at all, that might have indicated where he was going, if he mentioned travel, if he talked about anyone you didn't know…"

Her anger flared, frustration mounting. How many ways did she have to explain it to them? "We're done here." She pushed the screen door closed, but Agent Rodriguez stepped forward and stopped it with a hand.

"Ms. Lawson," he said sternly. "We are federal agents, and this could be construed as hindering an ongoing investigation. Do you really want to get arrested in front of your little friends?"

Sara glared at him, stepping forward so she was right in his face. "I don't know you," she said quietly. "Your badge doesn't impress me and your threats don't scare me. You know how many times people have come up to me pretending to be who you're claiming to be? And every time, it's ended in me getting hurt, or shot at, or kidnapped. I won't be your leverage against him. Not ever again."

The agent stared back at her. He slowly reached into his jacket, and for the briefest moment Sara held her breath, afraid that he would call her bluff and pull a pair of handcuffs. But instead, he took out an ivory business card and held it in her face with two fingers.

"If you remember anything," he told her. "Or if he attempts to contact you."

Sara snatched it out of his hand.

"Let's go." Ferguson put his shades back on, and the two agents descended the cracked concrete stairs of the porch.

Only when they had reached the street again did Sara breathe a sigh of relief. She slammed the screen door closed and flicked the card away, sending it fluttering to the floor.

Camilla stood behind her, wide-eyed. "What the *fuck* was that about?"

"It's..." Sara was about to say "nothing," but then sighed and shrugged a shoulder. What was the use of lying? Wasn't that what destroyed what used to be her life?

"My dad used to be a spy," she said simply. "Apparently he's gone and done something stupid."

"I'm sorry, *what*?" Camilla blinked in shock. But Sara didn't answer. She headed for the stairs. She still had to get ready for work.

As she passed by the open doorway to the kitchen, she heard the lanky boy, Tommy, snicker. "This is too good," he goaded her. "Just wait 'til I tell Needle you had the damn Feds come looking for you..."

A tempest of anger swirled inside her. Before she knew what she was doing she spun, grabbed two fistfuls of Tommy's loose-fitting T-shirt, and shoved him backward against the refrigerator so hard it shook. The dry erase board with their names on it clattered to the floor.

Tommy yelped, his eyes wide in surprise and fear.

"Hey, get off him!" Jo shrieked.

"You think you can threaten me?" Sara hissed in his face—or rather, his chin, since she was a full head shorter than him. "You just remember that the only thing keeping me from kicking the unholy shit out of you is that it's against the rules, and I need a place to live. If I don't have that, then there's *nothing* standing between me and breaking your face. Not Needle. Not your girlfriend. Not your lawyer dad." She let go of him, picked up the dry erase board, and stuck it back on the fridge.

"Bitch," Tommy murmured.

Sara swung before she could even think twice. Her right fist connected with his lower jaw and lip. It wasn't a particularly solid blow, but Tommy wasn't used to getting hit in the face. His head snapped back and his body followed. He sprawled to the kitchen floor, holding his bleeding lip and staring up at her in pain and confusion as if she'd just shot him.

Jo stared too. Camilla let out a disappointed sigh.

Dammit. She'd just assaulted a roommate. One of Needle's three cardinal rules.

Without another word, she stormed into the bathroom and slammed the door behind her. She made sure it was locked and, her fingers trembling, pulled out the two pills she'd stowed in her pocket.

Stupid. Stupid. Stupid! she told herself as she set them on the edge of the sink and used the back of a hairbrush to crush them. If Tommy told the landlord what she'd done, she'd be kicked out for sure.

As she arranged the powder in a straight line with her finger, it dawned on her that her anger in the moment, when her fist was flying through the air toward his face, wasn't directed at Tommy. It was directed at her father. It was his fault. Those agents never would have shown up if not for him. She wouldn't even be here, in this mess, if not for him.

Somehow, no matter how far she ran or what she did to get away, she couldn't escape him. She held one nostril and inhaled the crushed pill, wondering if the ghost of her father and her past would continue to follow her forever.

As she stood there with her head tilted back and her eyes closed, a memory swept intrusively into her mind. When she thought about him, thought about her father, it wasn't a lying, killing secret agent that she thought of. She hardly knew him like that. No, the memories that she had were of him helping her with homework. Teaching her to ride a bike. Humming along to music as he cooked dinner. Pizza and movie nights.

She remembered them skiing in Switzerland. Sara had taken a nasty tumble, but come up laughing it off. The three of them, her and Maya and her dad, raced down the bunny slope together. It was the last time she could remember them being happy—but they had been happy. Before everything else. Before she found out that her mother had been murdered at the hands of someone whom her father, and her sister, and she had called a friend.

Sara looked at herself in the mirror and wiped away the single tear under her eye before it could fall. "You're done with him," she reminded herself quietly.

But she hoped that wherever he was, he was okay.

Chapter Twenty Five

Zero slept better than he could ever remember sleeping, a deep and content and dreamless slumber. Karina had been right; nothing outside their room existed. Only the quilt and her scent and her warmth beside him mattered.

But eventually, a dream came. A phone chimed in his mind, sharp and intrusive. He grimaced and pulled a pillow over his head.

There were words too, a soft female voice speaking too quietly to decipher.

He didn't open his eyes. Not yet. Instead he reached for her, feeling the soft quilt under his fingers. But where her soft skin should have been was empty. Karina was gone.

Zero's eyes snapped open and he sat up. She wasn't gone; she stood alongside the bed, pulling on a shirt. He quickly checked the time; it was barely five o'clock in the morning, still dark outside through the window.

"I'm sorry to wake you," Karina told him gently. "You looked so peaceful there. But I just received a text from Veronika. They are nearby."

He rubbed sleep from his eyes, feeling slightly irritated after being roused from what was likely the best sleep he'd had in a year. "Why didn't they just come here for us?"

"Because." She smiled down at him. "They don't know where we are. Come on, it's only a few minutes' walk."

He begrudgingly rose from the bed and pulled some clothes on. He collected the Sig Sauer from the nightstand and handed her the Beretta, and made sure everything else they had brought along was stuffed into the shopping bags before they headed out into the twilight hour. Karina led the way, using a GPS app on the burner to guide them as they headed toward the location that Veronika had texted to her.

Though his feet were dragging, with wishes of coffee swimming in his head, Karina seemed to have a slight bounce in her step. Clearly she was pleased at the prospect of finally connecting with her sister, with FIS, and returning to her home country.

As they walked, she slipped her hand into his. "Before we arrive," she said, "there are two things I must tell you. Now that I know I can trust you."

"I'm listening."

"The first is that the future of Ukraine is at stake. My country, my people, have been threatened again and again since the dissolution of the Soviet Union. Russia will not stop until they own what we have. The nature of the meeting between the presidents was the means by which Russia will do so."

Zero almost stopped in his tracks. It shouldn't have been much of a surprise to him that the new Russian leader would be another Ivanov, but it had been so long since the conspiracy was unearthed—a year and a half—that he could hardly believe that it was anything but over.

"We're going to stop them," Zero told her candidly. "And the second thing?"

Karina paused, still holding his hand, and she looked him square in the eye. She did not blink, did not falter, so that he would know she was not lying as she said, "There is a recording."

What?

"No. There couldn't be." Zero shook his head adamantly. "You have no device. Besides, how could you have possibly gotten something into the meeting without the Secret Service knowing it?"

Karina's free hand absently touched her left earlobe—and the pearl stud that clung there.

"The earrings," he murmured. Karina's pearl earrings had been a permanent fixture since he met her. The only time she'd taken them off was to shower...

Because they're a recording device. She couldn't get them wet.

"Yes," she admitted. "These earrings were developed by an FIS engineer, at my sister's request. Very discreet, and very high-tech. They cannot be picked up by metal detector or scan. But they can only work together; one of them picked up Kozlovsky's side of the conversation, while the other picked up Harris. As the interpreter, my voice is the only thread that ties them together."

Zero shook his head. "I don't believe this. We could have used it, could have gotten it to someone who could do something about it..."

"No," she said. "We couldn't. There is no backup. These cannot simply be plugged into a USB port. There is no way I am about to hand them over to anyone but the person who created them, back in Kiev. The audio on these earrings is all that matters right now." She lowered her voice as she added, "Even more so than my life."

He wanted to be angry; it felt like he should. But at the same time, he understood. He had kept secrets from those he was close to. Those he loved. Those he trusted. In fact, Karina had not lied to him. She had omitted the truth, but that was a tactic that he himself had used many times.

Besides, he realized, *if you had known about them earlier, you would have tried to do something about it.* He would have at least attempted to persuade her to turn them in to authorities other than FIS—or might have even tried to take them from her and take matters into his own hands.

"Are you angry with me for it?" she asked.

He shook his head. "No."

She leaned forward and kissed him gently. "Thank you for understanding." Then she consulted the burner and said, "We're not far. They are in a parking lot about a quarter mile away."

They walked hand in hand the rest of the way as the sun struggled to rise in the east, rousing just as stubbornly as he had, the sky turning a shade of deep purple as they neared the apothecary where Veronika's text claimed them to be.

At that early hour, there were hardly more than a few souls out on the roads, and it was easy to determine which car belonged to them. There was a black SUV sitting in the small gravel lot adjacent to the shop, the lone vehicle parked there.

It's always a black SUV, Zero mused to himself. *Hardly incognito.* He reminded himself that no one was looking for them there, and that they were nearly out of the woods now, and he almost told Karina that since she had gotten the idiom wrong earlier that day—but then a tingle went up the nape of his neck and he stopped suddenly, tugging her hand back as she tried to continue.

"What?" She frowned deeply. "What is it?"

He wasn't sure. His instincts had simply given him a warning jolt, like some sort of spy's sixth sense, a sensation that he had not felt in a long time. It was too quiet here. Too empty. The SUV sat there inert; no lights, no movement.

"Feels wrong," he murmured as he snaked a hand into his jacket for the Sig Sauer. "Stay here." He took a breath and headed toward the SUV, gun drawn. Anyone who was inside would clearly see him coming, yet no doors opened. No windows came down. No one called out to him or even pointed a gun in his direction.

Something isn't right here.

His gaze tracked left and right, checking the surrounding buildings. Windows. Balconies and ledges. He saw no signs of movement.

To his chagrin, Karina did not stay put as he'd asked. She crept along behind him just a few paces, tiptoeing, her body tense. "Do you think ...?" she started to ask.

"Shh."

The windows of the SUV were tinted too dark to see inside. Zero reached for the door handle, hoping against hope that it wasn't a trick or a trap.

He yanked the door open. It took him only about a half a second to register what he found there, and as soon as he did he spun around, arms reaching for Karina to pull her away before she too witnessed it.

But it was too late. She was right behind him, and in that instant she too saw it.

The woman whom Zero had known as Emilia Sanders sat in the driver's seat. The woman whom Karina knew as Veronika, as sister, was suspended upright by a seatbelt, even though her head lolled to one side, facing the window. Facing them.

Her face was ashen, drained of blood. The back of her head was missing, and its contents were sprayed on the car's ceiling and seats.

Zero tried to reach Karina in time, but she had already seen it. He reached her as she crumpled, catching her with one arm as her legs gave out.

A shrill shriek of horror rang out in his ear. Karina's screams. He tried to pull her away from it but she pushed against him, as if she needed to get to Veronika. As if there might be something that she could do for her.

"Stop," he said hoarsely. "There's nothing you can do." But his voice was drowned out by her screams. And so were the footfalls of the man who came for them.

Chapter Twenty Six

Zero saw him almost too late. The man came rushing around the side of the SUV; all Zero saw was a blur of movement in his periphery. He released Karina and she slumped to the gravel, unaware of anything but her sister's body in the SUV.

Zero spun, the Sig Sauer in hand, but before he could fully get it around a beefy hand closed around his and forced the gun upward and away from him. At the same time the assailant twisted his body, and Zero's arm was suddenly locked painfully behind him at an odd angle. He groaned, knowing that the man had the drop on him, that any moment now could be his last—

"Don't shoot me," Alan grunted.

He released his grip and Zero staggered back two steps, utterly astonished. "Alan ... what? How?" His gaze went past his friend to the body in the SUV. "What are you doing here?"

Alan put his hands up defensively. "I just got here, I swear it ..."

"You!" Karina's voice was a tremulous growl rife with anguish. When Zero turned he saw that she had the Beretta in both hands, aimed at Alan's thick midsection. "You sold us out to Interpol!" she accused.

"I didn't!" Alan insisted. "The forger was careless and got busted on his way to meet you—"

"Did you kill my sister?!" Karina demanded, her voice high and tight.

"No." He put both hands up level with his head. "No, I swear I didn't. But we really shouldn't be hanging around here."

"Karina," Zero said gently. He reached for her and put his hand on her arm, and then her hand, and then the gun as he slowly pushed it down and out of firing range. "Alan didn't do this. Trust me. You said you do, right? Trust me now."

Tears rolled down both her cheeks as her gaze floated toward the SUV once more. "Someone betrayed her. I will kill whoever it was."

"We will, I promise. But this was done as a message—specifically to us. And we cannot stick around here, do you understand?"

Karina looked at him as if he'd slapped her face. "I can't just leave her like that!"

"We have to." He shook his head ruefully. "I'm sorry. But we have to." He turned to his old friend. "Alan, do you have a car?"

"Of course."

"Then let's go."

"Wait!" Karina hissed. "We're not honestly going to go with him, are we?"

"Yes," Zero said simply.

"Give me..." Karina wiped her eyes. "Give me one moment. Please?"

Zero nodded, though he knew it wasn't a good idea. There were people out, more by the minute, and the sun was rising. It would not be long before pedestrians and passersby noticed the body in the SUV.

Karina approached the driver's side slowly, her hands shaking as she did. "*Sestra,*" he heard her murmur, and then something brief and under her breath; a prayer, he imagined. She reached for Veronika's eyelids and gently pushed them closed.

Zero glanced over her shoulder surreptitiously. There were two other bodies in the SUV—both in the backseat, but no one in the passenger side. If he had to guess, whoever had originally been in that seat had betrayed the other three.

"Zero," Alan said softly behind him. "We should go..."

Zero was still bewildered by Alan's sudden presence, which wasn't made any easier by occurring only moments after finding Sanders/Veronika dead, but he didn't have time to ask.

Sirens whooped in the distance.

"This wasn't just a message," he said quickly. "This is a trap…" No sooner did he say it than there was a screech of tires, and two black sedans whipped around the corner not more than fifty yards from them. "Karina, we have to go, *now*!"

Chapter Twenty Seven

Karina looked up at him sharply, her eyes wide in surprise. Despite everything that had happened in the last two minutes, she seemed to understand. Her feet scrambled forward as Alan pointed toward the parallel street.

"This way!" he called to them, leading the charge. Two pedestrian gawkers stopped suddenly as they walked by, staring at the trio as they sprinted away from the small parking lot where the SUV sat, the body in the driver's seat clearly visible, and two cars giving chase.

Alan took a set of keys out of his pocket and rounded to the driver's side of a tiny black compact car.

"Are you kidding?" Zero muttered.

"It's Italian," Reidigger replied as he wedged himself behind the steering wheel.

"Come on, get in the car," Zero urged Karina. He yanked open the passenger side door for her; she was still shell-shocked from seeing her sister's body. He guided her in and then slid into the backseat, his knees practically around his ears in the tiny space.

"Hang on." Alan shifted gears and the car took off like a shot. Karina sucked in a breath as he weaved out onto the street, skirting between two cars expertly. "Relax," he told her. "I'm an excellent driver."

Zero glanced behind them. The source of the sirens—presumably the Belgian cops—hadn't arrived yet. But the two black cars had careened out the other side of the apothecary's parking lot and were gaining quickly.

"Yeah, I'm on it." He up-shifted and slammed the accelerator down. The little Italian car surged forward, gaining some distance between them and their pursuers.

"I know you're good at multitasking," Zero said, "so how about you drive and explain?"

"Where to start?" Reidigger grunted. He zipped around a truck and made a sharp right. The car responded perfectly, the tires barely losing traction. "Your pal Strickland came to pick me up. Said Maria sent him. He called me Alan. I had to get out."

"Did she sell you out?" Zero asked incredulously.

"Turns out…no. I was just being a tad bit paranoid," Alan admitted.

"How do you know? And how did you find us?"

"Uh…" Reidigger didn't want to admit that part. He yanked the wheel to the left, the car fishtailing slightly as it barely made the light.

"Do you know where you're going?" Karina screeched, holding onto the door handle tightly.

Reidigger ignored her. "Okay, so about two months ago or so, I put a chip in Maria's cell phone."

Zero blinked. "Why?"

He shrugged. "To steal CIA secrets?"

"Jesus, Alan…" Zero pinched the bridge of his nose.

"*Anyway*, the chip copies all of her data to an online server. All her calls, her texts, her browser history, all of it. After I fled, I checked the server. I saw that she hadn't actually sold me out. But I also saw that she was tracking Russian phones—specifically Kozlovsky's attaché." He paused for a moment before adding, "They're here, Zero. They're here in Belgium. I followed the trace to that SUV."

"They did this," Karina said venomously. "They will die for it."

Alan turned sharply left, and then a block further made a quick right. Zero glanced behind them; it looked like they lost the two black sedans.

"They'll pay for what they did," Alan told Karina, squeezing her shoulder gently as Alan slowed the car to traffic pace, trying to blend in. "And we'll do that by getting the recording into the right hands."

"There's a recording?" Reidigger asked.

"Yes," said Zero.

"No," lied Karina at the same time.

"That's great news," Alan said. "If you have it on audio, we can get it out there and clear your names."

"Not exactly," Zero muttered. "The recording is in a pair of earrings."

"And they are going back to Kiev," Karina added forcefully.

But Zero was no longer sure about that. The Ukrainian government would want to hear what was on that recording; but they would certainly not be happy to harbor international fugitives who had three dead FIS agents on their hands. He rubbed his forehead, feeling as if he was struggling to think straight.

"Karina," he said gently, "I think it's time to reconsider our options—"

Suddenly a phone rang out, interrupting him. Karina frowned and dug in her pocket. It was the burner, the one she had used to contact her sister.

She stared at it in disbelief. "It is Veronika," she murmured.

"Don't," Zero commanded. "It's Veronika's phone. If the Russians have it, they can track us with a call…"

But Karina did not heed his warning. She pressed the button to answer the call. "You killed my sister," she hissed into the phone. "And for that you will…" She trailed off, her furious expression going lax. "What? Artem?"

"Who the hell is Artem?" Alan asked.

Karina put the call on speaker, and Zero heard a man panting breathlessly through the receiver. "Artem, where are you?"

"Karina," the man wheezed. "Karina, I am so sorry, I ran, I didn't know what else to do…"

"Slow down. Tell me where you are."

"They knew where we were. They ambushed us. The Russians. Veronika covered, and I… I ran for it…" The man on the other end of the call, this Artem, held back a choking sob. "They are all dead. I'm so sorry."

"We ... we saw," Karina told him. "We are in Liège. We can come for you. It is not too late."

"Get out of there," Artem warned. "The Russians are there. They tracked us somehow." He paused for a moment before asking, "Do you still have it? The recording?"

"Of course I do," Karina told him. "Where can we meet?"

"There is a French commune a few miles southeast called Chaudfontaine. Meet me at the Chateau des Berges. It is safe there. And Karina—be careful."

"I will. See you soon, Artem." She ended the call and murmured, "I don't believe it."

"Who is Artem?" Zero asked.

"My sister's partner in FIS," Karina explained. "I never met him in person, but she talked about him often to me. She trusted him. He saved her life on several occasions."

But ultimately she paid for it with hers, Zero thought. He remembered the empty passenger seat of the SUV, coated in Veronika's blood where she had been shot.

Alan glanced at him in the rearview mirror, only briefly, but just long enough for Zero to know what he was thinking. They had been partners, years earlier in the CIA, and had saved each other's lives several times over. Either one of them would have done the same for the other.

"We must go to Chaudfontaine," Karina declared. "We will retrieve Artem, and he will contact our people in Kiev."

Alan spun the wheel and the car slid into the next right turn. "Southeast it is."

Karina sat up straighter and wiped her eyes. There would be time to mourn, but for now she seemed determined. There was still hope of getting the recording into the right hands.

She twisted slightly in her seat to look at him, and he smiled at her in what he hoped was a reassuring manner. "We're almost out of the woods."

No sooner did he say it than a siren whooped twice behind them. He twisted in his seat and saw two Belgian police cruisers, each a white Ford Mondeo with three blue stripes down the side and blue flashers on the roof, tailing them from less than three car lengths and closing in.

"On second thought," he muttered, "maybe we just can't see the forest for the trees."

Chapter Twenty Eight

Alan wrenched the wheel. The sprightly Italian car reacted instantly, making a sharp left that would have had any SUV rolling on its side.

"Were you followed?" Zero asked him. It was the only thing he could think of in the moment, that Reidigger had been tailed. But Alan was more careful than that… at least he had been in the past. Maybe it wasn't just Zero who was out of practice.

"Of course not!" Reidigger hissed through clenched teeth. He directed the car toward downtown Liège. "It's just a couple of cop cars. They must have been in the vicinity when—"

A black sedan darted out from between two old stone buildings, trying to cut them off. Reidigger swore as he swerved to avoid it, but he overcompensated on the pull. "Hang on!" he roared, and then he yanked the emergency brake as he counter-steered.

Zero was thrown to the other side of the back seat as the Italian car spun, wheels screaming in protest, turning a full three hundred and sixty degrees before aiming straight again. Alan shifted and slammed the accelerator and they darted forward, leaving the black sedan in the dust.

Zero looked out through the back windshield. One of the black car's windows was down, and behind it he saw a man in a suit speaking into a radio. *Not just the cops.* Could have been Interpol. Or the CIA. Or even the Russians.

Whoever it was, it meant they were in much more trouble than previously realized.

Karina pulled out the Beretta. Zero opened his mouth to protest—to remind her not to shoot at police or unidentified authorities—but the image of Veronika's dead, ashen face was burned into his consciousness. He had little doubt the people chasing them would do the same to them given the opportunity.

Zero glanced back again to see that it wasn't just the two cop cars chasing them. The second black sedan they'd eluded had joined in the hunt, as well as a man on the back of a motorcycle.

"That's not good..." he muttered as the sports bike roared ahead of the other pursuers. "Alan, company!"

"I see him!" Reidigger swerved left and right on the boulevard, cutting off the motorcycle as it tried to get alongside them. The dark-helmeted driver pulled an automatic pistol, steadying the bike with one hand.

"Let him get up next to us!" Zero instructed, one hand on the door. Alan did so, straightening the Italian car and letting the motorcycle come up on their right bumper. "Brake!" he shouted, and at the same time he threw the door open. Reidigger stomped the brake pedal; the motorcycle crashed into the rear passenger door, tearing it right off the side of the car. The driver hurtled off the bike, limbs flailing as he sailed about twenty yards before smacking into the pavement so hard the helmet cracked in two.

Alan spun the wheel as he shifted and punched the gas again, now heading in the opposite direction—directly toward the three cars tailing them, playing a game of chicken as they spanned the road, blocking them from passing.

Karina sucked in a breath. Zero closed his eyes and reminded himself that he trusted Alan with his life.

Reidigger grunted again and yanked the steering wheel. The responsive Italian car careened sideways, righted itself, and flitted down an alley so narrow there was barely six inches of room on either side.

"You are insane," Karina said breathlessly as she watched stone facades fly by her window. "You know this?"

"It's been said." They zoomed out onto the parallel street. Luckily traffic was light, or else the small car would have been obliterated as Alan skidded out and crossed two lanes. Zero glanced around; they were in the oldest section of Liège, where medieval architecture and cobblestone still stood against the test of time.

They'd evaded the police cars and the black sedan, but the flashing blue lights behind them told him that there were plenty more on the way. "We've got two more cruisers on our tail," he warned.

"On it." Alan piloted the car artfully as they crested a small hill, the front wheels leaving the asphalt for a moment, and down again toward a roundabout. "One of you two want to do something about our guests…?" he suggested as they entered the circle.

Zero rolled down the window and pointed the Sig Sauer at the oncoming police cars with his left hand. As they rounded the curve that put them parallel to the cruisers, he fired three times, aiming for the tires.

The shots threw up sparks as they hit pavement or metal. His aim was off. *Guess I'm a little out of practice firing from moving cars.*

Karina muttered something in Ukrainian as she rolled down her own window, a line that generally translated to, "If you want something done, do it yourself." She climbed halfway out the window, practically sitting on the door frame as she aimed the Beretta over the roof of the Italian car.

Alan weaved skillfully in and out of the two lanes of traffic, cutting off other vehicles as they honked and shouted at him in French and Dutch. He smashed down the accelerator so that they came up on the cruisers' tail, rather than the other way around.

The Beretta barked once, then twice, the report of it alarmingly loud even from outside the car. A shot hit the rear tire of the closest cruiser; the car wobbled and spun, smacking into the other police car. They both skidded sideways. Alan swerved into a controlled skid and they slipped past them, even as the two cop cars whirled in an about-face. Oncoming traffic screeched their brakes, some cars slamming into the cruisers while others jumped the curb to avoid a collision.

Alan took the next exit out of the roundabout and sped off down the street.

"Nicely done," Alan said as Karina climbed back into her seat.

"Thank you." And then lower she added, "My sister taught me to shoot." She twisted in her seat to make sure no one else was pursuing them before asking, "So, what is the plan now?"

"Don't look at me," said Reidigger. "I'm the driver, not the plan guy. You'll have to defer to the back seat for that."

Zero was still trying to get over his three missed shots. He wasn't bitter that Karina had done it herself, but that his aim was so off.

"Well?" she asked him pointedly. "Plan? We cannot simply drive to Chaudfontaine in this car. We'll need another, something inconspicuous."

"Yeah," Zero murmured. But he was barely paying attention. He was looking between the seats, through the front windshield.

About a hundred yards ahead of them and closing fast, a man was crossing the street. He stopped halfway, as if oblivious to the car speeding rapidly toward him. "Alan, watch for that guy…"

"I see him." Reidigger gripped the wheel, ready to swerve around the guy if necessary.

But as they drew nearer, the man turned directly toward them, and hefted something up to his shoulder.

"Down!" Zero shouted. He ducked low and covered his head with his hands as a burst of automatic gunfire pounded the car. The windshield shattered. Bullets smacked the hood and broke the headlights. Reidigger cried out in pain and surprise.

The tires shrieked as the car slid sideways. The assault kept up, glass from broken windows raining down over Zero as the man in the street emptied a full clip into the tiny Italian car. He dared to look up just as the firing stopped—just in time for the car to slide to a stop, the rear bumper smacking into their assailant with a bone-crushing impact that sent him bouncing across the pavement twice.

Zero breathed hard. His heart pounded in his chest as he looked around. It didn't seem like there was anyone rushing toward them; no shouts, no guns firing, no footfalls smacking the asphalt.

"Alan! Are you hit?" he asked urgently.

"Yup," he grunted. One thick hand was clamped near his shoulder, blood eking between his fingers. "Not too bad though. I think it bounced off my collarbone."

"Broken?" Zero asked as he tore off his jacket.

"Probably."

He passed the jacket to Karina, who leaned over Alan and tied it around his shoulder and midsection in a makeshift sling.

Zero pushed the car door open and climbed out carefully, Sig Sauer ready in his hands. Sirens screamed from a short distance; they had a minute, tops, to get clear. He looked around desperately, and then pointed. "There! Let's go."

Across the street from them was an ancient cathedral, its stone façade almost white from centuries of sun-bleaching, two tall spires rising from either side of a dome-shaped ceiling.

Zero helped Alan out of the car as Karina covered them with the Beretta.

"Wait!" Alan protested. "The trunk. There's a bag of gear."

Zero hurried around to the back of the car. The impact of striking the man in the street had thrown the trunk open. He noted with a grimace the bloody dent in the rear fender as he hefted a black duffel bag from the trunk.

Nearby, the man who had fired upon them groaned. Zero paused; he couldn't believe the guy was still alive after taking a hit like that.

"*Ty*..." the man stammered. There was blood leaking from his lips, his nose, his ears. Judging by the state of his impacted torso, there was a lot of internal bleeding going on. "*Ty sobira*..." He coughed violently and gasped in pain.

Russian. The man was speaking Russian, or trying to. "I'm going to what?" Zero asked him.

"Zero!" Karina shouted as she helped Alan to the cathedral steps. "Let's go!"

The man sneered as he spat in Russian: "You are still...going to die."

Zero fired the Sig Sauer once. His aim was spot-on this time as the bullet entered the man's forehead, more to put him out of his misery than to silence him.

He quickly followed the others toward the cathedral entrance. Over his shoulder he saw the flashing blue lights of police cars. He doubted they'd be alone.

As he passed through the stone archway, he glanced up toward the sharp spires that reached for the bright mid-morning sun. He tried to tell himself that they would hide here, just for a short while, long enough for the police and the Russians and whoever else was after them to move on.

But he knew that wasn't true. This was where they'd have to make a stand.

Chapter Twenty Nine

Zero pushed the heavy door closed behind him with a resonant boom and hurried across the narthex to the wide nave, its vaulted ceiling high overhead painted in a Biblical scene that he didn't have time to appreciate. Instead he surveyed the layout. It was a fairly standard cathedral; beautiful, to be sure, but built in accordance with the rules by which such places were built in its time. The entrance faced the west. The chancel, which held the altar at the far end of the nave, was to the east. Projecting to the north and south were stubby transepts, wings of the nave that formed the cross-shaped floor plan on the cathedral.

It was less than ideal, but it had been a spur of the moment decision to take cover in there. It was open, with few hiding places but fewer places to be ambushed.

Karina and Alan were nearly at the front of the church, jogging past rows and rows of wooden pews far older than either of them, heading toward the slightly raised chancel. The altar was a simple one, a table bearing a gold tablecloth and adorned with a few dozen candles in holders that might have been expensive once, but were now mostly obscured by dried melted wax.

Behind the altar was an enormous mural of the crucifixion, twice as tall as Zero was. *How apt,* he thought wryly.

"This way," Karina panted, tugging on Alan's sleeve. "There may be a back door..."

"Ow! Stop pulling," Alan grimaced.

"Wait," Zero said as he jogged after them. He stopped between the elevated chancel and the first row of pews and set the heavy black bag down. "Alan, let me see that wound."

"Eh. I've been shot plenty before." Reidigger tried to wave it off, but winced in pain.

"Shut up, let me see." Zero carefully peeled aside the jacket-turned-sling and checked the shoulder. It looked like Alan was right; the bullet had broken skin and definitely cracked bone, possibly even fractured it, but it wasn't bleeding badly and nothing major had been penetrated. "You're lucky."

"Lucky?" Alan scoffed. "I'm the only one that got shot…"

"*Excuse* me!" Karina interjected. "Can we please find a way out now?"

Zero shook his head. "We can't risk it. They're going to have us surrounded in moments. They'll be watching every street. They'll search every building."

"Then what did you have in mind?" Karina asked.

He unzipped the bag and nodded appreciably. There was an array of gadgets in the duffel, but right on top was a most welcome sight—a Heckler and Koch MP5, a German-designed submachine gun that fired 9x19-millimeter Parabellum rounds with an effective firing range of two hundred meters.

"You must be joking," Karina said flatly as he hefted it. "Here? In a *church*?"

"I don't see much of a choice otherwise. We make our stand here. If we can punch a hole through whoever's coming for us, we can get out." He almost believed his own lie. If there was any chance of escape, it would be Karina and Alan making the run for it while he caused the distraction.

"What do you mean, 'whoever' is coming for us?"

"That guy outside with the AK was Russian," Zero said. "And that other car likely was too. I don't know who's out there, but it's not just local Belgian cops."

"Great," Karina muttered. "Give me a gun. I'm almost out."

"No." Zero shook his head firmly. "You need to find a place to hide until you can make a run for it—"

"My sister is dead by their hands," Karina said forcefully. "And I *will* fight."

"Hand me one too," Alan grunted. Zero opened his mouth to protest, but Alan waved a hand. "Save it," he insisted, shouldering him aside and stooping for the bag. "These are my toys, anyway."

Zero grinned. He knew that Alan wouldn't just sit idly by. "Looks like you raided Bixby's lab."

Alan shrugged. "I might have."

The grin disappeared. *I was joking,* he was about to say. But then he heard a soft gasp from behind them and spun. The MP5 was up instantly, and he very nearly squeezed the trigger on the unsuspecting cleaning lady that stood in a doorway near the north transept. She was at least seventy, her hair white and tied in a bun, her hands still in yellow rubber gloves.

"*Pardon,*" she murmured quickly as her eyes fell on the gun in Zero's hands. Sorry. She took a small step backward as she said in French, "I will just go ..."

"Wait," Zero called back in her native tongue. "Is there anyone else in here?"

"*Non.* J-just me." Her voice was tiny and terrified, but echoed through the wide nave.

He gestured toward the door she stood in. "What's back there?"

"Only the vestry. And restrooms."

"*Merci.*" He pointed toward the main entrance to the cathedral. "Go. Hurry."

She nodded fervently and scurried along the edge of the nave toward the rear of the church, keeping her head low and muttering a prayer. Zero watched carefully as she reached the door, and he craned his neck to see outside as she pulled it open.

His line of sight was obscured, but he definitely saw a multitude of blue flashing lights and men scurrying about. He heard a few shouts as the police surrounded the building and got into positions.

They know we're in here.

He dashed to a tall stained glass window in the south transept and peered out through a yellow pane. Outside there were no fewer than five police cars blocking the street—but they weren't alone. Several black sedans and SUVs had arrived as well.

Always black, he noted dismally. *Why are they always black cars?*

Men in suits and sunglasses spoke heatedly with the Belgian police, gesturing with their hands toward the building. Zero wasn't sure who they were, but it looked like they were attempting to pull rank. Then he saw that nearby, milling about the black cars, were men with dark hair and dark jackets and blatantly armed.

He didn't like to stereotype, but he could make an educated guess of who they were just by the look of them. *Bratva*—Russian gangsters. Kozlovsky's people.

How did they find us so quickly? he asked himself in frustration. The only solution was that everyone was watching everyone—the CIA, the Russians, Interpol, anyone else who might be looking for them. No one trusted anyone, even those who were supposedly on the same or similar sides.

It didn't matter now. In moments they'd try to get inside.

"Karina," Zero said as he turned away from the window. "Take a position near the south transept. Watch that door." He pointed to the dark archway past the southern end of the chancel; it was the only other door that could have led to another exit.

"Alan, I want you near the front pew," he instructed. "Take cover and watch the main entrance."

"Aye aye, captain." Alan grunted as he knelt behind the first set of wooden pews, an automatic pistol in his left hand.

Zero stepped up onto the chancel and took a position behind the tiered pulpit. It was chest-high and made of sturdy wood, possibly oak. It would stop a few bullets, it seemed, but it wouldn't last long against an assault weapon.

"Return fire," he told them, "but don't shoot to kill. We've got a lot of misinformed cops out there that have families at home." He caught shadows slinking past the stained glass windows to the south. "Karina…"

"I see them." Her grip tightened on the French carbine she'd grabbed from Alan's bag.

His gaze flitted around the huge, empty cathedral as he thought about what he would do in their situation, if he was the one outside.

The back door is their only option. No way would they risk an assault through the main entrance. And they would have to avoid destroying any part of the centuries-old church.

He knelt behind the pulpit and angled his aim toward the dark doorway that led to the rear of the cathedral.

Any moment now.

He heard Alan chuckle lightly. "In a weird way... this is kind of nice."

Zero blinked. "I'm not sure that's the word I'd use for it."

"No, I mean... us. The two of us, back together again. It's been a long time, but it feels right." Reidigger paused and added, "Other than the bullet wound."

"No, that feels about right too," Zero quipped. "I'm glad you're here."

"Boys," Karina said sharply. "Perhaps we can save all this until *after* we've survived and escaped?"

"Sure," Alan muttered.

"Sorry," Zero added.

Silent seconds ticked by, the MP5 directed at the dark archway. He listened intently, but heard nothing—even the shouts from outside seemed to have ceased. He couldn't help but notice that the aches and pains he'd been feeling in his limbs had subsided, dulled by adrenaline and the thrill of the fight.

Karina let out a short, frustrated sigh. "What are they waiting for?"

Zero shook his head. "I don't know—"

The sound of glass shattering echoed through the vaulted nave. Zero spun left and right, tracking the MP5 as he quickly scanned for the source of the sound. *The back door? The vestry?* He saw nothing.

Karina was on her feet, gun pointed, confusion etched on her face as another window smashed elsewhere.

And then all hell broke loose.

Chapter Thirty

Zero whipped the MP5 around, certain that the second crash had come from the doorway that led to the vestry, where the old cleaning lady had appeared. As his grip tightened around the barrel, there was yet another stupendous shattering—and this time he saw its source.

He watched in stunned silence as a tall stained glass window of the Virgin Mary collapsed inward with the force of a projectile. Eight-hundred-year-old glass rained across the nave floor as a green canister bounced into the pews.

Across the cathedral, a translucent portrayal of St. Peter broke with the force of another canister. There was a bright flash from each, and thick white smoke plumed from the grenades.

"Tear gas?" Alan shouted.

"No." Zero recognized the canisters—they were M-18 smoke grenades, typically used for signaling or riot control. "Smoke!" *Which means…*

A muzzle flash lit like lightning in a thundercloud from within the smoke, accompanied by the deep thrum of an automatic weapon. Zero threw himself down behind the pulpit as bullets pounded the wood.

"Contact!" He heard the high-pitched whine of Alan's automatic pistol as he returned fire into the dense cloud.

Zero held his position, waiting for a brief enough reprieve to fire back. He could hardly believe they had stooped so low as to destroy even a part of such an ancient and historic building. *It's my fault,* he realized. He'd chosen this place.

"Coming in the back!" Karina shouted from somewhere in the cathedral. The chancel and altar were hazy like fog, slowly transitioning into an opaque white cloud only a few pew rows back. From somewhere in there, Karina unloaded the French carbine at the men attempting to enter through the rear entrance.

Zero dared to edge out from behind the pulpit, just enough to sight in on the MP5. He fired three-shot bursts at fifteen-degree angles, almost robotically, hoping to hit something. From within the cloud, someone yelped. Then a voice cried out in Russian: "The pulpit!"

Shit. He crouched and covered his head as a fusillade of bullets struck the wood in front of him. It wouldn't hold for long. A thick piece near his right shoulder broke and splintered, flying past his face.

Zero leapt out from behind the pulpit, staying low to the ground and tucking into a roll. He crouched behind the altar, the table with the gold tablecloth, quickly noting that it would do absolutely nothing to shield him from bullets.

"Sorry," he muttered to whatever power might be listening, and then he flipped the table onto its side. The candles crashed and scattered. Then he shouldered the upended table forward, using it as a shield as he slowly pushed to the edge of the chancel.

Bullets punched holes through his cover easily. *Can't stay here.* He shoved the table aside, drawing fire in its direction as he vaulted the opposite way, rolling again and almost colliding right into the front row of pews.

From a few feet away, Alan sprayed a dozen rounds into the thinning cloud of smoke and then dropped back down, somehow grinning from ear to ear. "Just like old times, huh?"

"Unfortunately, yeah." Zero dropped to his side and peered under the pews. He saw a pair of boots rapidly approaching up the center aisle. He aimed and fired off several shots, blasting out the assailant's ankles. The man screamed and fell.

"Listen, I don't mean to be a pain," Reidigger said. He fired off the rest of his clip. "But I'm empty. Grab the bag, would you?"

Zero groaned, but tossed Alan the MP5. "Fine. Cover me." He shimmied toward the chancel on his stomach, as if he was on a frozen lake, until he could reach a strap of the black duffel and pull it toward him. As he dug through it to find a spare clip, the shooting waned, pausing long enough for a voice to call out to them.

"Come on out, Zero!" The voice was male, and while he didn't recognize the speaker, it was undoubtedly American. "It's only a matter of time before those cops outside try to get in. You want their deaths on your hands too?"

"CIA?" Alan whispered as he swapped the MP5 for the freshly loaded pistol.

Zero shook his head. "With Kozlovsky's people? Doubtful. More likely on loan from Harris." They could have been Secret Service, or mercenaries like the ex-soldier unit The Division. It hardly mattered in the moment; they were there to kill him.

He jumped as the chug of a shotgun startled him, blowing a square foot out of the pew mere feet from his head. Splinters slapped at his face and arms.

He heard the thrum of the French carbine from somewhere in the dissipating smoke that still hung like a morning mist over the nave and knew that Karina was still alive. Reidigger returned fire as Zero pushed a new magazine into the MP5, and then he dug into the bag while Zero fired through the new hole the shotgun had made.

He saw shapes moving about in the haze, barely more than silhouettes popping up like targets at a carnival game and spraying bullets in his direction. There were at least four, possibly more.

"Psst." Reidigger held up a silver palm-sized cylinder. A flash-bang.

"No," Zero said immediately. Karina was out there somewhere; he had no idea if she'd held her position or not. "It could get her killed."

"Sitting here and hoping for lucky shots could get us *all* killed," Alan argued. "Let's survive first and apologize later."

Zero didn't like it, but Alan was right. Without something to give them an advantage, they were outgunned and would run out of ammunition sooner than later. "Fine," he said tightly.

Reidigger didn't hesitate. He yanked the pin and tossed the stun grenade over their shoulders, into the rows of pews beyond. The two of them ducked low to the floor, squeezing their eyes shut and hands clamped over their ears.

He didn't see the flash, but he still heard the bang, felt it deep in his chest as if someone had fired a gun right next to his ear. But he was ready for it; it didn't have the deleterious effects it would have on their assailants. He and Alan were up in an instant, guns in hands and tracking for movement.

Zero rounded the first row of pews and dared to head up the center aisle. The man he'd shot in the ankles was lying there, his face contorted in agony as he writhed. Zero kept going, staying low, knees bent, the MP5 tight against his shoulder.

There were three others that he could see, all dazed and floored by the flash-bang. He kicked away a shotgun and then an AR-15 as Alan relieved the third of his weapon.

"Karina!" he hissed into the suddenly silent nave. "Karina, where are you?!"

He didn't hear anything... but he saw a flash of movement to his left and whipped around, barrel tracking with him. A man dashed forward from the doorway south of the altar, a pistol in his hands. As Zero pulled the trigger, the man leapt forward into the pews. The rounds hit nothing but ancient wood.

"More incoming," Zero told Alan urgently. "Get these three secure!" The effects of the stun grenade wouldn't last long.

He surged forward, running down the man who had dived behind the pews—and then skidded to a stop in his tracks as he heard Karina cry out from somewhere.

"Karina?!"

"Zero..." He saw her as she stood, her dark hair, her face, her arms out in front of her, the gun gone from them—and behind her, gripping a fistful of her hair and pointing the pistol at her temple, was the man he'd been gunning for. He was blond, clean-shaven, with a deep-creasing sneer as he spoke to Zero in Russian.

"Drop your weapon, or I blow her brains out."

The MP5 was already up, but he didn't have a clean shot on a good day, let alone the way his aim had been lately.

"Do not," Karina said firmly. There was a small trickle of blood running down her neck from her right ear. It was as he'd feared; the flash-bang must have disoriented her long enough that the man had reached her and found her unarmed.

"Zero!" Alan hissed. Behind them, from the door to the vestry, came two more men. They stopped suddenly when they saw the standoff. Reidigger hesitated as well; both he and Zero knew that once a shot was fired, Karina was as good as dead.

"Well," said one of the newcomers. Another American. "Looks like we came at just the right moment."

Zero kept his aim directed forward at the Russian and Karina, but his gaze flitted over his shoulder. Reidigger had his pistol aimed at the two men in the doorway, but the three who had been blasted by the stun grenade appeared to be coming around.

They didn't have enough guns to hold this many people off for long.

"Hey," said the second man, "those cops aren't going to wait forever. If the shooting's stopped, they might try to get in here."

"You're right. Keep on the fat one." The first American edged his way closer to the nearest stained glass window, several panes of which had been broken in the firefight, and pointed his weapon through it. "Here's how this is going to go, Zero. You and your pal are going to put down your guns. Or else my Russkie friend here is going to kill the girl, and my other pal is going to kill this guy. Me, I'm going to start plugging cops. And since they think we're CIA, all of that is going to come down on your head."

"Don't do it," Karina said softly as her arms lowered to her sides.

"What's the play here?" Alan grunted.

Zero couldn't think straight. Any way he cut it, someone was going to get shot.

If he shot at the Russian, he might hit Karina. And they'd open fire on Alan.

But if they gave up and dropped their weapons, all three of them would undoubtedly be gunned down anyway.

"I'll give you to the count of three," said the American, with his assault rifle pointed out the window.

Zero's eyebrow rose as he saw Karina's left hand reaching for her waistband, creeping along at a snail's pace. *The Beretta.* She still had it.

"*Ne faites pa cela,*" he told her. Don't do it.

"One..." said the American.

Karina's hand crept along toward the back of her pants.

"Two..."

"It was real," she said quietly to him in French. "You and I. You know that, right?"

"Yes." His breath caught in his throat. "But please..."

"Thr—"

Karina pushed forward suddenly, away from the Russian, and twisted her head around to wriggle free of his grip. At the same time she pulled the Beretta and whipped it around.

Zero instantly twisted his body and dropped to one knee. He fired half the magazine into the two Americans, even as their own guns roared indiscriminately.

The trio of unarmed men in the pews jumped as the shooting began. Alan jutted out his good elbow, striking the closest one in the face, and fired into all three of them.

It took all of three seconds. But when it was done, he panted as if he'd just sprinted a mile. Karina stood over the dead Russian with her back to Zero. Alan kept his aim pointed downward as if the dead men would somehow stand again. Outside the cops shouted to each other and dove for cover.

But they'd done it. A moment earlier he was certain they would all be dead, yet they'd managed to eke out a win.

"Alan?" he asked.

"I'm okay."

"Karina?"

She turned to face him.

Blood blossomed from two entry wounds in her chest, soaking the fabric of her shirt as the color drained from her face. The Beretta fell loose from her fingers.

"I… I'm… I'm hit."

Chapter Thirty One

Karina's knees buckled. Zero couldn't feel his own legs as he rushed forward, unaware that he'd dropped the gun until he was catching her in both arms.

"It's going to be okay," he whispered quickly. "You're going to be okay." He said it over and over again, as if the mantra would make it true. "It's going to be okay."

She'd been shot twice, once near the navel and once higher, dangerously close to her heart. He tried to press his hand over it, but every beat pumped more blood out of the wound.

The sounds of men shouting from outside were lost to him. Or maybe it wasn't outside; it could have been Alan shouting right in his ear for all he knew or cared.

"You're going to be okay."

Karina stared back at him, her eyes wide and afraid, one hand gripping his neck tightly.

"It's going to be okay."

Then there was another hand on his shoulder, a stronger one, forcing him to turn and look up. It was Reidigger, his face red with exertion, shouting at him: "We have to go, Zero! Now!"

He looked around. The nave was empty except for the three of them and the bodies. All of those bodies. He couldn't let Karina just be another corpse in his wake.

Because that's what you do. You kill, or you get people killed.

Several booming thuds echoed through the cathedral. The police were at the door, shouting through it, warning whoever was inside of their arrival.

We have to go.

"Take her." He stood with Karina in his arms.

"Zero, we can't—"

"Just take her!" he shouted in Reidigger's face. Alan relented, slinging Karina's arm over his good shoulder. They both groaned in pain as he held her up.

He glanced around quickly. *Where…? There.* The AR-15, lying on the floor of the church. He snapped it up and fired several shots at the closed door of the church. The police on the other side shouted and scattered.

"Back door." Zero strode quickly toward the rear exit, pausing only to grab up the black duffel bag and sling it over his shoulder. He led the way with Alan and Karina limping along behind him down a short dark corridor to an old wooden door. He rooted around in the bag, knowing that Alan would have brought…

A-ha. A fragmentation grenade.

"Christ, Zero, what are you going to…?"

Before Alan could finish the question, Zero yanked the pin and released the lever. He pushed the back door open just a few inches and tossed the grenade out. Then he slammed the door shut and waited.

The explosion rocked the foundation and shook dust loose from the ceiling, but Zero didn't flinch. He shoved the door open again and stepped out into a plume of dark smoke, the assault rifle to his shoulder.

Right. Two men stood near an SUV, armed but reeling from the grenade. He took them out quickly with two squeezes of the trigger.

"Get her in the back," he told Reidigger as he spun to check his six. A gun fired as he did; a bullet grazed his arm, tearing the flesh of his bicep, but he barely felt it. *Up.* The shooter was on the balcony of the building behind the cathedral. Zero fired three shots into him and the man tumbled forward, plummeting to the street below.

Shouts. Police came running around the corner at the sound of the explosion. Zero dug into the bag and pulled out another grenade—a second flash-bang—and lobbed it at them. They split off in a hurry as the stun grenade exploded.

Alan was already behind the wheel as Zero jumped into the back seat with Karina. They sped off before the door was fully closed.

Karina lay on her back, hissing breaths through clenched teeth. "*Hnnn… hnnn… hnnn…*" Her dark eyes met his. "Hold… hold my…"

He gripped her hand tightly as he stared back desperately. "Alan, we need a hospital!"

"Zero." His voice was eerily calm for someone driving sixty-five miles an hour through a downtown area, swerving around traffic. "You know I love you, and I would do just about anything for you. But you need to listen to me. There's nothing we can do for her."

"Alan, she's dying!"

"I know," he replied slowly. "So does she. We need you to know it."

He looked down into Karina's face, searching her eyes. She nodded once tremulously. "He… he's right," she said breathlessly. The SUV bounced over a rut in the road and she cried out.

"Dammit," Alan muttered. A black car was coming up on them fast. "Hang on." He swerved out of the lane, letting the car come up alongside them. Zero saw the window rolling down, a man leaning out with a gun—

Alan wrenched the wheel, steering the SUV into them. They pushed the car right off the road and sent it crashing through a storefront.

Karina's other hand reached for him, gripping the back of Zero's neck. "Listen," she said in a hoarse, ragged whisper. "Listen to me. Take… take the phone."

"What?" He frowned as he looked down at the rectangular lump in the front pocket of her jeans. The blood from her wounds had fully soaked the front of her shirt, down to the hem of the pants. He reached for it and pulled out the small black burner phone. "But…"

"Take it." She gasped in pain, and then added, "Earrings. Get them to Artem. He will know… what to do."

“Don’t try to talk,” he told her. “We’re going to get you help. We’re going to help you. We can help you ...” He was rambling now, saying anything and everything that he thought she might want to hear. “Just don’t go. Not yet.”

He felt her grip on his hand weakening. Her fingers were cold, shock-white. Her other hand on the back of his neck pulled gently and he let it, let it pull him down to reach her. She kissed him softly and he tasted a tinge of iron from the blood on her lips.

“It was real,” Karina told him, her voice breathy in his ear. “It was real.”

And then she said nothing.

Chapter Thirty Two

Zero sat on the rocky embankment, idly tugging weeds from the ground as he stared at the SUV parked beyond and slightly below him. It was cool, almost cold in the shade and the chilly October air, but he didn't notice. He would have felt cold anywhere.

As soon as Alan was certain they weren't being tailed, he'd driven straight out of Liège headed due east for some miles. Zero had no idea how far they'd gone, but they were in a rural area of Belgian countryside. Alan had found an old covered bridge over a nearly dry creek and drove the SUV down the embankment, parking it directly underneath. No one would be able to see it from the road.

Zero looked at his hands. He'd tried to wash the blood from them in the meager trickle of water that remained of the creek, but he could still see it in dark red crescents beneath his fingernails, smudges in the fleshy spots between his fingers, on his arms. The blood on his hands would never fully wash off.

"Zero."

"Yeah," he said flatly.

"We can't stay. We need to go."

He said nothing in response, but continued staring straight ahead at the SUV, the back seat of which still held Karina's body. "She didn't deserve this, Alan. This wasn't her fight."

Alan groaned slightly as he crouched in front of Zero so that he was forced to look him in the eye. "I'm your best friend," he said, "which means the responsibility falls on me to tell you things that you don't want to hear, but need to hear. The moment Karina learned what was happening between those two presidents, she was a part of this. She chose to be a part of this, and did what was necessary to fight it. Sometimes we lose people. We always have. But the job isn't over. So right now, I need you to snap the hell out of it and help me form a plan."

Zero rubbed his face with both hands. Alan was right; the job wasn't over. "We need to go to Chaudfontaine. Link up with the FIS agent there, Artem. Get the earrings to Kiev, back to their creator."

Alan looked dubious. "Zero, we could take them elsewhere. The United Nations, for example? Or ... or we call Maria, explain what happened here ..."

"No," Zero snapped. It wasn't because he was still angry with Maria; he wasn't. He could hardly concern himself with any of that at the moment. But if they contacted Maria, the CIA would know where they were—and if the agency was being puppeteered as well, they would never let her come for them personally. Zero might trust the earrings in Maria's hands, but *only* in Maria's hands, and simply the knowledge of Zero's whereabouts could potentially put her in direct danger.

Besides, Karina had given her life to get the earrings back into the hands of her people, so that's what he was going to do. And he was not going to leave the sole surviving FIS agent behind to be found and killed by the Russians. "We go to Chaudfontaine. Rendezvous with Artem. FIS was always the plan. It's still the plan."

"Okay," Alan relented with a sigh. "But we can't go anywhere in this car."

Zero knew what he meant; not only was it likely flagged by the Russians, but it was battered and dented, easily identifiable—and had a body in the back seat. "We'll torch it, right here. We'll find another ride and get to Chaudfontaine."

He rose slowly to his feet and instinctively put a hand in his pocket to ensure that the two earrings were there. He'd gingerly removed them from Karina's ears after her final breath, his hands trembling.

In his other pocket was the burner phone. She had insisted that he take it with him, but he didn't understand why. Veronika was dead, and Artem would be utterly foolish to have kept the phone on him after making the call. What purpose would the phone serve now?

He pulled it out and inspected it. Part of the screen was slightly smeared with blood from his thumb. Karina's blood. He tapped a button on the phone; the screen lit up, and Zero immediately noticed something strange. Right there on the home screen, an unfamiliar app had been downloaded to the phone.

He frowned and opened it. It looked like some kind of third-party calling app ... and stranger still, the only number it had been used to call was the burner's own number.

Why would she make a call to her own phone ...?

He sucked in a breath as he realized the answer. *Clever.* The only reason Karina would call her own phone's number would be to leave a voicemail.

He checked the messages, and sure enough there was a single voicemail waiting in its inbox.

"Zero," Alan prodded. "We can't stay here ..."

"Hang on a second," he murmured.

"What? What is it?"

But Zero ignored him and put the phone to his ear as he played the voicemail message.

"Zero."

His heart broke anew at hearing the sound of her voice, knowing that her body was lying mere yards from him.

"If you're listening to this message, it likely means I'm dead. It also means that I probably didn't tell you everything. But I'm going to tell you now. Here's what you need to know: Kozlovsky has some kind of serious dirt on President Harris. I believe he may have been a part of the US cabal against Iran, and I think the Russians helped get Harris elected. In the meeting between the two, Kozlovsky asked two things of Harris. The first was that the US withdraw from NATO. That part is already happening. The second was that Harris order the disarming of American missile systems in Eastern Europe. That may have already happened; it wouldn't be public knowledge. It seems to me that Kozlovsky is intent on finishing Ivanov's work and annexing Ukrainian assets. Possibly even planning a full-scale invasion. I don't think I need to tell you the ramifications of this. Kozlovsky may have a bigger aim in sight: triggering a new world war. Not only would it inspire patriotism to his side, but if the US allied with him it would make the perfect pretense for seizing assets and territory from other countries."

His hand again touched the small lumps in his pocket that were the pearl earrings, the recording. That's what she had captured. The two conspiring presidents, one of them intent on finishing his predecessor's work and the other commanded to sit idly by.

Karina's voicemail paused for a moment before continuing: "I trust you to do the right thing and put a stop to it... even if I'm gone. You've gotten this far. Wherever you are, I hope that you're well. And... thank you. You came for me when I needed you. I've never met anyone quite like you, Zero. *Au revoir.*"

He slowly lowered the phone, a lump forming in his throat. Karina had died so that so many others could be saved. They had to get to Chaudfontaine as soon as possible, before the Russians caught up with them. But first...

Zero looked toward the SUV and felt a stab of guilt. They didn't have time or tools to bury her, and torching the car was not exactly a funeral pyre. But he felt that she would understand he had little choice. And when he looked around, noting the fresh air and the miles of fields and narrow, gently bubbling creek, he couldn't help but think that there were far worse places one could be laid to rest.

Alan seemed to understand what he was thinking. He tore off a strip from the jacket/sling around his shoulder and stuffed it in the open hole of the gas tank with the end trailing. Then he handed Zero a book of matches.

He struck one and held the burning tip to the fabric. It took several seconds, refusing to catch quickly. "Goodbye," he murmured.

Then he hefted the black duffel bag, and he and Reidigger crested the embankment away from the vehicle.

They were only a few yards away from the covered bridge when the tank caught and exploded. Neither of them looked back.

They walked together in silence. Zero couldn't help but wonder if in another life, things might have been different for them. If they could have been happy together—the history professor and the interpreter. If they might have taken vacations to places like Liège or Chaudfontaine, instead of harboring international secrets that would get them killed. He wondered what his daughters would think of her, and decided they would both like her. She might have taught them how to speak Ukrainian. They might have taken trips abroad to meet her family, her sister Veronika, and see her native country.

Zero felt Alan's hand come to rest on his shoulder and squeeze it gently as they hiked across the field toward a farmhouse in the distance. He appreciated the gesture, but in the moment he didn't want solace or sympathy. He wanted answers, and more than anything he wanted to personally ensure that Karina did not die in vain.

Chapter Thirty Three

After hiking from the covered bridge and crossing about a mile and a half of Belgian countryside, they came to a small farm with a barn that housed an old pickup truck, a couple of decades of wear under its hood and likely just used to run supplies across the acreage. But there was no one around, and its age only made it easier for Reidigger to hotwire it. The engine was slow to turn over, but they just needed the old truck to get them the fifteen miles to their destination, and it did that without incident.

"Pretty place," Alan noted.

"Sure is," Zero agreed. "Too bad we don't have time for sightseeing."

Chaudfontaine was a breathtakingly beautiful French commune in the heart of Belgium, rife with heritage and historical sites, situated along the edge of a small river. At least that's what Zero noted at a glimpse, which was all he could afford in the moment.

They parked the truck on a street at the edge of town and asked a local where they might find the Chateau des Berges. The man they asked was around Zero's age, wearing owlish glasses and a tie knotted at his throat. He chuckled lightly and told them in English, "It is only a short distance that way. Trust me, you will know it when you see it."

The two of them got back in the truck and headed in the direction of the chateau, the name of which translated roughly to "castle on the banks." It was easy enough to discern which building was the Chateau des Berges as they approached; he guessed it was the downright palatial estate house they were quickly approaching, built in gray stone with dark shutters on every window, with several gables bearing statues of angelic forms.

Alan parked the truck at the edge of the property and they sat there for a long moment, inspecting the front of it. The trees that dotted the front of the property made it difficult to see if anyone was waiting for them.

"So," Alan said casually. "If this doesn't work, what's our backup plan?"

"We'll have to flee," Zero said candidly. "Get out of Europe and get somewhere non-extradition until we can figure out what to do next."

If there's anything that can be done. They were killers, both of them. Not CIA, not spies, not even law enforcement. Their choices were prison or be on the lam.

"I know a guy in the Malé Atoll in the Maldives," Alan said with a thin, sad smile. "Could be nice. Do some fishing, some snorkeling."

Zero smiled despite himself, but it evaporated quickly. They were heading into this blind, with no idea who this Artem fellow was and if he was followed—and worse, they were unarmed. Zero had dropped the Sig Sauer at some point, likely in the cathedral shootout. "I don't suppose you've got any more guns in that magic bag of yours."

Alan shook his head ruefully. "Fresh out. But I do have something else…" He searched in the bag again and came out with precisely what Zero hoped he wouldn't suggest. "We'll just have to make it count."

He handed Zero what looked like a flash-bang, a silver canister with a pin and lever. But it wasn't quite like any stun grenade he'd seen before. "What is this?"

"Not entirely sure, to be honest," Alan replied.

Zero scoffed. "You really did raid Bixby's lab, didn't you?"

Alan shrugged. "That guy really needs to update his security."

It was better than nothing. Though not by much.

They got out of the truck and crossed the front lawn, Zero keeping his eyes on the windows of the enormous estate house. But he saw no movement. The two of them entered the reception area, an opulent foyer with tall ceilings and an enormous crystal chandelier hanging overhead. To the left was a check-in counter, but there was no clerk or concierge.

In fact, as far as Zero could tell, they were alone. There were no sounds, no talking, no people around at all.

This doesn't feel right. He reached into his pocket and pulled out the stun grenade, hiding the narrow canister as best he could in both of his palms with his hands clasped in front of him.

"Anyone home?" Alan dared to call out.

"Hello." A male voice floated to them. They both looked sharply to their right to see a man coming down an old winding staircase just off the foyer, his hand gliding along the black iron railing. He was young, perhaps a full decade younger than Zero, well-built, with short dark hair and a passive expression, seemingly blasé in a way that made it hard to tell what he might be thinking.

"Are you Artem?" Zero asked cautiously.

"I am. And you must be Zero," he said with a small nod as he reached the bottom of the stairs. "But who is your friend? And where is Karina?"

"Karina is somewhere safe," Zero lied, though it pained him to say it aloud. "With the earrings. Come with us. I'll take you to her."

Artem hesitated. "She was supposed to meet me here…"

"She is afraid for her life," Zero replied. He knew in that moment that his instinct had been right. This Artem was too calm, too composed for someone who was supposedly on the run from murderous Russians. "She was right to be, wasn't she?"

Artem shook his head. "I don't know what you are talking about…"

"Indeed she was." A new voice, stronger, deeper—and speaking Russian. A man stepped into the round, cavernous foyer from an adjacent room. It was a man that Zero knew, or at least had met briefly once before. He was tall, his features bland, and his right hand was heavily bandaged. Zero did not need to see the wound to know that he would have only three fingers remaining on that hand, two of them having been shot off by Karina Pavlo.

President Aleksandr Kozlovsky scrutinized both Zero and Alan, a thin, almost reptilian smile on his lips. "It took us quite a while to locate you."

"Who's this guy?" Alan murmured.

"I'm surprised to see you here in person, Mr. President," Zero told him in Russian.

"Well, as the saying goes, if you want something done, you must see to it yourself." He glanced over his shoulder and said loudly, "*Uviydit.*" Come in. Three *Bratva* entered from different directions, corridors and adjacent rooms to the round foyer, each silent and armed with automatic weapons and most definitely not friendly.

"You sold out your own people in FIS," Alan growled at Artem.

The traitorous agent shook his head. "I was given no choice. It was this or be killed."

"That's still a choice," Alan countered.

Zero stared at Kozlovsky, his clasped hands sweating around the silver canister. It was this man's fault that Karina was endangered in the first place. This man's fault that she was dead.

"Enough talk," Kozlovsky commanded in Russian. "We know now that the interpreter had a recording device in that meeting, hidden in her earrings. We also know that she is unwilling to hand them over to anyone but her people in Kiev. You can tell me where she is now, or my people will torture you for the information."

Alan narrowed his eyes angrily and said in Russian, "We're not going to tell you anything."

Kozlovsky sighed irritably. He turned to the nearest Russian thug and barked an order: "Shoot the chubby one."

"Wait!" Zero stepped in front of Alan. "Wait. Don't shoot. I have them. I have the earrings."

"Zero, we can't!" Alan protested.

"We have to," he said to his friend. In a whisper he added, "Trust me."

This is insane. But so was everything else he'd done so far. Louder, to Kozlovsky and his companions, he said, "I have them here." He cradled the grenade in his two hands in front of him, hidden in his palms, and slowly pulled the pin, making sure the thin safety lever was pressed firmly against the grenade's body in his sweaty palm. One small slip of the wrist or wiggling of fingers and the lever would release.

Zero held out his hand to Kozlovsky. "Here."

The Russian president gestured to Artem. "Give them to him."

Zero nodded tightly. He held out his fist and opened it over Artem's waiting hand.

The FIS agent looked down and frowned. The object in his palm was not the earrings. It was the pin of the grenade.

"What…?" he said in confusion.

Zero opened his other hand and the silver canister rolled out of it, clattering to the floor as the lever released and sprang away. Kozlovsky frowned, his mouth dropping open. Two of his armed *Bratva* recognized the grenade and their eyes widened in shock.

Zero grabbed Alan and they leapt to the floor, both of them hitting the deck and clamping their hands over their ears before the stun grenade went off.

But as Zero had noted earlier, it wasn't quite like any stun grenade he'd seen before.

Chapter Thirty Four

Even through his clenched eyelids and facing the floor, Zero still saw a blinding shock of light, as if someone had turned on the sun itself right in front of his eyes. The resonant blast that followed shook him to his core, roiled his insides, a wave of intense nausea washing over him. For what felt like several moments he could hardly move, couldn't even take a breath.

The stun grenade that Alan had grabbed from Bixby's lab must have been one of his experimental weapons. The intensity of it was easily five times that of an ordinary flash-bang. Even as Zero opened his eyes again he saw dark spots in his vision, and had to hold himself steady with both hands on the floor until the nausea and dizziness passed.

"Alan," he said hoarsely. "Are you okay?"

"Nope," Reidigger groaned. He sat up as well, wavering slightly with the loss of equilibrium. "Christ. I don't know what the hell that was, but I want five more of them."

At last Zero got to his feet, shaky as he was, and staggered over to where the others had just been standing. They were laid out on the floor, all five of them, including Kozlovsky. The Russian president was on his back, his eyes wide and unblinking, bleeding from both ears.

"Is he … dead?" Alan asked carefully.

"I don't know—"

Suddenly Kozlovsky sucked in a deep, ragged breath. At the same time one of his arms shot upward, groping at nothing in particular, his thin fingers clawing at the air.

"I can't see!" he moaned in Russian. "I can't... I can't..." His voice sounded odd as well. "I cannot hear! Someone help me!" He groped aimlessly, trying to roll over and faltering with his lack of balance.

Zero could see that the others had been similarly affected as their cries joined Kozlovsky's. He didn't know if the blindness and hearing loss would be permanent or not, but he certainly had no compassion to offer them.

"Zero!" Alan shouted behind him.

He spun to see Artem staggering toward the exit. Apparently the FIS agent had also tried to protect himself in the instant that the stun grenade had gone off, and was now attempting an escape. Alan lunged for him, but teetered off-kilter and rolled to the floor, his balance not fully restored.

Zero dropped to one knee and snatched up an AK-47 from one of Kozlovsky's foot soldiers. He put it to his shoulder and aimed at the fleeing FIS renegade. But just before he took the shot, he remembered his faulty aim from earlier and tracked the barrel just slightly to the left.

He pulled the trigger, firing off a three-shot burst. All three tore into Artem's back. The Russian mole yelped and fell forward on the lawn.

For Karina. And for Veronika.

"Nice shot." Alan climbed to his feet again and shook his head gruffly. "I'm still a bit shaky on my feet."

"We need to get out of here quick," Zero said urgently. "Someone will have heard those shots."

"And they probably heard that flash-bang in Brussels," Reidigger noted wryly.

Zero ditched the gun, not wanting to be spotted carrying an automatic weapon, and the two of them hurried back out across the lawn to the truck. Sirens wailed in the distance, but Reidigger kept it at the speed limit as they drove away from the Chateau des Berges. Zero glanced back occasionally to make sure they weren't being followed.

They were less than a full mile away when Alan voiced the concern that was on both their minds. "That was a bust," he muttered. "What do we do now?"

Zero didn't have an answer for that. FIS was compromised; so was the Secret Service. If the Russians had gotten to them, they could have people anywhere—Interpol, the CIA, possibly even disguised as police.

I thought I was over that sort of paranoia, he mused. But it wasn't just paranoia; besides the man in the truck with him, there was no one Zero could trust. There would be no getting across borders. And to make matters the absolute worst, he was keenly aware that he might have just permanently blinded the president of Russia.

"Zero?" Alan pressed. "We need a destination, pal."

Suddenly Alan's suggestion of the Maldives was looking attractive. But when he rubbed his tired eyes, he saw her face behind his closed lids—he saw her the way he wanted to remember her, lying beside him in an inn in Liège, smiling, her hair hanging down over one shoulder with her head propped in her hand.

He couldn't give up now. He had the earrings. That was all that mattered.

"FIS is out," Zero said, working it out aloud. "We can't risk the contacts we know. No CIA, no Interpol. No UN either; politicians can be bought."

"NATO headquarters is in Brussels," Alan offered, "but the US has announced its withdrawal. We won't get any amnesty there." He scoffed at himself and added, "Then again, we won't get amnesty anywhere."

But Zero barely heard it. At Reidigger's mention of Brussels, a memory streaked through his mind, one he hadn't thought about since his mind had been restored.

"Wait a second," he murmured. "Alan, do you remember about five years back or so, we were on an op in Brussels? We were undercover, trying to find the client of a Belgian weapons smuggler."

"Yeah, I remember. What about it?" Then Alan's eyes widened under the brim of his trucker's cap. "Are you thinking about Sutton?"

"Yes."

Alan shook his head. "Are you insane?"

"No. Maybe."

Back then, a little more than five years earlier, the CIA had lent the two of them, Zero and Reidigger, to United States European Command to assist with finding the arms smuggler's customers before they received their purchase, a powerful warhead. They had liaised specifically with four-star General Raymond Sutton, whom Zero recalled as an impressive yet thoroughly apolitical military leader.

And if he's still running things there…

"What makes you think he'll listen to us?" Alan asked.

"Because…" Zero started. Because back then, the two of them had discovered that the arms smuggler's clients were a pair of AWOL American soldiers suffering from PTSD and delusional episodes. Zero and Reidigger had detained them, and the CIA wanted them brought directly to H-6. But Sutton saw it differently. He appealed to Zero himself to defy his agency and keep the men at Chièvres Air Base in Belgium, where they would be under lock and key but also get the help they obviously needed. "Because," Zero said, "I believe he's a man of integrity. This is an issue of potential war, and if he's still the man I remember, then he may be the best shot we have at getting someone to listen to us."

"Uh-huh," Alan said lowly, clearly hesitant. "Zero…you understand that would require us to turn ourselves in, right?"

"Yeah." He looked out the window as the Belgian countryside rolled by. "I do."

Chapter Thirty Five

Sara didn't like this part of town. It was the type of neighborhood that Camilla would call "super sketch." The kind of place where stories of girls like her getting grabbed and stuffed into vans and never heard from again were prevalent.

But she needed it.

After the altercation with Tommy, the threat of being kicked out of the co-op loomed heavily over her head. If she got the boot, she would be homeless. There were no two ways about it. She barely had any money to her name. She'd be on the streets.

She'd begged Camilla for the name and address of her guy. Camilla didn't have enough on her. Sara's nerves were jangled; she needed more.

She found the address even though one of the numbers on the front of the house was missing, a white silhouette in its place. She stepped up three creaking steps to a porch that held, for some reason, a rusted washing machine. The siding was grimy with age and algae. The screen in the door was torn and hanging half out of the frame.

She knocked.

A dog barked from inside, a deep and threatening woof.

"Shut up," warned a male voice. Then the door opened, and the guy scowled down at her. He was tall, taller even than lanky Tommy, wearing a tank top over heavily tattooed and well-muscled arms. He had a wispy, unruly beard and a bruise under his left eye.

"What you want?" he demanded.

Sara cleared her throat and straightened her back as she said, "I'm looking to buy."

"Buy?" He scoffed at her. "Buy what, fuckin' Girl Scout Cookies? Fuck outta here, little girl." He started to close the door in her face.

"I'm a friend of Camilla's."

The dealer paused. "You know Camilla?"

"I'm her roommate." *Though maybe not for long.*

He thought about it for a moment, the door half-closed. "Yeah, all right. Come on." He pushed the door open again and she stepped inside. "You best not be a narc."

"I'm not," Sara assured him. She was standing in a small living room of the rowhouse, the brown and well-worn carpet a sharp contrast to the huge flat-screen TV and video game systems. There was a game paused on the television, a controller sitting on a black leather sofa whose arms had been chewed up, presumably by the dog she'd heard earlier.

"What you need?" he asked.

"A few grams," she told him.

"You're gonna have to be more specific than that. You want an eight-ball?"

"I... I don't know what that is," she admitted.

The guy grinned. "Where the fuck Camilla meet you? The high school?"

"I dropped out," she told him flatly.

He nodded. "Yeah. Me too. Went and got my GED. Way easier than dealing with that shit."

Sara almost rolled her eyes. She could just imagine what Maya would say if she learned that her little sister's drug dealer had gotten his GED when she hadn't yet.

"An eight-ball is three and a half grams," he told her. "It's called that 'cause it's one-eighth of an ounce."

"Um. Okay. Yeah, then that."

"Stay right there." The dealer disappeared into the adjacent room, which Sara could see was a small kitchen. A drawer slid open; there was some clanking, and then he came back with a tiny baggie. "I know it don't look like much, but I stand by all my stuff. It'll do it for you, I promise."

He was right; the baggie didn't look like much, but it would have to do. Sara reached into her purse for her wallet. "And how much …?"

"It's two hundred."

She balked, and then immediately felt a deep sting of guilt for all the drugs she'd let Camilla give her. "Shit," she murmured. "I don't have that much."

"You need to hit an ATM or something?"

She shook her head. "No. I've got about forty bucks to my name right now."

The dealer sucked air through his teeth. "Sorry, girlie. But forty ain't enough to get you there."

Sara sighed. The thought of going home with nothing made her skin crawl, made her hands tremble. But she said, "Okay. Thanks anyway," and turned defeatedly toward the door.

"Hang on a sec." The dealer rubbed his wispy chin. "There might be something we can do. You know this area pretty good?"

She nodded. "Yeah, pretty well. I work at the Swift Thrift, so sometimes I do pickups for them. All over town."

He looked her up and down in a way she did not at all like. "Young white-bread lookin' girl like you, all innocent. I think we could cut a deal."

She frowned. "What kind of deal?"

"Nothing big. You move some stuff for me. Pick it up here, bring it somewhere else. They give you money, you bring it back here. That's all."

Trafficking, she thought. *He's talking about trafficking.* Just the very thought of the word sent a shiver down her spine and the cold memories of the Slovenian traffickers that had kidnapped and nearly killed her. It was almost enough to make her want to turn and walk right out of there.

Almost.

"… Cops are always suspicious 'bout a guy like me." She hadn't even realized the dealer was still talking. "I get hassled just going down to the corner to buy smokes sometimes. But you? You could get anywhere. Even some of them higher-end type of people, the downtown folks."

"And what would that get me?" she asked.

"I'll give you a cut. Five percent. And if you want product, we'll take it out of that."

She thought about it. Five percent on the eight-ball she was going to buy would only be ten bucks; hardly worth it for running all over town. "Ten percent," she countered, "and I'll do it."

The dealer scoffed. "You think this is a negotiation? I'm making an offer, and that's that."

"Then no thanks." She turned and reached for the door.

"Seven and a half," he said behind her. "And I'll pretend not to be pissed off every time I have to use my calculator to figure that shit out."

She paused, pretending to consider it, and then turned back to him and nodded. "Deal." She stuck out a hand. "I'm Sara."

"I'm Ike." He shook her hand, and then held the eight-ball out to her. "Consider it a sign-on bonus."

Chapter Thirty Six

Reidigger parked the old truck a short distance from the gated entrance to US Army Garrison Benelux. The location of the small base was technically Brussels, though the capital city proper rose about a half mile in the distance.

Zero inspected the layout from behind his closed window. It was a far cry from the types of military installations he was more accustomed to seeing, places in the desert with twelve-foot-high fences topped with barbed wire, guards armed to the teeth, anti-aircraft weapons always at the ready to stall some threat. The Brussels base was comparatively pleasant, surrounded by a simple chain-link fence, beyond which were grassy fields and paved pathways, stout red barracks, and a beige administrative building which, if he recalled correctly, was where they would find General Sutton.

"Are you sure about this?" Alan asked. He too was craning his neck toward the window, watching a platoon jog in formation in fatigue pants and Army-tan tees.

"No," Zero replied honestly. "So let's go do it before I change my mind." He pushed out of the truck, and Reidigger followed, albeit with a heavy sigh.

The base's entrance was a one-lane-wide gap in the fence, a small guard booth, and a tollbooth-style lever arm painted cautionary yellow. A young MP peered out of the booth at them. He had a sidearm, but made no motion for it as they approached. Instead he took a step out of his small booth and held up a single hand.

"Hold up, please." He looked them both up and down. Zero couldn't imagine how they must have looked to him, dirty and bloody and bruised. "This is a US military installation, sirs."

"We know, son," Alan said, amused. "That's why we're here."

"We need to speak to General Sutton," Zero told him. "It's an urgent matter."

The MP frowned deeply, and for a moment Zero's heart sank. It had been too long; this was no longer Sutton's post.

But then the young soldier asked, "What sort of business do you have with the general?"

"None yet," said Zero candidly. "I need a message delivered to him. I need you to tell him that Agent Zero is standing at the gate."

"Who?" The soldier glanced from Zero to Alan and back again.

"It's not that hard, son." Alan took a step forward, smiling politely. "Pick up that phone in there, and tell General Sutton that Agent Zero is here to see him. Trust me. He's going to want to hear this."

"I don't believe this." Four-star General Raymond Sutton stroked his smooth chin, shaking his head in disbelief as he stared down at the two tiny pearl studs in his opposite palm. He looked almost the same as Zero remembered; tall, proud, barrel-chested, well-maintained despite his fifty-plus years. But at the moment, he looked conflicted.

"Believe it, sir." Zero sat beside Reidigger on a bench seat in Sutton's austere office, against a far wall. Both of them had their wrists cuffed in front of them, and two armed MPs stationed directly on either side of the bench.

Even though he had already recounted the episode to the general, Zero repeated: "Those are recording devices, sir, and on them is a conversation captured by the interpreter of the secret meeting that was held between Harris and Kozlovsky."

Sutton closed his fist around them gingerly. "Let's just say that I believe you for one minute. Why in the hell would you bring them here? To me?"

"Because," Zero said simply, "a few years ago, we worked together briefly. You proved yourself to be trustworthy; to do the right thing over blindly following an order."

"Yes," the general said distantly. "I remember that. I remember you."

"When we found ourselves with no other options, your name came to mind," Zero explained. "So we're surrendering to you, and you alone. What happens next is in your hands."

"Literally," Reidigger added, gesturing toward the earrings in the general's fist.

"You should know that this has already been called in," General Sutton informed them. "The CIA and the government are aware that you're here."

"We understand, sir. But we cannot let those earrings fall into anyone else's hands—"

The door to the office flew open as an overzealous soldier practically spilled through the door, cutting Zero off. "Sir! There's a call for you on line two. Urgent. It's... well, it's the president."

Sutton blinked. "The president?"

"Yes, sir. President Harris, sir."

Sutton exchanged a glance with Zero, and then rounded his desk and plucked up the phone. "This is General Sutton." His gaze lowered to the floor. "Yes, sir. I understand, sir. That is correct, sir." Then Sutton frowned deeply. "... What Russians, sir?"

Russians?

Sutton stretched the cord of the phone as far as it would go as he yanked the blinds open over his office window.

Reidigger let out a low whistle. Outside the chain-link fence was a veritable convoy, Humvees and SUVs and sedans, rolling to a stop just beyond the gate of the small base.

"Yes, sir," Sutton said, his voice quiet, and then he hung up the phone. He glanced down at the pearls in his palm once more. "The president," he told them, "has just ordered me to turn you, and these earrings, over to the Russian government." He glanced out the window again at the cavalcade of vehicles that had scattered themselves outside the base. Men were pouring out of them, but lingered, staring inward at the base and making no attempt to hide the weapons they carried. "He told me that you attacked the Russian president. Blinded him."

"Yes," Zero said honestly, "we did. But only to avoid being killed by his people."

"To refuse that order and continuing to harbor you here could be considered an act of war," the general stated plainly.

"What the Russians plan to do will be an act of war," Reidigger countered.

"Sir," Zero added, "we came to you because of your integrity as a leader." He shook his head. "I'd hate to be proven wrong."

"Then you have to give me something more than just your word," Sutton persisted. "Something tangible. Right now I'm holding a pair of earrings that you're telling me are spy gadgets, with more than fifty armed and pissed-off Russians about to storm my gates. We don't have artillery or air support here; all of that is down at Chièvres. Why should I risk my people and my career for you? There must be something else."

Alan shook his head. "The only person who could have told you more is dead. Everything else is there, in that recording."

"Wait," Zero said suddenly. That wasn't true; Karina had left him her posthumous voicemail, in which she *had* given him more. "I do have something. In the meeting, Kozlovsky told Harris to order the disarming of American missile systems in Eastern Europe. That wouldn't be something that only American military would be aware of, right?"

Sutton frowned, but nodded. "That's right."

"There would be no way for me to know that unless I knew it from that meeting—the interpreter that was in it," Zero said quickly. His gaze flitted to the window; the Russians outside were gathering at the gate, the single MP there holding up both his hands as fellow American soldiers approached behind him.

There wasn't much time.

"Is there a way that you can confirm that, General?" Zero asked.

Sutton nodded. "All right," he agreed. He stuck a finger in the air to punctuate his point as he said, "But you had better be right." He threw open his office door and barked at the soldier who had burst in before. "Get me Eastern Command on the line. I want to speak to General Fitzgerald." To the two MPs flanking them, he ordered, "Keep an eye on those two." And Sutton vanished through the doorway.

All Zero could do was sit there, cuffed, and wonder if he had made the right decision or not. Either way, he was bound to face the music for what he had done to get that far; but if it meant that Karina and Veronika had not died in vain, and that no one else would have to, it could be worth it.

"Hey," Reidigger said gently, as if reading his thoughts. "We gave it our best try."

"Not out of the woods yet," Zero murmured, glancing through the window at the veritable powder keg that was the Russian force. He imagined that Kozlovsky had been amassing people in Belgium the moment he learned that Zero and Karina were here, and they appeared to have arrived in force.

And they had already proven they were willing to do just about anything to get what they wanted. It was strange that he had to hope that Harris had indeed already ordered the disarming of the missile systems, even though that would inevitably mean that Russia marched one step closer to potential war.

"Leave us." General Sutton's commanding voice jarred Zero out of his thoughts as he appeared in the doorway again, his expression grim. The two MPs murmured a "yes, sir" and left the office as Sutton crossed the floor, standing in front of Zero and staring down at him.

The general held out a fist. "Hold onto these for me." And he deposited the earrings into Zero's waiting hand.

"Sir…?"

But Sutton did not reply. Instead he rounded his desk, plucked up the red phone, and said, "Get me Chièvres Air Base. This is General Sutton at Garrison Benelux. We have a hostile force at our gates and require immediate air support."

Zero let out a sigh of relief. He had put his trust in the right person.

"I can buy you some time," Sutton told them, "but not long. We'll need to get that recording off of those earrings and broadcast it out."

"The only person who can do that is in Kiev," Zero told him. "And we don't know who he is."

"That might not be true," Alan said. "We know a certain engineer at Langley who might be able to help."

Zero nodded. If they could conference with Bixby from CIA headquarters, he just might be able to help them obtain the recording. But to do that they would first have to contact Maria.

There was a sound then, barely more than a hum at first but quickly growing louder. Zero glanced out the window to see the shapes soaring closer, several of them, speeding rapidly from Chièvres and flying toward the base. A half-dozen Black Hawk helicopters converged on the small Army base, hovering over the amassed Russians beyond the gates. Their shouts were inaudible as they scrambled back to their vehicles, but they didn't dare fire a shot. The combined might of the Black Hawks could obliterate them in seconds.

"Thank you, sir." Zero stood from the bench, his hands still cuffed but the earrings secured in his fist.

"My pleasure, Zero." Sutton nodded to him. "Now let's go figure out how to tell the world what you already know."

Chapter Thirty Seven

The audio of the meeting between US President Harris and Russian President Kozlovsky was broadcast on every news channel, every radio station, every website and blog on the entire planet with even the least bit interest in political stories.

Maya had heard it so many times by now that she could almost recite the meeting's exchange herself. They aired it unabridged, with the interpreter speaking between the two presidents in both Russian and English.

She followed the story intensely over the three days that it unfolded. First the news that the interpreter of the meeting had been killed, murdered by a Russian hitman in Belgium. Almost immediately after came the release of the audio file, through a joint effort between the CIA and American forces in Belgium. The audio was analyzed and picked apart every which way; professional translators were brought in from far corners of the world to ensure the accuracy of every statement while technology gurus were consulted on whether or not the recording might have been faked.

The consensus was almost overwhelming that the two presidents had gotten caught in yet another cabal. On the eve of the second day after the recording was released publicly, the Senate called for an emergency vote on the subject of three matters: for the United States to reenter NATO, to renew the arming of missile defense systems in Eastern Europe that Harris had secretly had disarmed, and the third, in which they unanimously opted to impeach—the first time in American history and, if anyone had their say, hopefully the last as well. For good measure, the vice president was dismissed as well pending an investigation, but Harris would face the full brunt of the law.

The United Nations was investigating Russia and the new administration, but Kozlovsky himself was nowhere to be found. His last known public whereabouts had been that his plane landed in Dusseldorf in Germany, but after that he seemed to have simply vanished. The CIA was on it, though, as were Interpol and a dozen other law enforcement agencies in Europe.

Maya had followed all of it over the course of the three days since the story broke, but it wasn't until the afternoon of the third day, between two classes and sitting at a bench outside of the academy, that she took out her phone and made the call. The weather was turning; even with a sweatshirt it was chilly, but she ignored it as the phone rang.

"Hi," Maria answered, sounding surprised to hear from her. And rightly so, she imagined.

"Hi," Maya replied. But in that moment she seemed to have forgotten everything she wanted to say. Words suddenly failed her like never before.

I'm nervous, she realized. *I'm nervous to even talk about him, let alone* to *him.*

"He's not here," Maria told her, as if reading her mind. "We, uh…we're not together anymore."

"Oh." That came as a surprise to her, but she decided not to press further. "That's…I'm sorry to hear that. But I wasn't calling to talk to him. I was calling to talk to you."

"Really?" Maria asked.

"Yeah. I've been following what's happening, and…"

She heard Maria's light, breathy chuckle through the phone. "Yes. It was him."

"And, uh…" She cleared her throat. "Is he okay?"

"He's okay," Maria confirmed. "A little banged up, like usual. But he's okay."

"Good. Good. Are you going to, maybe, see him sometime?" Maya asked.

"I will. He's actually coming back to work." Maria added slowly, "Though he doesn't know that yet."

"Good. I think that'll be good for him. He needs it, you know."

"He needs you too," Maria said plainly.

Maya bit her lip. She had promised herself she'd be done, done with all of it, with him, with that old life and the lies.

But I miss him so much.

She felt tears sting her eyes as she said, "Can you tell him something for me? When you see him?"

"Of course, Maya. Anything."

"Tell him…tell him I said I'm really proud of him." A tear tried to fall down her cheek, but she swiped it away before it could. "And, uh, maybe I'll visit again sometime. On my next break or something."

"You know you could tell him yourself. If you wanted."

Maya shook her head, even though no one could see it. "I'm not sure I'm ready for that. Just tell him that for me?"

"I will. I promise."

"Good. Thanks, Maria. Bye." She ended the call quickly, before her voice might crack and betray her. But she regretted it as soon as she did, because then she was alone, completely alone, sitting on a bench in October under a gray sky with no one, no one but herself.

She wiped her eyes once more and dialed another number. She just needed to hear a friendly voice. But instead of Sara's phone ringing, she heard a recorded message:

"The phone number you are trying to reach is not currently in service. Please try your call again later. Thank you." And then the call was automatically ended.

Maya frowned at the phone. She knew that Sara had fallen behind on her bills now and again, but was she so late on her phone bill that her service had been shut off?

She checked the time; she had to get to her next class. But she made a mental note to call Todd Strickland and have him check it out when he was able.

Maya stood then, stretched, and turned to head back toward the dormitories when she spotted a very unwelcome sight. Heading across the quad toward her was a group of boys—all of whom she recognized, and at the front of which was Greg. The other boys walked side by side, so that her path would be blocked if she tried to walk back that way.

Undeterred, Maya headed straight toward them. She tried to skirt around the bunch, but one of the boys sidestepped, blocking her.

"Move," she growled. The boy only laughed at her.

"Let her pass," Greg told him, and he stepped out of her way. Maya shoved past, resisting the urge to hurl an insult their way.

"But hey, Lawson?" Greg called to her. She paused, but didn't turn. "You might want to watch your back. I hear things are getting pretty tough around here for girls like you."

The boys laughed again as she strode away angrily. They could say whatever they wanted; she wouldn't let them get to her. But even as she told herself that, she couldn't help but glance up at the sky and think that there was a storm brewing over the academy—and that she might be at the eye of it.

Chapter Thirty Eight

It was three days before Zero was allowed to go home from Belgium. General Sutton granted him and Alan amnesty—and much-needed medical attention—in the wake of the recording's release, letting them sleep in the military barracks while the whirlwind of what had occurred whipped around the world.

On the third day, Sutton called him out to the field behind the administrative building, and the two of them watched as a black chopper came into view—a Bell AH-1 Cobra if he wasn't mistaken.

The wind whipped around him, tearing at his clothes as the helicopter descended and landed right on the grass. Zero watched as a shape hopped down from the cabin.

She spotted him, and he saw her, and for a long moment neither side moved.

Then Zero put both hands up slowly, showing they were empty, and placed them on his head as Maria Johansson strode toward him.

Maria scoffed at him. "Put your hands down, Kent."

"... You're not here to arrest me?" he asked, fully expecting it.

"No."

"Oh." He let his arms fall by his sides.

She stared at him for a long time, almost imperceptibly shaking her head. "You're a mess."

"I know."

"But you were right," she sighed. "About everything. I should have believed in you."

"I know," he said again, this time with a small grin.

Maria reached into her blazer and pulled something out, something black and rectangular and barely more than palm-sized. She slapped it against his chest.

He caught it before it fell to the ground. It was a document holder, and when he opened it he was astonished to see that it was his own identification staring back at him—in a way.

It was the CIA credentials for Agent Kent Steele.

"I convinced the right people that uncovering another international conspiracy was a much better story than a rogue former agent going on a spree," she told him. "So this whole time you've been working as an undercover operative under me and Spec Ops Group. It's either that or a hole at H-6. I'll let you pick."

"Doesn't seem like much of a choice," he muttered.

"Good. Then it's settled." She forced a smile. "Welcome back to the CIA."

"Are you sure you don't mind?" Zero asked her two days later. He had a cardboard box in his hands, a heavy one filled with books, as he stood in the open doorway to the basement steps of the Craftsman-style bungalow that he and Maria had once shared.

"For the last time, I don't mind at all," she insisted. Maria had been more than gracious in the process of him moving out, even going so far as to let him store whatever he needed in the basement until he got a bigger place. "After all," she added with a shrug, "it's not like I'm using a half-finished basement…"

"Funny," he said flatly.

He started to head down the stairs, but Maria stepped forward from the kitchen. "Hey."

He paused, sensing that she was about to say something serious. He set down the box and faced her.

"You don't have to do this. You know… we could still coexist without being… you know."

He smiled at her. Maria was one of the most direct people he knew; for her to be roundabout and vague only meant she was feeling vulnerable. "You have plans," he told her. "And you need to see those through. I want to see them happen. I'm not going to hang around here and get in the way of that."

She nodded appreciably. "Thanks." Then she stepped forward and wrapped him in a tight hug. "We're going to be okay, you and me."

"Of course we are." He had taken the first decent apartment he'd found, a fairly pleasant two-bedroom in DC, and signed a one-year lease before he could change his mind. She was right; they were going to be okay. But only if they gave each other some space.

"I'll never not be your friend," she said in his ear. "We've been through too much for anything to change that."

"I know." They separated before he casually added, "Except now you're my boss, so I guess we'll have to see."

"Hey," Maria shot back, "out of your last two bosses in the CIA, one was shot in a basement and the other was actively trying to start a war, so I think I'll be an improvement."

He smiled at that. He was coming back; there was no other way about that. And he wasn't alone either. Alan Reidigger had very reluctantly agreed to sign on as a CIA asset to avoid serious prison time. He refused outright to return as a full-fledged agent, but he would do what Maria needed when she needed it.

Zero could think of far worse options than returning to work with his best friend. That much was certain.

On the return flight from Belgium, he and Maria had plenty of time to talk. He'd admitted that he'd slept with the interpreter; no, that was unfair to suggest. He'd admitted that in the barely two days that they knew each other, he'd had intense feelings for Karina. He'd cared for her, and her death was still a huge weight on his shoulders that he couldn't shrug off.

It would be for a long while.

He and Maria both knew and acknowledged that they wanted different things, but not being in each other's lives wasn't an option. So he took the apartment, and she kept the house, and they would see each other at work and—who knew? Maybe beyond that, eventually.

He reached for his box of books again as Maria checked her phone. "Is that the time? I have to go!" She scurried to gather her purse and belongings.

For the first time in American history, the Speaker of the House was moving up into the Oval Office. It was a bewildering turn of events, one that had never happened in the history of the office, and there was a lot of trepidation surrounding it and the Speaker's ability to run the country—but laws were laws, and he was being sworn in that afternoon. Maria had scored a seat at the inauguration, on account of publicly being the woman who ran the "op" that uncovered the collusion between Harris and Kozlovsky. The latter of those two, the Russian president, had not yet regained his eyesight, though the doctors at H-6 believed it would be return over time. And when Kozlovsky's sight returned, he would find his new surroundings to be a five-by-five cell of packed earth for all he had done.

"You're sure you don't want to come?" she asked for what must have been the fifth time. "I can bring a plus-one."

Zero shook his head. He'd had his absolute fill of presidents, enough to last a lifetime. "I really have to move the rest of this stuff today. But thanks."

"Suit yourself." She hefted her purse, tucked her phone in it, and then quickly kissed him on the cheek.

Then her face turned beet-red as she realized what she'd just done. "Sorry. Force of habit."

He grinned. "It's okay. It'll take some getting used to."

"Yeah. It will." She headed toward the front door. "Lock up after you leave? Oh, and Kent."

He craned his neck toward the foyer to see her.

"Keep the key. Just in case."

Then she scooted out the door.

He chuckled to himself as he reached for his box once again. But he was halfway down the stairs before he realized the full intent of the statement.

She's still holding out hope that it'll work for us.

And then he doubted if the kiss was accidental at all, or the invite for him to stay and "coexist" was as innocent as it sounded.

And then he sighed heavily, because he was returning to the CIA and she was going to be his boss but also his friend and his former team member and his former lover, and all of that meant that nothing was less complicated than before. If anything, it was more so.

"Someday you'll get your shit together," he muttered to himself.

He set the box down with the others and glanced around the partially finished basement. He had to admit that the work he'd done looked pretty damn good. If only he'd had the drive to keep going, to finish the job.

It was a work in progress.

It was rough. It wasn't pretty. But when it was finished, if it was ever finished, it would be beautiful.

There's a metaphor in there somewhere... he thought wryly.

His phone rang in his pocket. It was Todd Strickland—possibly to congratulate him on his return to the agency. He smiled as he answered it.

"Hey, Todd."

"Zero." Strickland did not sound congratulatory or even pleasant. "We need to talk."

"Uh... sure. What's up?"

"I can't locate Sara."

Zero blinked. "What do you mean?"

"Her cell service has been cut off. I called her roommate at the co-op where she lives, and she hasn't seen her in two days. She's been looking too. No one has seen her."

A pit formed in his stomach. "I thought you were keeping tabs on her."

"I was!" Todd protested. "But last time I saw her, she got angry. She shouted at me, demanded that I leave her alone, so I backed off for a bit, and then this happened..."

"Todd, slow down," Zero told him. "Has Maya talked to her lately?"

"She tried, but no answer."

He remembered all too well his visit to Florida: Sara calling the police on him. Shrieking at him to get out and leave her alone.

Her admission that she'd been doing drugs.

"I need you to text me her home address," Zero instructed. "And tell me whatever you know about that's been going on with her."

Strickland was silent for an uncomfortably long time.

"Todd!"

"Okay. I'll tell you," said the young agent. "But... you're not going to like it. What are you going to do?"

Zero was already up the stairs and had his keys in hand. "I'm going to the airport."

Now Available!

ASSASSIN ZERO
(An Agent Zero Spy Thriller—Book #7)

"You will not sleep until you are finished with AGENT ZERO. A superb job creating a set of characters who are fully developed and very much enjoyable. The description of the action scenes transport us into a reality that is almost like sitting in a movie theater with surround sound and 3D (it would make an incredible Hollywood movie). I can hardly wait for the sequel."

—Roberto Mattos, Books and Movie Reviews

When a mysterious ultrasonic weapon attack may be the preamble to something greater, Agent Zero sets off on a

global manhunt to stop the ultimate devastation before it is too late.

Agent Zero, trying to come up for air on the heels of the President's impeachment and Sarah's close brush with danger, wants to retire from the service and try to get his family back together. But fate has other choices for him. With the safety of the world at stake, Zero knows he must follow the call to duty.

Yet his memories are shifting, and with it, new secrets are flooding back. Tormented, at his low point, Agent Zero may be able to save the world—but he may not be able to escape from himself.

ASSASSIN ZERO (Book #7) is an un-putdownable espionage thriller that will keep you turning pages late into the night. Book #8 in the AGENT ZERO series will be available soon.

"Thriller writing at its best."
–Midwest Book Review (re *Any Means Necessary*)

"One of the best thrillers I have read this year."
–Books and Movie Reviews (*re Any Means Necessary*)

Also available is Jack Mars' #1 bestselling LUKE STONE THRILLER series (7 books), which begins with Any Means Necessary (Book #1), a free download with over 800 five star reviews!

ASSASSIN ZERO
(An Agent Zero Spy Thriller—Book #7)

Made in United States
Orlando, FL
10 June 2023

33997271R00157